JULIE KENNER

D0042562

Even bad boys
have weak spots.

Aphrodite's Flame

$6.99 US
$8.99 CAN
£5.99 UK
$14.95 AUS

FIRE & ICE

Mordi focused on Izzy. She was frowning at the Henchman she'd frozen solid with her superpower, concern etched on her face.

But was it really concern? Or was it all an act? He didn't like it: the woman was the most intriguing he'd ever met, but he still couldn't discount the possibility that there had been no other attacker, and that Izzy was simply trying to cover her own tracks.

Inside the auditorium, applause crescendoed. They were running out of time. "Call in a retrieval team," he said. "And be ready."

While she watched, binder cuffs at the ready, he gathered his power, took aim, and—quite literally—fired. The Henchman defrosted, first blinking, then writhing about, bellowing at the top of his massive lungs. By that time Izzy had snapped the cuffs on him and jumped back. She looked at Mordi, her gorgeous eyes wide, and mouthed one word:

"Fire."

He nodded. "Ice," he said, referring to *her* power. And he didn't have to say that the two didn't mix.

Aphrodite's Flame

JULIE KENNER

LOVE SPELL NEW YORK CITY

To KP, for always reading the "Mordi bits."

LOVE SPELL®

August 2004

Published by

Dorchester Publishing Co., Inc.
200 Madison Avenue
New York, NY 10016

ISBN 0-505-52575-5

The name "Love Spell" and its logo are trademarks of Dorchester Publishing Co., Inc.

Printed in the United States of America.

Visit us on the web at www.dorchesterpub.com.

VENERATE COUNCIL OF PROTECTORS
1-800-555-HERO
www.superherocentral.com

Protecting Mortals Is Our Business!

Official Business

Hieronymous Black
Outcast
Internet Delivery; Location Unknown

Greetings and Salutations:

The Venerate Council of Protectors is in receipt of your Form 849-7A (filed in triplicate) seeking re-assimilation into the Council and eradication of your status as an Outcast pursuant to the Outcast Re-Assimilation and Immunity Act (codified at Part III, Title 9 of the Protector Code of Conduct).

As you are most likely aware, all Outcasts seeking re-

1

assimilation shall be assigned a Re-Assimilation Counselor; you will receive notice of the date, time and location of your initial Meeting and Assessment (along with your counselor's name) within ten business days. Please complete the following forms and bring them with you to the initial meeting with your counselor.

- Form 26Q(3)(a)—Affidavit of Intent re Non-Recidivism;
- Form 297-T (please complete the top portion only; the bottom portion may be retained for your records)—Statement of Purpose and Rationale Behind Decision to Seek Re-Assimilation;
- Form 26Q(3)(b)—Chronology of Events and Activities Undertaken As An Outcast. Remember, only truthful Outcasts will be re-assimilated! and
- Form T-26—Request for Pardon.

It is highly recommended that you read Circular 147B, *So You Want To Be Re-Assimilated!* Further information may be found on the Council website, *www.superherocentral.com*, on the Re-Assimilation Procedure page. Prior to sending questions or comments to the Council, we suggest you check the FAQ section to see if your situation has been covered.

Again, thank you for your interest in returning to a productive and helpful life as a Protector.

Sincerely,
Phelonium Prigg
Phelonium Prigg,
Assistant to Zephron, High Elder

jbk:PP
enclosure

Chapter One

"Nothing but bills today," Burt Foster said, smiling as he handed Isole Frost a stack of mail. The mailman's skin was baked to a golden brown, a testament to the recent beautiful weather that had soundly defeated whatever rain, sleet, snow, or hail might otherwise have tried to keep him from his appointed rounds.

Izzy took a good look at him as she fingered the bundle. Burt was about forty, with a round face and a receding hairline. His wife had passed away three years ago after a lingering illness, and when Izzy had met the man at the beginning of the summer, he'd seemed haunted and alone, giving off the scent of mild depression with just a hint of restlessness.

Now, though, she was picking up happiness combined with—what? She lifted her chin, sniffing slightly. *Ah, yes. Self-satisfaction.* The conquering hero. Virility mixed with tenderness.

No doubt about it. Mr. Foster had got himself a girl.

Izzy put on her work face, determined to hide her smile. "Thanks for bringing this up to the house," she said, sounding casual. She'd ease him into a discussion of his love life. No sense being pushy. "Of course, you

3

could have thrown in the *TV Guide*, too. It's my last day of vacation, you know. I plan to veg out and do some serious channel surfing." *That* was a far cry from the ice-cold professional veneer she clung to at the office, but at home with her father she could be herself without any repercussions. And today, "herself" wanted to lounge about in sweats.

A frown cut across Burt's features. "Aw, now, that's a shame. We'll be sorry to see you go. So will your dad."

Izzy nodded. Leaving her dad was the hard part. She'd taken the entire summer for vacation, spending lazy days on his Colorado property, just reading and watching him tinker. But while she'd enjoyed vacation and spending time with her father, she was thrilled about going back. A new job, new responsibilities. She couldn't wait.

She leaned forward, happy to share her news, even if Burt couldn't know *all* of the details. "I'm actually excited about going back," she said. "I got a promotion!"

The mailman beamed. "Congratulations! You're some sort of counselor, right?" He didn't wait for an answer. "They *should* give you a promotion. A woman as perceptive as you. Hell, they should give you your own TV show."

"Thanks for the vote of confidence." It meant a lot, actually, that Burt believed in her. Other than her father and her uncle, it was hard to find someone in the hallowed halls of the Venerate Council who believed Izzy knew what she was doing . . . much less that she was good at it. So, even though Burt couldn't know all the details—or, really, *any* of the details of her life or job—Izzy was glad for his support, and a little saddened that she couldn't tell him the truth. But, unfortunately, a girl simply didn't confess to the mailman that she was, technically, a superhero.

And tomorrow, she was stepping into her new job as

a Level V Re-Assimilation Counselor—a much-coveted position, and a significant promotion for her. She'd jumped straight from an entry-level position to the highest rank, skipping entirely that annoying middle ground—much to the consternation of her peers.

She'd worked her tail off for this promotion, though, to prove that she was worthy. But no matter how hard she worked or what accolades she won, she knew the whispers about her would never stop. Her peers would always look at her with wonder, jealousy, and a hint of contempt.

Well, too bad for them, Izzy thought, mentally lifting her chin in defiance. She deserved this promotion, she was damn good at what she did, and she didn't need anyone's approval or help. For that matter, she didn't need anyone.

Except, maybe, her dad.

She blinked back tears. She really did hate to leave him.

"We'll miss you around here," Burt said again, and Izzy picked up on the unspoken thought—*I'll* miss you.

She hid a smile, grateful that she'd been able to help him. "Did you talk to Janey?" She leaned forward conspiratorially, even though she already knew the answer.

A deep red flooded his neck, coloring his face even under the leathered bronze of his skin. "Well, yeah. I did." He shifted the mailbag on his shoulder, and focused on his shoes. With his head down like that, Izzy could see that the blush had spread to his scalp, visible under his thinning hair.

She smiled. A flush that intense could mean only one thing. "You took her the daisies."

He shrugged, looking up to meet her eyes. "Janey loved them. She was all smiles, and she looked at me like I was some kinda hero. She told me daisies were her favorite flower, and that I must've read her mind."

Izzy flushed. "She said that? How funny."

Burt cleared his throat. "We're, um, going out again on Friday night. That'll make two dates."

"Oh, Burt, that's wonderful!" She knew she shouldn't—it was *technically* against regulations—but this was a good cause, and so she reached out and grabbed his hand, disguising the gesture as a friendly squeeze.

She'd touched him once before, three months prior, when she'd seen the desolation that was in his heart. Now, though, the storm of emotions, thoughts, and images that zipped through her senses held only happiness and the wonder of a budding relationship, confirming the impression—the smell—that had already tickled her mind and nose. She gave his hand a little squeeze, tinged with just a hint of self-satisfaction, and let go. "I'm so happy for you," she said.

"Yeah, well, I've got you to thank." The red had faded, but still colored his cheeks a bit. "Especially since you're the one who told me I should talk to her in the first place."

Izzy rolled a shoulder in a half-shrug. "Woman's intuition."

"More than that," he said. "How *did* you know she'd like daisies? How'd you know she'd like *me*?"

"Oh, Burt—what's not to like?"

"I'm serious," he said, standing up straighter, an invisible shield of male pride clinging to him, just waiting to be pierced. "You didn't go into town and, well, *talk* to her, did you? I mean, you told me her favorite flower. Her favorite restaurant."

The possibility clearly mortified him. "Dugan's is my favorite restaurant, too. It's not like we've got a lot of choices around here." Hardly a booming metropolis, Izzy's hometown of River Run, Colorado, lacked the big-city amenities she'd gotten used to in New York. Like restaurants, coffee bars, and twenty-four-hour grocery stores.

"But the daisies," he said. "Are they your favorite, too? Or did you talk to her?"

"Actually, tulips are my favorite." She looked him in the eye, then drew a cross between her breasts. "And no, I didn't talk to Janey. I swear."

The perfect answer. Because she absolutely *hadn't* talked to Janey. Izzy hadn't said one single word to the cashier at the Larkspur Grill. Was it her fault their hands had brushed as Janey handed Izzy her change?

That one unexpected touch was all it had taken. For just an instant, she'd been Janey, watching Burt from afar, wondering if he'd ever say anything, *do* anything. And fantasizing that one day he'd walk into the restaurant bearing daisies.

Izzy couldn't just sit back and do nothing. Not with such a grand romance in the making.

And it was only a little bitty violation of the rules. And for a very good cause . . .

"—is that?"

Izzy realized she'd tuned Burt out. "Hmm? I'm sorry. What?"

"That noise. What is it?"

For the first time, she heard the *pound, pound, zip, whrrrr!* "Daddy," she said simply. The noises filtered up through the floor from the basement workshop below, but Izzy barely noticed. She'd grown up with her dad's banging and rumbling and tweaking and tightening. The man was forever working on some new and exotic invention, and after twenty-seven years of hearing his hammering, a few metallic bangs and well-placed curses were hardly enough to distract her.

Bang! Ka-chung! Ching! Pow!

"I should have known," Burt said. An ardent inventor, Izzy's dad had never quite risen to the level of his idol, Thomas Edison. Or anywhere close, to be exact. But he kept on trying, and the folks in town didn't mind his idiosyncrasies. Especially when Harold Frost was single-handedly responsible for keeping Main Street Hardware in business.

"Well, anyway," Burt continued, "thanks for suggesting the daisies." He gestured over his shoulder. "I'd better get going."

They said good-bye, and Izzy headed back inside, flopping down onto the couch and switching her laptop on. She clicked straight to the Council website, *www.superherocentral.com*, entered her password, and started scrolling through the news, wanting to see if the announcement of her new position had made the Daily Update. And if so, if anyone was posting nasty gossip about it on the Council's message boards.

The promotion had come from the High Elder himself, and it was just a coincidence of birth that Zephron happened to also be her uncle. So while some Protectors might look down their noses at her skills and whisper that she received special treatment, Izzy was determined not to be cowed; she deserved this promotion, and she intended to prove it.

For the last two years, she'd worked with low-level Outcasts—interviewing them, analyzing their psych profiles, and using her innate abilities to judge if they were worthy of returning to the fold. Starting tomorrow, though, she'd be dealing with the rogue Protectors who'd undertaken a lot more serious offenses. The promotion was exciting, yes, but also a little bit scary. Not that she'd ever admit *that* to anyone.

She scrolled down, staring idly at the colorful screen, but not really seeing. Her job was tough, no doubt about that. A lot of Protectors simply didn't want Outcasts reentering the fold, and Izzy could understand their reasoning. After all, as superheroes in the mortal world, the Protectors' sworn duty was to watch over mortals. Outcasts, though . . .

Most Outcasts had managed to break that sacred trust, and they'd paid the price by being shunned, stripped of their right to use their powers. Not that the censure stopped the truly nefarious Outcasts; they just continued in secret their evil plotting against the mortal race.

And it was precisely because of those plotting, scheming, conniving Outcasts that so many Protectors were against re-assimilation. And while Izzy knew where they were coming from, she also knew that *some* Protectors had been outcast for only minor infractions. Or for breaking some tenet of Protector law in order to serve the greater good. Or—

She cut her thoughts off with a sharp shake of her head. The fact that she could completely empathize with how a Protector could be outcast for a low-level offense was precisely the reason she had this job in the first place. Her primary Protector trait was empathy, and that was the skill she relied on primarily for her job. She picked up emotions in scent: a handy trait if she ever needed to know if someone was trying to pull the wool over her eyes.

She was also adept at mind reading; just one touch, and unless she'd had time to put up some heavy-duty mental blocks, she'd find herself awash in another person's specific thoughts, not just vague feelings. The skill was handy, but also draining. Even more, since Regulation 976B(2)(d) required a mind warrant or full disclosure (which re-assimilation candidates were required to give) before reading another Protector, Izzy tended to use her touch power only during the last phase of re-assimiliation.

Reading mortals was forbidden, too, and the regulations spelled out specific censures for any mind-reading Protector caught in the act. Izzy knew she shouldn't have meddled in Burt and Janey's romance, but some rules were meant to be broken. And considering how happy Burt now seemed, she could hardly regret her breach of protocol.

Her finger slid over the trackball as she scrolled through the boards, looking for a reference to herself. Nothing. Well, good. Maybe nobody was gossiping about her. After all, her skill had earned her the promotion. *Not* her family connections.

She repeated the thought, trying to make herself believe it. She knew she was good; knew her talents were real. Unfortunately, that didn't necessarily mean that she should have been admitted to the Council in the first place.

No.

She pushed the familiar doubt from her mind. So what if she'd received special dispensation? All Halfling applications were scrutinized, and they'd let her in because she was good—*not* because the High Elder happened to be her uncle.

Besides, that had been a long time ago. She'd pulled her own weight since then, and this promotion was no exception. She was going to ace this job, and she was going to prove to one and all that her uncle's confidence was justified.

No matter what, she'd—

"Fire! Fire!" The unfamiliar voice filtered through her mishmash of thoughts, and she shot to her feet, realizing that the banging and pounding had stopped, replaced by an ominous silence. *Her father!*

Jumping Jupiter, was he okay? What had he done now?

She raced to the back door and threw it open, revealing a stocky little man who vaguely resembled a hamster. She had no idea who he was, and she really didn't care. "Fire? Where?"

"Down there!" He stabbed at the air, pointing up rather than down, but it didn't matter. Izzy could see gray puffs of smoke rising into the air. The house was built into a hill and, as she leaned over the railing for a view of the basement window, there was a horrible clatter as the window blew out in a flurry of glass and flames.

"Daddy!" Izzy shrieked. Without thinking about the hamstery stranger, she bounded over the railing, jumping the two stories to the hard and dusty ground. She landed in a crouch, dropped into a roll, then sprang to her feet, never missing a step as she raced for the door.

She might not fight bad guys in the field, but at the moment her semi-rusty Protector skills were serving her just fine, thank you very much.

As she reached the now-decimated basement window, she heard the sound of someone slipping and sliding down the craggy slope behind her. Hamsterman, no doubt.

She didn't bother to see if her guess was right. Just waved away the dust and smoke and peered inside the workshop.

She'd expected a huge conflagration. Instead, she saw a lot of smoke, some charred feathers, and other unrecognizable bits of flotsam and jetsam smoldering in the various corners. Glass bottles, plastic flasks, screws, nails, wires of all colors. Even a collection of deep purple fountain pens, scattered like Pick-up Sticks in a puddle of green goo.

And, thank goodness, her father was there, too, huddled in the corner, worrying at a large metal box with an oversized screwdriver. His white hair stood straight out in all directions, and black streaks marred his face, giving him the appearance of a rather baffled, and somewhat incompetent, soldier in camouflage.

As far as Izzy could tell, he hadn't yet seen her. For that matter, he didn't even seem to realize there'd been a fire. Much less that bits of trash were still smoldering around him.

"Daddy!"

He looked up, blinked owlishly behind his thick glasses, and then smiled. "Izzy, my girl, I think I've finally got it!"

"Got it?" She swiveled, her gaze taking in the workroom that looked more or less like the aftermath of a tornado. "Got what?"

"Doesn't matter, doesn't matter. Far too complicated to go into now." He climbed to his feet and started dusting himself off, for the first time squinting around the room. "Hmmmph. Going to have to find something less flammable than gunpowder for the starting reaction, *that's* for sure."

He wasn't talking to her, and so Izzy just watched as her father patted himself down.

"Pencils, notes. Ah, yes. Here. Now then." He frowned. "Where are my glasses?" He swiveled, his gaze sweeping in an arc over the floor.

"Daddy . . ."

"Just a minute, sweetie. I'm looking for my glasses."

"They're on your head, Daddy."

"They are?" He looked cross-eyed, obviously focusing on the bridge piece. "So they are!"

She shook her head, fighting a smile. Her father was a dear, and not really *that* absentminded. He just had a tendency to lose himself in his work. After two or three hours away from the basement, he'd be good as new.

"Come on, Daddy. Let's make sure this fire is out and then head upstairs. I'll fix you lunch, and you can tell me what happened."

"Oh, no, no. I couldn't go now. I'm right on the verge!"

Izzy looked dubiously at the collection of wires and circuits on his worktable. "Uh. Yeah."

"It's just a matter of tweaking the design, so I don't overload the transmitter or the receivers. Oh, Mr. B is going to be delighted. Just delighted!" He actually clapped his hands together, and Izzy couldn't help but grin.

"Who's Mr. B?" she asked.

"Oh, my dear, you're going to love him. He's been an inspiration. An absolute inspiration. We've been working together now for a year, and I swear, the man has insight into my work that's simply—"

"Help! Get it away from me! Help!"

"Oh, my goodness gracious, the servo-bot!" her father cried.

Izzy swung around in time to see what she'd thought was a pile of tin cans and rubbish grab Hamster-man. Apparently the thing was some sort of robot, and now it stood tall, tin-can head twisting this way and that, as one hinged arm swung upward, Hamster-man dangling from a viselike grip that served as a hand.

"Help me! Put me down!"

The servo-bot (whatever the heck *that* was) didn't seem inclined to cooperate; and instead of releasing the poor man, it simply started spinning—going round and round on the roller-skate wheels that served as feet—while its poor prisoner screamed and screamed for the metallic creation to *put him down.*

"No, no," her father shouted. "Mr. Tucker, *please* don't speak. The voice reactor node is damaged. The bot thinks you're saying '*around.*' "

"I am *not,*" cried the little man. "Put me down!"

But that just got the bot riled up some more, and around and around he turned, while Mr. Tucker's complexion shifted through various shades of green.

"Daddy!" Izzy cried. "Where's the control? Shut that thing off before Mr. Tucker gets hurt." Even as she spoke, she was racing to the far side of the room, toward the spinning robot and the flailing Mr. Tucker. Ideally, she'd use her innate Protector power of levitation to lift the robot off the floor and stop him from spinning. Then she could get Mr. Tucker loose before putting the robot safely out of harm's way.

Unfortunately, she didn't *have* any innate Protector power of levitation. That was her dirty little stigma—the fact that she'd been admitted to the Council even though, as a Protector, she was truly subpar, unable to pass an examination of even the most rudimentary Protector skills.

"It's not functioning," her father yelled from behind her. "Ah, blasted thing!" She could hear him whacking the controls against something hard, curses flying from his lips.

In front of her, the bot was still spinning and Mr. Tucker's eyes were beginning to bulge.

Well, she might not be an ace at levitation, but she still had strength and agility in her repertoire, and it was time to put them to good use. But as she started to jump into the fray, the bot's head began to spark, the little flashes dancing around his head like lightning bugs.

"The CPU," her father hollered. "It's flammable. One of those sparks catches, and—"

Kabloom!

The bot's head shot straight off, but losing his head didn't mean losing his grip, and the now headless and flaming robot was still holding tight to Mr. Tucker.

"That's just the beginning," her dad cried, still banging away at the remote. "Oh, dear, oh dear, *where* did I put that fire extinguisher?"

Just the beginning? And then Izzy realized. The bot

14

was writhing in a mass of electricity, shaking as if being attacked by a thousand electric eels. The entire thing was going to blow, and if the force of the first explosion was any indication, Mr. Tucker was going to be in serious trouble when the even more massive robot torso lit up like a Roman candle.

With no time to waste, Izzy stood stock-still in the middle of the room, ignoring all the sound, and especially ignoring Mr. Tucker's screams to please get him down *now*. She couldn't afford the distraction. Couldn't afford to mess up. She had one shot and one shot only.

And then she heard it. A faint electrical crackle as the CPU ignited. She wasn't ready—hadn't let her power fully fill her—but hopefully she was ready enough.

With one quick movement, she lashed out, sending a shower of icy sparks flying from her fingertips. Her aim was dead-on . . . and her timing was perfect. Just as the bot started to explode, Izzy's ice storm enveloped it, essentially dousing the flames and leaving nothing but the gentle sizzle of steam rising to fill the room.

"I . . . what . . . who . . . help . . ." Mr. Tucker's weak cries filtered through the haze, and Izzy picked her way to him, then pried open the bot's viselike hands so that the little man could fall, uninjured, to the ground.

"Oh, good job, Izzy." Her father rushed up behind her, clapping his hands. Then he reached down and helped Mr. Tucker to his feet, and began shaking the little man's hand vigorously. "Mr. Tucker. So very, very good to finally meet you. As you can see, things can get a little out of control here in the lab. But that's the exciting life of an inventor."

"I, yes. Yes, I see that." Mr. Tucker squinted at him. "You *are* Harold Frost?"

"Of course. Of course. And this is my daughter, Izzy."

15

She wiggled her fingers in a little wave. "Hello."

"But who . . . how?"

"Another one of my inventions," Harold lied. "Izzy's testing my, um, my . . ."

"Freezing beam," Izzy said helpfully. "Top secret. Government. Very hush-hush. Do keep it quiet."

Mr. Tucker nodded, looking absurdly proud to have been rescued by a top secret device. "Of course. Of course. But what a pity it's a secret. Something like this would liven up the speech considerably."

Izzy frowned. "Speech?" She looked between her dad and Mr. Tucker, finally settling on the newcomer, who smelled of self-importance. "Who are you?"

"Why, I'm here to interview your father, of course. The ceremony is just days away!"

"Ceremony?"

"But of course. Your father is receiving the prestigious Thomas Edison Award from the North American Inventors' Association. Of course there will be a ceremony. In Manhattan, no less. The chairman asked me to speak to your father and then write his speech for the presentation."

"Daddy!" Izzy threw her arms around her father, who managed to hug her back with equal enthusiasm while still maintaining a humble aura.

"Why didn't you tell me?" she demanded, wishing her skills worked on her father so that she could simply see into his soul and share his joy. Her entire life, her father had been trying to make something out of himself and his inventions. She knew the last year had been really good for him, but she'd had no idea he'd done so well. And to now be receiving such a prestigious award, it was . . . well: "It's fabulous, Daddy. I just can't believe it."

"I wanted to tell you, sweetie. But I thought it would

be more fun to surprise you. No one knows. Just me and Mr. B."

She frowned. That was the second time her father had mentioned this person, and she had no idea who he was.

Mr. Tucker apparently wasn't at a similar loss. "Ah, yes." He pulled a notepad out of his front pocket and flipped a few pages. "Your mysterious benefactor."

"Not so mysterious," Harold said. "More inspirational."

"Who?" Izzy asked.

"About a year ago, I met the most remarkable man," her father said. He gestured toward the door, then started walking that way, leaving the broken remains of the bot and his other experiments behind. "Let's go have a spot of tea and I'll tell you all about it."

"Daddy!" Izzy stayed rooted to the spot. "Just tell me *now.*"

Her father adjusted his glasses. "Well, there's not much to tell. He's provided me with some financial backing, which, as you know," he said, turning to Mr. Tucker, "is so very important." He turned back to face Izzy. "But mostly he provided me with a sounding board. Someone to discuss my theories with. He always said he wasn't an inventor himself, but I don't believe him. The man has a remarkable head on his shoulders. Remarkable."

She was still confused. "So, this man just popped in and gave you money? Why?"

"Well, because he supports my work, of course." Her father grinned. "And he's commissioned me to invent a few things for him, too."

"Things? What things?"

"Oh, this and that." Her father waved a hand. "It doesn't matter. The point is that Mr. Black has been a wonderful support." He turned back to Mr. Tucker. "I'd have to credit his inspiration on equal par with my daughter's support. Be sure and mention both of them in that speech, will you?"

"Of course," Mr. Tucker said, taking notes furiously. "And you'll need to write a speech, too. The members will want to hear from you after you've accepted the statue."

"A speech," her father murmured, practically preening.

Izzy barely noticed. Her brain had stopped back when her father had said two nerve-wracking little words—*Mr. Black.*

. "Daddy?" she asked, then realized that her throat hadn't worked quite properly. She tried again. "Daddy?"

"Hmmm?" He and Mr. Tucker had moved a few feet closer to the door, and now they stopped and looked back at her. "Yes, dear?"

"Uh, this Mr. Black. Is he . . . that is, do you know his first name?"

"Oh, of course," her father said. He turned back to Mr. Tucker. "But that reminds me. He insists on being an anonymous benefactor, so you'll have to call him Mr. B in the speech. Not Mr. Black."

"Mr. B," Mr. Tucker said, scribbling furiously. "Right."

They started walking again.

"Daddy!" .

"Hmm? Oh, yes. His name. Fascinating, really. It's Hieronymous. You hardly ever hear a name like that, you know."

No, Izzy thought, as her blood ran cold. She didn't suppose mortals did hear a name like that very often.

She did, though. Because Hieronymous was the most notorious Outcast of the whole Protector race.

And for some reason, Hieronymous Black was helping her father.

She had no idea what was really going on, but she did know one thing—whatever it was, it couldn't be good.

Chapter Two

Mordichai perched on top of the Empire State Building. The wind had kicked up, and even now in the middle of August, the air this high was chilled. Mordi hardly noticed, though. His favorite propulsion and invisibility cloak was wrapped tight around his shoulders, a barrier against the elements and a shield against prying eyes.

Of course, *this* high the only prying eyes would be the tourists with their zoom lenses peering straight up or passengers in low-flying aircraft looking to see if King Kong was home. For a moment, he amused himself by picturing the faces of those passengers if he decided to shapeshift into the giant ape, hang on to the building's spire, and beat his chest.

He bit back a grin. Fun to think about, but probably a little too flamboyant for a stakeout. Better to sit quietly and invisibly up here and wait for his quarry to appear below.

And so he waited. And waited. And waited some more. He was thrilled to no longer be on probation, to be a full-fledged one-hundred-percent member of the

21

Council. But he had to admit that on some days a life of legitimacy could be exceedingly dull.

Not that Mordi had any regrets. He didn't. He'd walked away from his father and from the Outcast life, and he wasn't about to look back. A little tedium was worth the price for knowing that now, finally, he was doing the right thing. And besides, the moments of tedium were usually counterbalanced by unexpected flurries of pure adrenal excitement.

He stifled a yawn. At the moment, some of that excitement would be most welcome.

Forcing himself to focus, he once again aimed his binocs at the street below. There'd been many a time when he'd envied his cousin Zoë, whose superpowers included super senses, but never more so than times like these, when he was on a stakeout and could really, *really* use super hearing or super vision.

Lacking either, he instead adjusted the high-powered binocs, aiming them at the street. For three days, he'd been following Clyde, an Outcast who was wanted by the Council for violating not only the strict prohibition against Outcasts using their powers, but also for seeking to inflict harm on a mortal.

Several mortals, actually. Before he went on the lam, Clyde had been Hieronymous Black's right-hand man, doing much of the bigwig Outcast's dirty work.

It was Hieronymous's firm opinion that mortals were a substandard race, and that Protectors who sought to protect them were short-sighted and foolish. In Hieronymous's mind, Protectors were like gods, and those measly little mortals should bend to his will. If the mortals didn't like that plan . . . well, then too bad. Hieronymous would have no trouble at all simply exterminating their entire race.

Mordi stifled a shudder, recalling some of Hieronymous's more extreme plots. So many times the brilliant Outcast had almost succeeded. Scary, really. And now, with the Council and the mortal governments renegotiating the Secret Mortal-Protector Treaty of 1970 . . . well, Mordi supposed it was a good thing that mortals didn't know just how many times they'd come *that* close to extinction or enslavement. If mortals knew how much some Outcasts had it in for them, and how possible it was that any Protector might turn Outcast, they'd probably be supremely leery about signing a treaty with *any* of super blood—even the good guys.

And for every stunt that Hieronymous had pulled, Clyde had been right there. He was the muscle enforcing his commander's will. The perfect soldier, ready to do whatever Hieronymous might ask.

Mordi stifled a grimace, wishing he could keep his thoughts in little boxes so he wouldn't keep thinking about Hieronymous. Or, barring that, he wished he could think of Hieronymous *only* as an Outcast.

He tried; really he did. But no matter how much he attempted to wrest some control of his thoughts, eventually Mordi's mind returned to the facts: who Hieronymous was—*his blood, his sire.* Hieronymous was Mordi's father.

Frustrated, he twisted on the building's spire, his gaze taking in the full length of Fifth Avenue. He and Hieronymous might share the same blood, but that didn't mean they were related. Not anymore. Yes, there was a time when Mordi leaped when his father said "boo," but that time was long gone.

He'd never once managed to please Hieronymous, and now he wasn't even trying. Mordi had moved on. He'd found a place among the Council. A place where not only was he useful, he was *appreciated.*

His mind wandered to his recent conversation with Zephron, in which the High Elder had asked that

Mordi and Mordi's cousin Zoë participate in the ongoing treaty renegotiations. After all, Halflings were half-mortal; Zephron thought their presence at the negotiating table might ease the mortal ambassadors' minds.

An ironic twist of fate, all things considered. Hieronymous had always scorned Mordi's Halfling status. Now that very status had elevated him to the upper echelons of the Council. Instead of being scorned, he was needed. And that, frankly, had been a long time coming.

Right now, though, he was determined not to think about his father or the negotiations. He was here to watch Clyde. And by doing so, Mordi would catch himself yet another traitor. Lucky thirteen this one would be. And Mordi couldn't wait.

As if his thoughts had conjured the man, Clyde appeared on the street below, his hulking form emerging from one of the office buildings and loping toward Thirty-fourth Street. Mordi's fingers tightened around the binocs as he wondered if today would be the day.

As a member of the Protector Oversight Committee, Mordi had been privy to recent intelligence suggesting that a certain well-placed Protector had been assisting and passing information to Clyde and other Outcasts.

But it wasn't Clyde that Mordi was after. No, the Outcast was proving too useful at ferreting out spies and traitors within the Council's organization.

Today, Mordi was hoping to catch Romulus Rothgar in the act.

A Protector First Class, Romulus was the last person that anyone would think was a traitor. Anyone, that is, except Mordi.

He'd been watching Romulus for months. Watching his face in particular. And his shuttered expression

Mordi recognized. He'd seen it before, on the faces of his father's comrades, and on his own reflection before he'd finally come to terms with who he was and what he truly wanted.

No, Mordi had no doubts at all. Romulus had something to hide, and Mordi intended to figure out what it was.

Unfortunately, on this mission he was on his own. He'd sought approval from his supervisor, but Elder Bilius had turned him down. Romulus had a perfect record and an upstanding family, and that knowledge enveloped him, a solid blanket of protection.

So now Mordi was here unofficially, gliding through the sky, his propulsion cloak set to silent mode as he followed Clyde, hovering a good twenty feet above the Outcast and at a respectable distance behind him. If Romulus *did* meet with Clyde, then Mordi was golden; interaction between Protectors and Outcasts-on-the-lam was a punishable offense. Mordi was certain a meeting would take place . . . and he intended to be there when it went down.

Clyde moved with deliberation down the street, and Mordi hoped that he didn't descend into one of the subway stations. No such luck, for after a few more blocks Clyde did just that, disappearing into the subterranean bowels of Manhattan.

Damn it to Hades! This was most inconvenient.

Mordi swooped down, still invisible, leaving in his wake a rush of wild air. The stairs were narrow, and he brushed against a woman, her startled cry from being thrust aside by something solid and invisible echoing through the corridor.

As soon as he reached the inside of the station, he stopped, glancing around until he saw Clyde, who was biding his time on the platform.

Romulus, however, was nowhere to be seen. *Hades and damnation*, surely Mordi wasn't off on a wild-Outcast chase!

In the distance, a train started to rumble. Mordi leaned against a tiled pillar and waited, foot tapping. As soon as Clyde got on that train, Mordi would follow. He'd follow the Outcast all day if he had to; he had no intention of failing.

The floor and walls seemed to vibrate in time with the train's approach, and Mordi stood up a bit straighter, frowning as he realized that a blond woman clutching a baby was staring in his direction, her mouth hanging slightly open in a less than attractive manner.

Forgetting he was invisible, he frowned at her. "Yes?"

"You . . . you're see-through!"

Uh-oh. Mordi glanced down and realized that she was right. The power cell on his cloak must be fading, because its power of invisibility was fading right along with it, leaving him looking like some sort of specter.

He nodded politely to the woman, then moved to the far side of the pillar. As he walked, he shifted forms, turning himself into a sleek black Labrador retriever. There didn't seem to be any policemen around for that to be a problem.

He padded back out, this time finding Clyde more by scent than anything else. He loped in the Outcast's direction, realizing but not really caring that the blond woman was slowly backing out of the station, her baby pressed tightly to her breast.

Mordi plunked down on the cold concrete and started scratching. In front of him, the approaching train rumbled to a stop. Mordi tensed, preparing to follow Clyde onto the train.

But Clyde stayed perfectly still, and soon, Mordi saw why. Romulus, tall and blond and dressed in jeans and a black T-shirt, a backpack slung casually over one shoulder, stepped off the train and onto the platform.

Mordi's tail wagged. He'd been *right*.

As Mordi watched, however, Romulus did nothing suspicious, didn't even glance in Clyde's direction. Instead, he checked his watch, then looked at the newly installed electronic board that dutifully announced the next train would be arriving in seven minutes, preceded by an express that wouldn't stop but simply zip through the station at high speed.

With what sounded like a sigh of annoyance, Romulus crossed to the pillar near Mordi, pulling out a stick of gum as he walked and popping it into his mouth. As soon as he reached the pillar, he dropped his backpack on the ground. Mordi fought the overwhelming urge to lift one leg and mark the thing.

No. Dignity, remember? In all things, dignity.

Romulus stood and unfolded a street map of Manhattan, holding it up to the light and twisting and turning. Mordi yawned, a deep doggie yawn, but neither Romulus nor Clyde seemed to hear or otherwise notice him.

Clyde walked toward the pillar, then reached into his pocket and pulled out an old candy wrapper. He dropped it into the nearby trash can. And, Mordi noticed, he did a little bit more than that. In fact, had Mordi not been watching the two of them so closely, he doubted he would have caught the subtle act. But right after dropping the candy wrapper, Clyde dropped a single slip of paper into the now-open backpack.

Then Clyde kept on walking, right toward the stairs that led out of the station.

The tempo of Mordi's tail-wagging increased. A bone-deep desire for revenge urged him to follow Clyde. The Outcast had always looked down on him and, petty though it might be, Mordi could think of little more satisfying than sinking his canines into Clyde's gluteus maximus.

But, no. That urge could wait. He was only one dog, after all, and his self-appointed mission was to catch Romulus in an act of treason. Romulus might not have directly acknowledged Clyde—thus deftly dodging *that* violation—but the note passed from Clyde might just prove the link between the two.

Mordi needed to get that note.

Romulus hadn't moved, so Mordi assumed the Protector intended to hop the next train and get out of the station that way. Fine. Mordi could simply follow him on. There didn't seem to be any transit police around; the odds that anyone would try to apprehend a dog on the subway were reasonably slim.

The station started to fill with the distant rumble of the approaching express train. Romulus picked up his backpack and started to move toward the edge of the platform. Mordi didn't hurry to follow. This train, after all, was an express. It was the next that Romulus would be catching.

Whoosh, rumble, rumble, whoosh. The deep bass of the train filled the station, and Mordi wanted to howl against the sound grating on his canine ears.

To the right, a pinpoint of light broke the darkness that filled the tunnel, growing larger as the train approached, until the headlight bore down on the track, illuminating the way into and out of the station.

The train drew closer, not slowing at all, but instead of staying behind the yellow line demarking the safe area of the platform, Romulus moved over it. By the time Mordi realized what his quarry intended to do, it was already too late. Romulus jumped, leaping with perfectly timed precision to land right in front of the train.

The speeding express never stopped, didn't even

slow down, and Mordi's howls of frustration harmonized with the squeal and clatter of the train along the tracks.

He trotted forward, nose sniffing the air as he tried in vain to pick up the scent of the vanished Protector.

Nothing. Damn it all to Hades, his quarry was truly gone.

Frustrated at himself for letting Romulus get away, Mordi paced back and forth on the platform, his four doggie legs moving in an instinctual rhythm. That's what was driving him—instinct. And his hunter's intuition was telling him that the game wasn't over yet.

Plunking his rump down again, he lifted his nose into the air, trying to make some sense of the odd mishmash of scents that were accosting his olfactory nerves.

Rotting food. Dead vermin. Stale perfume. Grease. The sharp scent left by metal scraping metal. Cinnamon.

Cinnamon?

Mordi got up on all fours again, searching for the source of the smell even as his mind rewound to the memory he was seeking—Romulus stepping onto the platform, tucking a strip of gum into his mouth and sauntering over to the pillar.

Smells conjured memories and, in this case, Mordi was certain. The gum had been cinnamon-flavored. And the scent that he now caught belonged to Romulus.

But where was he?

The one thing that Mordi's initial research had failed to turn up was Romulus's personnel file, and now the absence of that information frustrated him. If he only knew what the Protector's special powers were, he might have a better idea where the man was hiding.

Because he *was* hiding. By now, Mordi was certain. Not only had his trusty nose put in a vote, but the distinct absence of any guts and goo on the rails below more than suggested that Romulus had not leapt to his death.

Think, Mordi, think.

He paced, tail wagging in thought, ears plastered back in frustration, haunches moving with a sure and steady motion.

And then he realized. The answer was so simple, it had to be right.

If Romulus hadn't left, then he must still be there. Mordi simply couldn't see him. But with a little bit of persuasion, Mordi was certain he could convince the rogue Protector to show himself.

Three mortals had wandered onto the platform, waiting for the next train that, according to the display, was due to roll into the station in four minutes.

Well, there was nothing Mordi could do about them. Hopefully the MLO would be able to concoct some sort of spin, planting a story in the papers designed to make Mordi's less-than-normal activities seem perfectly explainable.

He couldn't execute his plan in dog form, and so he loped back to the pillar, circling it once more and this time emerging in his usual form. His clothing always transformed with him—the cloth changing into fur, or another outfit, or whatever was appropriate—and now he emerged in one of the tailored suits he favored.

Not that he was going for fashion here. He raced toward the platform and leaped over the edge, letting flames engulf his entire body, gathering them as he soared through the air to land beside the train tracks.

Behind him, mortals screamed, but Mordi ignored them. He sent a wave of fire dancing along the tracks, flames tickling every surface—both seen and unseen.

His ploy worked.

As waves of flame rolled over the beams of the train tracks, another shape emerged from between them, a lumpy shape, defined only by the fire that clung to it.

The fire rose up in the shape of a man, and Mordi knew he'd been right—Romulus had the power to make himself invisible. Either that, or he had an invisibility cloak. And somehow he'd realized that Mordi was on to him and hidden in plain sight, carefully avoiding the third rail as he crouched on the track. Now, though, Romulus was running, a streak of pure flame taking off into the depths of the train tunnel.

Mordi raced after him, shifting back into canine form as he did, since a superhero dog with four legs tends to be faster than a superhero with only two.

He could hear the gasps and overloud whispers coming from the platforms, and a headline flashed through his head—*circus performers attempt double suicide.*

Might work.

He didn't have time to ponder further journalistic possibilities, however, because Romulus was picking up speed.

Oh, no, you don't. Mordi leaped, landing on the rogue's back and knocking him to the ground. Romulus groaned, letting out a short, breathy *oof* before rolling over and, finally, materializing.

"You're in so much trouble," Mordi said. Then he realized that, since he was once again a dog, his words would sound like only so much barking to Romulus.

Apparently, though, his captive got the drift. His shoulders sagged in defeat, and Mordi felt the thrill of victory trill through his veins.

The thrill was short-lived. Only seconds later, Romulus was looking at him, pure contempt burning in his eyes.

"Well, if it isn't Mordichai Black."

Mordi shifted back to his human form, surprised Romulus managed to spot him through his canine disguise. Some Protectors, though, had the ability to see

31

past a shapeshifter's change, and that must have been how Romulus had clued into Mordi's presence in the first place.

"So it is," he said. "And you're under arrest."

"Hypocritical little puppy, aren't you?" Romulus sneered.

Mordi crossed his arms over his chest and tried to maintain an air of authority. "Wrists. Now."

Romulus jutted his arms out, wrists together, and submitted to the binder cuffs. Mordi gave them a tug, testing to make sure they were secure, then slipped an immobility lariat over his captive.

No, Romulus wasn't going anywhere.

With the rogue Protector secured, Mordi bent over and plucked the man's fallen backpack from the train tracks. He rifled through, finally finding the paper that Romulus had dug out of the trash can. He opened the note, then frowned at the nonsense written there:

Holmes says: The game's afoot.

What the hell?

He waved the note under Romulus's nose. "What's this mean?"

The Protector snorted. "Give me a break," he said. "You think you're hot stuff just because you're Zephron's newest tattletale? You're nothing, Mordichai. *Nothing.* And I'm not telling you anything."

"Fine. We'll see if you talk in a holding cell." Mordi flipped open his holopager, taking his time to dial in the correct frequency to summon a retrieval team. This might have started out as an off-the-books mission, but the circumstances and the note were enough to engage Mordi's authority to arrest.

"You little worm," Romulus continued, his voice rising. "You're just like me, and you know it. Who are you trying to fool? Zephron? That old fart's an artifact."

Mordi stiffened, stifling the urge to punch his captive in the face.

"You'll see," Romulus sneered. "You of all people should know Zephron's on the outs. The whole Council is. You should be working with us, not against us. It wasn't so long ago that you were on the winning side, Mordi. You're just like me. You've just forgotten."

A thousand snappy comebacks sprang to Mordi's lips, nice-sounding words about honor and duty and the Protector's Oath. He didn't say a one of them.

Because Mordi hadn't forgotten. Hopping Hades, he could *never* forget. Try as he might, his heritage would follow him—plague him—forever. The Halfling son of Hieronymous Black would never have an easy time of it.

And even though he'd proved his worth to the Council time and time again, Mordi knew that he'd have to go on proving himself, over and over for the rest of his life.

Chapter Three

Down, down, down.

As the elevator dropped deeper and deeper, Izzy paced the small compartment counting how many steps wide (three) and how many steps deep (two). She tugged idly at the hem of her jacket, and considered her theory that elevator cars were really nothing more than vertical caskets.

Stop it!

She fisted her hands at her sides, determined not to freak out. Yes, she was in an elevator. Yes, it was taking her deep into the ground under the Washington Monument. Yes, she was going to end up in a room with only circulated air to breathe and not a window in sight and absolutely no way to escape if the fans suddenly stopped turning, leaving everyone to die slow, painful deaths from asphyxiation.

Okay. She really needed to get herself under control here.

One more deep breath.

Then another.

Okay. *Okay.* Yes. Right. Things were improving. Her

skin wasn't quite so clammy, her breathing was normal, and her heart was no longer racing.

Try again.

Yes, she was going to be underground, but the secret Protector headquarters under the Washington Monument had existed without incident since the 1970s. Certainly it would manage to hang in there a few more years.

Yes, the air was circulated and the room was windowless, but the staff was comprised primarily of superheroes. If the fans quit turning, she was quite certain that at least one staff member could bore through the earth and concrete and lead them all to safety.

Yes, she had horrible claustrophobia, but she'd been fighting it for years, and she could fight it again today. She'd never once heard of a Protector with a debilitating phobia, and Izzy didn't intend to be the first. She took enough ribbing for being a Halfling, and even more for being raised by a mortal father who hadn't even introduced her to her heritage through her mother until junior high.

And, of course, there was that whole business about the Council accepting her Halfling application even though she'd never mastered levitation.

Determined, she lifted her chin. She'd been tormented enough. She had no intention of giving her colleagues any additional ammunition by showing that she was scared of an elevator. She'd never lost her cool at the office, and she didn't intend to start now.

By the time the metal box ground to a halt and she stepped out into the polished lobby of the Venerate Council's D.C. headquarters, Izzy had completely pulled herself together. The steel doors of the elevator were polished to a shine, and she caught her own reflection. Shoulders back, spine straight. Suit perfectly pressed. Eyes clear and focused. Hair swept away from her face and pinned up in a no-muss/no-fuss style. All in all, the picture of professionalism.

Footfalls clattered on the marble floor, and a young Protector rounded the corner, clipboard held in front of him like a shield. "Oh, good. You're here. Right on time. Shall we? Elder Bilius is ready for you."

"Excellent," she said, lifting her chin and making sure to put the appropriate note of authority in her voice. "Let's hurry. I don't want to keep him waiting."

The guide straightened, and from his scent she could tell that he was used to responding to authority—and that now he saw *her* in that light. Good.

He turned briskly and led the way, marching down the hall with purpose. Izzy followed, her footfalls echoing as they passed through hallways lined with file cabinets and cubicles, each cubicle staffed by a mortal busy entering information into the vast Protector databases. There were dozens of mortals working as salaried employees of the Council (the health insurance was an especially nice perk). Other mortals worked with the Council on a project-by-project basis, most often employed by the Mortal-Protector Liaison Office to concoct some sort of cover story to keep all Protectors' activities secret.

Did a battle break out at Sea World, with Outcasts and Protectors streaking through the sky, throwing fire and talking with the cetaceans? Did a Protector leap from a Los Angeles skyscraper, then rescue a small boy from wandering into oncoming traffic? No problem. The MLO's mortal stringer would figure out a plausible explanation. And by the time the story was run in every major newspaper, even the eyewitnesses would begin to think they misremembered.

Needless to say, being a spin doctor for the MLO was a highly popular job.

She could use one of the spin doctors' talents now, that was for sure. As it was, she still hadn't decided what to do about the little bombshell her father had let drop yesterday.

He was actually working with Hieronymous Black!

She'd followed him and Mr. Tucker back into the house, asking just enough innocuous questions to confirm that her father had no idea that Hieronymous was a Protector, much less that he was an Outcast, currently wanted by the Council as a result of a lifetime of heinous acts culminating most recently in the kidnapping of a Halfling child.

No, all her dad knew was that the man had money (Hieronymous did) and that he had great insight into her father's inventions (Hieronymous was big into inventing things).

She'd almost opened her mouth right then to tell her father just who Hieronymous was. After all, her father had a right to know that he'd been working with villainous scum determined to end the mortal race. But in the end, she hadn't said a word. Right as she'd opened her mouth, Mr. Tucker had started his spiel about the success of her dad's newest inventions, and how honored they were to name him Inventor of the Year after he'd spent a lifetime struggling, and her father's eyes had sparkled and he'd held Izzy's hand and squeezed.

Her powers might not work on her father, but at that moment, she hardly needed them. This was what her father had been living for. How could she take that away from him?

She couldn't. She'd opened her mouth—once, twice, even three times—but no words had come out. Nothing except congratulations.

"Zephron will be in right after your meeting with Elder Bilius," the guide said.

Izzy's head snapped up in surprise, but she only

nodded curtly, taking care to make sure her expression held no hint that her mind had wandered . . . or that she was now worried. She'd had no idea her uncle was coming by. Did he already know about her father?

The guide was still standing there, as if he was expecting some sort of reaction from her. She waved her hand in a manner she hoped looked unconcerned, as if he'd just delivered old news and he should really quit boring her. "I thought I asked you to hurry," she said, just a teensy bit amazed that she managed to pull off an authoritarian tone. She really was getting good at this professional-woman-on-the-go thing.

His face flushed and he hurried off. She followed, her mind occupied by the irony of her current situation. Here she was playing the totally together counselor when the truth was, she could be Outcast at any moment.

Her stomach twisted with the thought, and she wanted to go home and hide, the covers pulled high over her head. But there was no escaping the truth. Her father had entered into a commercial arrangement with a known Outcast . . . and Izzy was aware of the situation. Regulations were crystal clear. Failure to immediately report such Outcast intervention in mortal affairs was an outcastable offense.

She *had* to report it.

But reporting it would devastate her father.

Her stomach twisted some more and the hall seemed suddenly very cramped.

The guard stopped, and Izzy almost plowed into his back, her professional façade starting to falter. "Conference room," he said, looking at her with a slightly furrowed brow. "Elder Bilius should be here soon."

"Right." She nodded in dismissal. "Thank you for the escort."

For a moment she thought he was going to say

something else, but in the end he simply left, pulling the door closed behind him. As soon as she heard the latch click, she relaxed, rolling her shoulders and glancing around the austere room dominated by a huge mahogany table surrounded by twelve chairs. The walls were bare, painted stark white and seeming to reflect back the overly bright lights, giving the conference room an otherworldy quality, as if its occupants had stepped into a cloud.

She'd been here twice before, and each time the room had intimidated the hell out of her. The first time, she'd been thirteen, a gawky Halfling doing nothing more than visiting a newly discovered relative, to say nothing of a newly discovered heritage.

The second time, she'd been less self-conscious and certainly less confused, but the intimidation factor had still been there. She'd been twenty-five, and the purpose of her visit was to go over her Halfling application for admission to the Council. Zephron had told her she'd been accepted despite her pathetic failings, and the bright light of the room had seemed like the light of a hundred angels singing the Hallelujah Chorus in perfect harmony.

That had been an amazing day. She'd been so certain that her application would be rejected. But Zephron had brushed off her doubts and quelled her feelings of inadequacy, telling his niece simply that her skills were needed.

Needed. She'd practically preened. To be part of the Venerate Council: that esteemed, secret organization dedicated to protecting mortals and making the world a better place. From the moment she'd learned of her heritage, that had been all she'd ever wanted. She'd fought hard, worked hard, and she'd gotten in. Her peers might turn up their noses and whisper of *nepotism,* but Izzy knew that she'd worked her tush off.

She deserved to be on the Council. She deserved her job. And she couldn't muck it all up by failing to disclose a known incident of Outcast Intervention in Mortal Affairs.

She had to speak up. Right here. Right now.

She knew that, and yet . . .

Frowning, she circled the table, her arm outstretched so that her fingertips brushed the polished surface of the walls. Her hands were probably leaving fingerprints, but she didn't care. For that matter, she barely realized what she was doing; she was too caught up in the memory of her father. In the recollection of that light in his eyes.

It was a light she rarely saw, and she would do anything to make sure it didn't fade. Including staying quiet.

Breaking a rule, yes. But hopefully she wouldn't get caught. After all, it was for a very good cause.

And she'd be careful. She'd keep a sharp eye on her father. If it looked like Hieronymous was up to any nefarious activities, then she'd report him and simply say she'd just found out.

Until then . . . well, so help her, she was going to keep silent. If that's what it took for the light to continue to burn in her father's eyes, then she'd stay quiet forever.

The door opened and Bilius strode in, a forest-green cape billowing behind him as he walked. He didn't look at her, merely perused a tablet held in front of him. Izzy stood on tiptoes, trying to appear unobtrusive, but also trying to see what the document said.

She couldn't see a thing.

He snapped the tablet down to his side and looked at her, his pale gray eyes seeming to absorb the light in the room. His face was harsh, all lines and angles, and she had to remind herself to stand up straight and not cower like a little girl.

"I want you to know I did not support the decision to promote you," he said without preamble.

"Oh." She reached out, steadying herself against the wall. She blinked, fast and hard. She would *not* cry.

He stared at her, as if expecting her to say something else. Well, he was going to be damned disappointed, because she was truly at a loss.

Finally, he sighed, then lifted his tablet again. He made a tick mark, and she imagined him putting a check by *Humiliate Isole Frost.*

She frowned, then sniffed, picking up subtle hints of Bilius's emotions. He hid his feelings well, but still she caught the edges: no-nonsense professionalism and a deep contempt. Contempt for her, of course. By now, she really ought to be used to it.

Bilius focused on her for a few more minutes, as if once again waiting for her to speak. She wasn't about to give him the satisfaction. He glowered, but finally spoke. "As I said, I do not approve of this promotion, but there is no doubt that your record—on paper, at least—supports it."

Izzy bristled, her entire body tensing at the suggestion that somehow her work record had been forged.

"Nonetheless," he continued, "I have only your record to work with, and the ultimate decision regarding promotions is, unfortunately, not up to me."

Great. She'd be reporting to a man who had absolutely no interest in seeing her succeed. This just kept getting better and better.

"The decision for upcoming assignments has been made, and you have been selected to evaluate a somewhat challenging candidate. Were it up to me, I would not leave the responsibility for such a vile Outcast in your hands."

She frowned, the scent of his contempt for this particular candidate almost overwhelming. The stench of his distrust seemed to fill the air; this was not an Outcast that Bilius wanted re-assimilated. Of *that*, she was certain. Who, though, could the Outcast be?

She was just about to ask when the elder continued. "The responsibility is too great to entrust it to someone with less than perfect credentials," Bilius said, as Izzy's cheeks burned with shame. "It is not, however, up to me. For that matter, I will not be your supervisor for this endeavor."

"Excuse me?" she said, sure she'd heard wrong. Bilius's absence was simply too much to hope for.

"My duties have become increasingly time-consuming as the treaty negotiations heat up. I am, therefore, temporarily stepping aside at the request of the Inner Circle of Elders." He paused and cleared his throat. "Zephron will be the interim director of the Re-Assimilation Program."

"Oh." This was good news. She tried to keep her face passive. "I understand."

"No," he said. "I don't think you do."

"Um." She focused on the floor, not sure what to say but decidedly relieved.

"Keep in mind that I am only stepping aside temporarily." She looked up and saw the steely glint of his eyes. "I will be returning."

She swallowed. "Of course," she said, then nodded deferentially. But as soon as he left and the door closed behind him, she let out a little cheer.

Her mini-celebration was cut short by the return of reality. Bilius might be temporarily handing over command to Zephron, but that didn't change the one inescapable underlying fact: Her own supervisor didn't believe she was worthy of this new job.

She sighed and rubbed her temples, all her insecurities returning to ride roughshod over her ego. When she'd received word of the promotion, she'd thought she'd finally found a place where she fit in and where they believed in her on her merit. Where they weren't whispering behind her back and saying she didn't really belong.

Apparently, she'd been wrong.

A tear clung to her lashes, then fell, landing with a plop on the polished wood. Before she'd been accepted into the Council, she'd had to make a decision, just like every other Halfling. She'd had to formally choose to join the Council, and she'd had to formally reject the process of mortalization.

She had done so, of course. She'd been awed by her uncle when she'd first met him, then blown away by the very existence of Protectors and their mission to protect and aid mortals. How could she have turned away from something both heroic and exciting? She couldn't, of course—but now she had to wonder if maybe she would have been happier living her life as a mortal after all.

Certainly her colleagues seemed to think she was no better than a mortal.

No. She was not going to think like that. Her record was stellar—so stellar that Bilius couldn't even believe it was true. But it was. And she'd show him. She might only have herself to rely on, but in the end, she'd show him. She'd show them all.

The door opened, and Zephron strode in, moving with the grace of one much younger than his long white beard would suggest.

"Uncle Zephron!" And then, remembering that this was an official meeting, she cleared her throat and tried again. "Zephron, sir. It's a pleasure to see you again."

She thought she saw a faint twitching at the corner

of his mouth. Then his eyes turned serious. "Bilius has many qualities," he said, "but tact is not one of them. You earned this promotion. Don't let his ramblings sway you to think otherwise."

Even though she'd been thinking that very thing only moments before, right then she was having a hard time believing in herself. So much for her bold plan to "show them all."

Apparently Zephron didn't pick up on her discomfiture, though. He was smiling at her, a broad, open smile that was almost paternal.

"What?"

"Your skills as a Level I Re-Assimilation Counselor exceeded even my expectations. You have a gift, my dear. As we all do, of course, but yours is particularly strong in this area."

She felt her cheeks warm under the praise. "Thank you."

"And while your excellent performance may have resulted in this promotion, I'm afraid it will also put you a bit on display. And perhaps even earn you some enemies."

"So I noticed. Though I suppose I should be used to it by now."

His eyebrow twitched. "Gossip is only gossip, my dear."

"Even when it's founded in truth?" The words came out more biting than she'd intended, and she took an involuntary step back, focusing on her shoes rather than on her uncle.

His deep sigh drew her back to him, and she looked up, noticing how deep the lines on his face had become in the years since they'd first met. "We've had this conversation several times now, Isole. I thought you finally understood."

She shrugged, feeling like an impudent child but unable to help it. Though she loved him, being with her uncle—the High Elder of the Council, a man who seemed practically omnipotent—always brought her own failings into stark relief.

A tender smile touched his lips. "We all have our weaknesses, Isole. Even me."

She grimaced. "I thought *I* was supposed to be the mind reader."

"Perhaps you're just too transparent," he said, his eyes twinkling.

"Or you're too good." She tilted her head back and sighed with frustration. "I can't even *levitate*."

"Did you know that I am completely incapable of discerning the approach of most mosquitoes?"

She blinked, then gaped at him, entirely confused as to where the conversation was heading. "You're what?"

"Six hundred hertz," he said. "I have a deaf spot for that particular frequency. I simply don't hear it."

At that, her eyes widened. "You? A weakness?"

He chuckled. "Shocking, I know. But, yes, it's true. Mosquitoes have sought and claimed my blood on many occasions . . . and I was unable to stall their nefarious advance."

Now she was laughing outright. "You're making fun of me."

He moved closer, pulling her into his embrace. "No, child, I'm not. I'm simply pointing out that we all have our weaknesses . . . and we all have our skills." He crooked a finger under her chin and tilted her head up until she met his eyes. "You are here because of your skill. There is no other reason."

She nodded, but her gaze drifted away. Here *today*, perhaps. But that didn't answer the question of how she got admitted to the Council in the first place.

Now, however, wasn't the time to argue. She *was* on

the Council, she *was* doing a good job, and she intended to continue doing just that.

Except . . .

She grimaced, realizing that by keeping the secret about Hieronymous, she was violating her oath.

Time for a reality check . . . and also time for the truth, no matter how much it would hurt her father.

She straightened, drawing her shoulders back as if the movement would give her courage. "There's something I need to tell you."

He waved her words away. "Isole, my praise of your job skills is sincere. However, you must learn when to be familiar and when that is inappropriate. We need to discuss your next assignment. You may address another topic, personal or Council-related, once our business is complete."

Her cheeks burned, but she merely nodded. "Yes, Zephron." She cleared her throat. "You were saying I'd be on display with my new assignment. Why is that?"

"The nature of your first Outcast," Zephron said. "We've never before had such a prominent Outcast apply for re-assimilation. The process will undoubtedly be covered daily in columns on the Council website, news and editorials in the *Daily Protector*, and, of course, gossip."

"Oh." It sounded horrible. Idly, Izzy wondered if it wasn't too late to request reassignment. Maybe working undercover as a lifeguard at some beach resort. A few daring rescues . . .

"Izzy?"

She licked her lips. "Sorry. I'm still here."

"You aren't going to disappoint me." It was a statement, not a question, and she couldn't help but smile at his confidence.

"No. I won't." She cleared her throat. "But, um, why me? I mean, if this Outcast is that big a deal, why not assign one of the Level-Fives that have been around for a while?"

"Under the circumstances," he said, "I thought that this assignment should go to you. I was able to persuade the other members of the committee to my point of view."

His gaze settled on her, his kind yet penetrating eyes. A chill seemed to settle over her, and she knew that she should ask what he meant, but somehow she couldn't manage the question.

He was watching her expectantly, but after a few moments of silence, he shifted his gaze back toward the door. He'd entered with a briefcase, now resting by the closed door, a portfolio peeking out of the top. He crooked a finger and the portfolio levitated, lifting free of the briefcase, then glided across the room to land in his outstretched hand. Izzy tried not to look jealous.

Zephron flipped pages. "Also under the circumstances," he said after a moment, "I thought it best if you had an assistant. I intend to assign someone to help you out."

She frowned, her forehead creasing. *An assistant?* Whatever for? "Who are we talking about?"

"The assistant?"

"The Outcast!" Her voice rose in frustration.

"Ah, of course. The Outcast, my dear, is Hieronymous Black."

She blinked, positive she'd heard wrong.

She opened her mouth to say something, but then closed it when she realized she had no idea what to say.

She tried again. "Hier—Hieronymous Black. Hieronymous Black? *He* wants to be re-assimilated?"

"So he says."

"Why?"

"He has seen the error of his ways, according to his application."

"And you *believe* him?"

Zephron smiled. "What I believe is immaterial, my dear. *You* are the one who will make the final recommendation to the Inner Circle."

"Oh." She rubbed her temples. "Oh."

"I will say that if he is sincere it couldn't come at a better time."

"The treaty negotiations, you mean."

Zephron nodded. "Precisely."

Izzy sank into a chair, her fingers tight on the leather armrests and her thoughts in a whirl. The first Mortal-Protector Treaty had been signed in 1970. It was a complicated document, but the basic deal was that Protectors would remain secret, but would do what they could to assist the human race. The treaty also created the Mortal/Protector Liaison Office, or MLO, which employed that handful of mortals who were aware of Protectors and what they did.

For years, Zephron had been lobbying to renegotiate the treaty so that Protectors played a more open role in society. The formal negotiations were to take place in two weeks—with lots of meetings and positioning and politicking going on in the meantime. At the moment, except for a few dissenters, it looked as if the mortal governments were leaning toward accepting full Protector disclosure.

She voiced all that to Zephron, and he nodded. "I'm pleased you've been following our efforts," he said. "In fact, the mortals' only real hesitation at this point centers around the Outcasts."

"I don't understand."

"The very existence of Outcasts disturbs some mortals. They fear that if the ban of secrecy is lifted, mortals may not trust *any* Protectors. They also fear that Outcasts would decide to ignore the rules and start a full-scale war with the mortals."

"They could have done that already," Izzy said.

Zephron nodded. "And the mortals well know it. They also know that Hieronymous is the most vocal of the Outcasts, the only one currently with the clout to band the others together."

"And they know that Hieronymous *really* doesn't want Protectors on par with mortals," Izzy said, finally getting it.

"Exactly."

"But if Hieronymous is out of the Outcast business, everything will be better. The mortals won't be as afraid, the negotiations will go smoothly, and the treaty will go off without a hitch."

"That, of course, is my hope," Zephron said.

Izzy nodded, still a little uncertain. Zephron knew more than anyone how deep Hieronymous's hatred of mortals went. Could he truly be turning over a new leaf? Or was Zephron grasping at the best hope he saw of pushing the treaty through? For years, Izzy knew, the renegotiation of the treaty had been her uncle's pet project. To have it now be so close . . .

As if reading her mind, Zephron spoke, his face clouded. "Of course, if it's all a ruse . . ."

She nodded, understanding. If it was a ruse and Hieronymous was merely trying to infiltrate the Council to further some nefarious plan, well, that would be disaster.

But if he was sincere . . .

Could he be sincere? The prospect was almost too much to hope for, and she wondered if she, like her uncle, was grasping at a foolish notion.

Because if Hieronymous Black was really coming

over to the good side, then there was no reason at all to reveal her father's deep, dark secret to Zephron. After all, re-assimilated Protectors could associate with whomever they pleased.

Which meant that, for the time being at least, she was justified in keeping her mouth shut.

Chapter Four

Mordi pulled his Ferrari up in front of the Los Angeles bungalow, and killed the engine. The sun was just starting to set, and so he sat in the car for a bit, watching the vibrant streaks of purple slice the sky over the trees.

He told himself that he was simply watching the celestial show. Of course, that was a lie. In truth, he was stalling.

He'd paged his cousin Zoë that morning, wanting to talk to her about their shared role as the token Halfings for the treaty negotiations. She'd insisted they meet here. At the time, Mordi hadn't thought anything of it. He'd wanted to meet; it was only fair they do it at her convenience.

Now, though, he had to wonder. Was she making an overture? Telling him without telling him that he was welcome back in the family? The thought pleased him more than he'd expected. For years, he'd told himself that it didn't matter. He'd done what he'd had to do, and if his family couldn't accept that, well, that was just too damn bad. He'd spent his whole life alone. He'd gotten rather used to it.

Julie Kenner

If that was really true, though, then why was he still camped out in the car wondering about Zoë's motives?

Frustrated, he yanked the door open, climbed out, and marched toward the house, noting for the first time the banner hung over the doorway of Nicholas Goodman's house:

Deena and Hoop . . . About Damn Time!

Mordi couldn't help but grin.

Deena and Hoop had been flirting with a serious relationship since before Mordi had met either of them. An artist, Deena worked part-time at the elementary school where Zoë used to work as a librarian, before her entry into the Venerate Council had taken her in another professional direction.

Hoop was a private investigator, a guy who pretty much fit all the stereotypes of a rumpled gumshoe. The man truly loved Deena, though, any idiot could see that, and Mordi wondered what had taken them so long to finally set a wedding date.

Then again, considering he himself had never once let a relationship with a woman get to such a serious level, he was hardly the man to criticize the speed—or lack thereof—with which Hoop had finally popped the question.

"Mordi!" Inside, across the living room, his cousin Zoë waved. He returned the gesture, then started walking that way through the crowd. "You look well," she said before moving closer and pulling him into an awkward hug. He patted her shoulder, figured that satisfied propriety, then stepped back.

"Thanks for meeting me here," she added.

"I didn't know I had a choice."

"Oh." She looked him up and down, frowning. "Sorry. I didn't realize it would be such a terrible or-

54

deal for you to come. I actually thought you might enjoy the party."

He opened his mouth to snap a retort, but closed it with a sigh. "We need to talk about this committee stuff."

She studied him, her expression earnest as always. "We know you were undercover," she said, and since that had nothing to do with their committee responsibilities, Mordi knew that he'd been right: His cousin was making an overture of sorts.

He almost kept silent, but if she was going to make an effort, then so would he. "Yeah. I wanted to tell you but, like you said, I was undercover." He hadn't been at first, of course, but Zoë knew that as well as Mordi.

She nodded, a tiny frown marring her serious expression. "And we know you stood up to your father."

"And so you up and invited me to Deena's engagement party?" He crossed his arms, feeling more manipulated than welcome. "Come on, Zo. I might be part of the family, but you and I know I've never really belonged."

"I just thought—"

He shifted his weight. In theory, he appreciated the overture. In practice, he felt as though he'd been thrust under a microscope. "Let's just get down to business, okay?"

He thought she was going to protest again, but instead she turned away, leading him across the room. The house belonged to Deena's brother, Nicholas, and his wife Maggie. And although he'd never been there before, he could see that this building was more than just a house—it was a home. A sharp contrast to the austere studio apartment he kept in Manhattan.

Zoë aimed them toward the buffet, and though Mordi expected her to continue past to some private room, instead she stopped. A man stood by a plate piled high with sandwiches, his back to Zoë and Mordi, and Mordi could see the straps of some sort of gear crisscrossing his back. The man turned, and Mordi realized who it was—and what he was holding.

George Bailey Taylor met his eyes. "Mordi. Good to see you." The words were polite enough, but Mordi didn't miss the way Taylor's hand moved to protectively cup the tiny head of a baby girl, swaddled in pink and snuggled into the papooselike pack that nestled against his chest.

"You haven't seen Talia since she was born," Zoë said, beaming at the sight of her daughter.

Mordi reached out a tentative finger, and the little urchin took it, her tiny finger closing tight around his. "She's so big."

"Time passes," Zoë said. She looked up at Taylor, who didn't move a muscle, but still Mordi was sure some silent communication passed between them. Zoë cleared her throat. "Listen, you can come by any time if you want. I mean, if you want to see the baby or something. We'd like to see you and all."

"Building bridges?" Mordi asked.

Her eyes flashed. "At least I'm trying."

She was, and Mordi had to give her credit. He nodded. "Well, thanks. I'd like that. Really." He drew in a breath, then cast around for a distraction. He wanted to talk about this committee thing. Wanted to get it over with and get out of there. But he'd brought it up twice now, and it was obvious Zoë intended to take her own sweet time.

He glanced around the room. "So, who's here?" Over the years, Mordi'd had run-ins with many of Zoë's friends. *She* might be gunning for a reconciliation, but he wasn't certain about the rest of them.

"Well, Hale, of course." She frowned as she lifted up

on her tiptoes and scanned the room. "But I don't see him."

Mordi exhaled, relieved. Hale was Zoë's half brother and also Mordi's cousin. Unlike Zoë and Mordi, though, Hale was a full-fledged Protector. He was also arrogant as hell and had a tendency to be unforgiving.

Considering Mordi had given Tracy—Hale's wife— a bit of a rough time a few years ago, Mordi rather hoped Hale didn't suddenly appear.

The clatter of toenails on the hardwood floor drew Mordi away from his thoughts, and he looked down as Elmer skittered up. The little ferret glared at him and started bouncing up and down, his tail straight up and his sharp teeth gleaming.

"Come on, Elmer," a disembodied voice behind Mordi said. "He's okay . . . *now*."

As Mordi turned toward the voice, the air seemed to shimmer. And then, without any fanfare Hale appeared, looking picture-perfect as usual.

The ferret scurried to Hale's pant leg, then climbed all the way up until he perched on Hale's shoulder, chattering wildly.

"Where's his collar?" Zoë asked. "I can't understand a word he's saying."

"Didn't wear it," Hale said, nodding to Mordi. "We were running late. He's saying he doesn't trust our cousin."

"For the love of Hera," Mordi began. "I don't care what the little rodent—"

"No, no. It's okay. *I* trust you." He rolled his shoulder, and Elmer struggled for balance. "This one will just have to get used to the idea."

"Why?" Mordi asked.

"Why? You mean why do I trust you?"

Mordi nodded.

Hale shrugged, then grimaced as Elmer's claws dug

in. "Zephron says you're one of the good guys now." Hale's steady gaze met Mordi's. "He's always right. Are you saying he was misinformed?"

"No," Mordi said firmly. "He's right."

"Well, then. You've got my vote until you screw up again." Hale held out a hand. "Welcome to the party."

Mordi purposely didn't shake. "Thanks."

Hale pulled his hand back and shoved it in his pocket, his eyes fixed on Mordi's. "See you around," he said, then turned and headed across the room. There Tracy was laughing with a woman with short dark hair.

Mordi turned back to Zoë. "I really didn't come here to—"

"I know. You came to discuss business." She shrugged. "Don't worry about the negotiations. I imagine Zephron will only expect you to sit there and look friendly and cooperative. After all, he only wanted us for our blood."

He had to agree with her. They were both Halflings, and Zephron wanted Halflings at the negotiating table. Someone with whom mortals would feel a kinship.

Well, if Mordi's blood made him useful, then so be it. For that matter, it would be the first time in his life his mother had ever done anything for him. Other than giving him birth, that is.

He frowned, Zoë words finally registering. "Expect *us*," he said. "You meant to say that Zephron will expect *us* to sit there and look friendly."

Her face shifted, taking on a determined yet embarrassed quality. "Well, the thing is—"

Little Talia let out a piercing wail, and Zoë immediately started fussing with her, finally quieting the little girl. "*She's* the thing," Zoë said. "I just don't feel right leaving her, especially not when the meetings are so erratically scheduled."

The import of her words hit him. "*Alone?*" It was bad enough wheeling and dealing with politicos, but to have to do it alone?

She shook her head. "Zephron said he'd appoint another Halfling to replace me."

Small comfort, but Mordi couldn't argue the point because Zoë lifted Talia out of the carrier, wrinkled her nose and sniffed in the general vicinity of the little girl's bottom, then took off, leaving Mordi quite alone.

Well, damn.

He poked at the buffet, piling crackers and cheese on a plate while his thoughts drifted to what Hale had said. *Yes*, he was one of the good guys. But when, exactly, had that happened?

When he'd first agreed to Zephron's offer to be a mole, Mordi's sole motivation had been self-preservation. In his mind, he hadn't actually turned away from his father. How could he have? He'd spent his whole life trying to meet his father's expectations, trying to wrest some hint of approval out of the man's cold, hard eyes.

It had never come.

Hieronymous had been his father by birth, but that didn't mean the man loved him. Mordi was a Halfling, and in Hieronymous's view, that made him an object of contempt and derision—hardly someone worthy of inheriting Hieronymous's empire, such that it was.

Idly, Mordi looked around the room for his half brother. Jason was a full-fledged Protector, and Hieronymous had been more than willing to pour love and glory on that son.

But Jason had wanted nothing to do with Hieronymous. Hieronymous had promised Jason everything that Mordi had ever wanted, and Jason had thrown it back in his face.

Mordi had thought his brother a fool.

Now, he saw Jason standing with his wife Lane, Taylor's sister. Both were chatting with Tracy and the dark-haired woman.

He inched toward Taylor, who, having been relieved of his infant burden, was sucking down a beer. "Who is that?"

Taylor followed the direction of Mordi's finger. "That's Maggie. Nick's wife."

That figured. As far as he could tell, everyone at the party was quite attached, bound to husbands and wives, starting families. They were each loved, and they each had someone to love.

Mordi grimaced. He hated sappy sentimentality, and yet here he was, being all sappy and sentimental. But the truth was the truth, and he'd never known that kind of love. Never had another human being—mortal or Protector—who cared about him above all others. And how could he, with the stigma of his father hanging over his head? Even free of the man, Mordi was still haunted by his presence.

"Mordi?"

He jumped. Zoë had come back and now had a hand on his shoulder.

"Are you okay?"

He shrugged away from her touch. "I'm fine. I'm going to go talk to Jason." He didn't wait for her to answer, just headed across the room until he was standing outside the little circle of people, slightly behind Jason. After a second, his brother realized he was there and turned.

"Well, well, the prodigal brother."

Mordi searched Jason's face, looking for a hint of emotion. There wasn't any, and he started to take a step backward. This was a mistake. After all, he and Jason had had the roughest patch of all, and if—

"Where the hell are you going?" Jason's fingers clamped down on Mordi's shoulder.

"Nowhere," Mordi said.

Jason studied him.

Mordi stood a little straighter. Since the first moment he'd met Jason, his brother had intimidated the hell out of him. Well, no longer. "I'm leaving," Mordi said. "Where in Hades did it look like I was going?"

To his surprise, Jason started laughing. "Hopping Hera, Mordi—you are so damn touchy."

Mordi started to argue, but then stopped himself. He *was* too damn touchy. Instead, he took a deep breath. "Sorry."

Jason looked him up and down for a moment, then stepped back to lean against the wall, his arms crossed over his chest. "So I guess congratulations are in order."

Mordi squinted. "Are they?"

"I skim the website," Jason said. "You've brought in thirteen traitors in as many months. Not a bad record."

"I'm proud of it," Mordi said.

"I'll bet."

Mordi frowned, not certain if the sarcasm he heard in Jason's voice was real or imagined. "What do you mean by that?"

Jason shrugged. "I just wonder if you're not trying too hard."

A chill ran down Mordi's spine. He ignored it. "I'm a Protector," Mordi said. "I'm just doing my job."

"Really."

"Yes," Mordi said. "*Really.*"

"So you're not out to prove that you don't care what Daddy Dearest thinks of you? You're really past all of that."

"Of course I am," Mordi said. "I don't care what he thinks about me at all." But that was a lie. He did care. He cared one hell of a lot. He'd simply pushed caring aside.

He sighed. He knew he'd made the right choice, taken the right path.

Why, then, was it always so damn hard?

Chapter Five

Izzy stood in the cafeteria line, bouncing a little as she checked her watch. She'd flown back to Manhattan from D.C. the night before, and she hadn't yet even made it into her own office. She'd received an e-mail from Zephron that morning, sticking her on some committee (as if she had time for that!), and she'd raced from her apartment in the Village all the way to the Council's headquarters under the U.N. She hadn't eaten since yesterday afternoon. She was starved. And if the line didn't start moving faster, she was going to be late.

Greedily, she eyed the last lemon poppy-seed muffin, safe and snug in the display case. She was eighth in line, and mentally she tried to calculate the odds that the muffin would still be there when she reached the counter—taking into account the fact that she was definitely picking up on some strong poppy-seed-muffin vibes from somewhere ahead of her.

No idea. Math had never been her strong suit.

Maybe she could shout out that she wanted the muffin and ask them to set it aside for her. Might not work, but it was worth a shot.

Besides, she was ravenous, and if she didn't get the lemon poppy-seed, she was stuck with zucchini (bad) or chocolate (worse). While she liked chocolate just fine, the idea of a chocolate *muffin* grossed her out. Cake, yes. Muffin, no. Some things were just plain sacred.

Inspired to lay her claim, she lifted her hand, trying to catch the clerk's attention. No luck. But the seven Protectors in front of her and the five behind all noticed.

A few turned away immediately, making a point of not looking at her. Two started whispering together, and though her hearing wasn't anything special, "that's the one" drifted unmistakably toward her.

She blinked, lowering her hand. She couldn't even stand in a stupid food line without getting stared at and whispered about. And she sure as Hades wasn't going to ask that the muffin be set aside now. Zeus forbid it look like she were the recipient of some special muffin privilege.

She could hear it now. *"Zephron's her uncle, you know. Not only did he get her on the Council, he arranged it so that the cafeteria makes special meals for her. Veal when we have chicken. Eggs Benedict while we choke back dried-out pancakes. Lemon poppy-seed muffins while we're stuck with those chocolate abominations. Privileged, undeserving little bit—"*

"Ms. Frost?"

Her head snapped up, eyes wide. She was sixth in line, the muffin was still there, and a familiar-looking man had sidled up next to her. She squinted, blinked, and then everything clicked into place.

"Patel! I didn't recognize you. You look great."

"Thanks." He held out a hand to shake, then, obviously remembering the rules and who he was talking to, awkwardly tugged it back and shoved it into his pocket. "Re-assimilation will do that to a person. I feel like a new man."

"You look like one." He did, too. Where once he'd been a bit amphibious, now he seemed lean and trim. He gave the appearance of a man freshly scrubbed, and she caught the scent of his aftershave: an odd brand that reminded her of newly minted pennies. Unusual, but charming in its own way.

His face, once sheltered, now seemed more open. Happier. There was still a shadow behind his eyes, but she supposed that living six years as an Outcast would do that to a person.

Patel had been her very first re-assimilation, and one of the first group of Outcasts who'd applied after the passage of the Outcast Re-Assimiliation Act. She hadn't been surprised that he'd slipped so easily through the system. He was the ideal re-assimilation candidate, the kind of Outcast for which the act was passed in the first place.

He'd broken the rule against public defamation of the mortal political process—an Outcastable offense but (in Izzy's opinion, anyway) nothing to get too worked up about. He'd been repentant, but it was a third offense, and the Council's three-strikes rule was set in stone. Examples had to be made, and Patel had been out.

"I've been assigned to Elder Armistand," he said. "Personal assistant."

"No kidding? That's great." They moved forward in the line. Only four people ahead of her now, and the muffin was still there. "I've actually got a meeting with him in a few hours. I've never met him. What's he like?"

"Oh, he's fabulous," Patel said. "Efficient, organized, no-nonsense. I've been doing a lot of work toward the treaty renegotiation." He shrugged. "The man knows politics."

"I suppose so," Izzy said. "He hired you."

Patel blushed a little. "Well, I like to think my re-assimilation essay played some role, but mostly I think you're right."

Izzy shrugged. There really was no sense sugarcoating the situation. Armistand had supported the act from day one. What better way to prove it was working like a charm than to hire the re-assimilated?

"And I get access to the elder spa," he said. "So that's cool."

Izzy bit back a grin. The elders and their staff had access to exclusive spa facilities on Olympus. She'd been there once, as Zephron's guest, and it had ruined her for every other spa experience.

From what she could see, Patel was taking full advantage of the facilities. He'd lost at least fifteen pounds, had a tan, smelled faintly of massage oil, and had been thoroughly cut, styled, and blow-dried.

Jealousy crested, and she made a mental note to schedule an appointment to have her hair trimmed and her nails done at Frederic Fekkai. Not Olympus, but not shabby either.

The line moved. Two people ahead of her now.

Patel shifted backward, clearly about to take his leave. "Anyway, I saw you and I just wanted to say hi and to tell you that I'm doing well. And it's all due to you. Thank you."

And then, even though she knew she shouldn't, she reached out and took his hand, hoping that the gesture looked casual, as if she was so moved by the spirit that she simply forgot the rules. But it was a stupid rule, and she had to know. Had to be sure. He was her first and now, with Hieronymous's re-assimilation dogging her, she just needed to *know*—with absolute certainty—that Patel was doing right.

That *she'd* done right.

His thoughts filled her, spilling into her head so quickly that she almost stumbled under the weight of him. *Honor, commitment, honesty.* Those things pervaded his brain. He was walking the straight and narrow, all right.

Izzy felt her smile broaden as she pulled her hand away. "It was great to see you," she said. "I'm so glad you stopped to say hi."

And then he was gone and she was the first in line. And, damn it all to Hades, the lemon poppy-seed muffin was gone.

Chapter Six

Elder Armistand had a stern face and an even sterner voice. Didn't matter. Even faced with the threat of Armistand's disapproval, Mordi was completely unable to concentrate on the elder's words. His attention was too taken by the woman sitting next to him.

It had been a long time since he'd been attracted to a woman. The complications in his life had left little time for romance, and Mordi had learned to simply quit looking. Why risk that tender tug at his heart if there was no way he could follow through?

And how could he? Even now that he was a full Protector, he still carried the stigma of his blood. He wasn't exactly eligible bachelor material, that was for sure.

This woman, though . . .

From the moment they'd been introduced, he'd been intrigued. Something about her manner, about the way she held herself. Something suggested to Mordi there was more to Isole Frost than she was letting him—or anyone—see.

Armistand had introduced her as Zoë's replacement. And now she sat beside him, looking prim and proper in a white linen suit, her blond hair pulled up into a perfectly coiffed knot. Her face was angular, all shadows and lights, and her piercing blue eyes reflected strength and an innate professionalism.

In sum, she was starkly beautiful and utterly distant. She'd given Mordi a quick glance when she entered, nodded briefly, then taken her own seat across from Armistand. Now she was taking copious notes, showing not the slightest bit of interest in him.

For the best, he supposed. She'd got his attention, that was for sure. But unless she was the world's best actress, she wasn't nearly as fascinated as him. Besides, getting involved with any woman would be a mistake. And considering this woman was showing absolutely no interest in him, he supposed that he was in no danger of having to extricate himself from a romantic entanglement.

Too bad.

He must have sighed, because suddenly both Armistand and Isole turned to look at him.

"Are we boring you?" the elder asked from behind the broad expanse of his oak desk.

"Sorry, sir. Something in my throat." He brushed his neck for effect, and Armistand grunted, then focused again on his notes. In the upholstered guest chair next to Mordi, Isole lifted an eyebrow, her expression suggesting that she saw right through him.

Armistand flipped two pages, grunted again, then looked back up, his gaze landing first on Isole, then moving quickly to Mordi. "So we are clear, then? You understand the role you're to play?"

Mordi's stomach twisted, and he had the sudden sensation of being back in boarding school, thrust to the front of the room to work a quadratic equation when he'd spent the entire class trying to surreptitiously levitate a pencil on the schoolmaster's desk.

"Mr. Black?"

Mordi swallowed. "Of course, sir. The Council—"

"—wants to reassure the mortal representatives that Protectors can be assimilated into mortal culture and that we are no threat," Isole said, sitting forward slightly and not looking at Mordi. "Because of our heritage as Halflings, Mordichai and I are already somewhat integrated into mortal society. We can provide a good face, if you will, for the Council and, hopefully, smooth the negotiations."

She sat back then and recrossed her legs. He tried to catch her eye, wanting to signal his thanks, but she studiously avoided him.

Armistand's eyes narrowed. "Thank you, Ms. Frost. However, I had meant to inquire of Mr. Black."

Her eyes widened, and she lifted her hand, pressing her fingers lightly over her mouth. "Oh, I'm so embarrassed. I didn't even think. I was just so excited about being a part of this endeavor that I—"

Armistand cut her off with a wave of a hand, his expression softening. Clearly, he bought what the girl was selling.

For someone who'd just embarrassed herself, though, she had managed to not even raise a hint of blush. Considering how fair she was, that was quite a feat indeed, and Mordi suddenly realized what was going on. She hadn't jumped in out of excitement. She'd jumped in to save his butt.

Maybe she was a little intrigued by him after all. . . .

"Mr. Black?"

He cleared his throat. "I think Ms. Frost did an excellent job of summarizing our role. I'd only like to add that it's an honor to be able to assist the Council in this matter."

Armistand's face didn't soften as it had for Isole, but neither did he challenge Mordi again. Not being a fool, Mordi took that as a victory.

71

"Very well." Armistand closed his portfolio. Apparently, the meeting was over. "We'll expect to see you at the next committee meeting. Plan to make a good impression on the mortal representatives. And it would probably be a good idea for you two to meet with the mortal liaisons beforehand. My assistant will make the necessary arrangements and e-mail you the date and location. That will be all."

Isole stood, and Mordi followed her lead. "Thank you, sir," he said, then turned to leave, holding the door open so that Isole could precede him through.

He'd expected her to wait for him, but apparently she had other intentions. By the time he pulled the door shut, she was already halfway down the hall, her heels clicking on the polished stone floor.

"Ms. Frost," he called, picking up his pace so that she wouldn't reach the elevator and disappear. "Isole!"

She stopped, and he saw her shoulders sag just slightly. Then she turned and faced him, irritation lining her perfect features. "I have an appointment in five minutes," she said. "Will this take long?"

Taken aback, Mordi stopped cold. "Don't worry. I won't take up too much of your precious time."

"Then I'd suggest you get on with it."

Mordi grimaced. So much for his fantasy that he might actually connect with this woman. She practically dripped icicles. "I got the impression that you meant what you said to Elder Armistand—that this project was high priority."

"I did mean it," she said, apparently unruffled.

"Then perhaps you could demonstrate it," he said. He gestured to himself. "We're both working on this project. Perhaps you could eke out a few minutes to discuss our game plan?"

She raised an eyebrow. "I don't think so, Mr. Black. If

you're not interested in paying attention during the Elder's presentation, I hardly intend to play tutor now."

He felt his face warm. "I appreciate you covering me in there."

"Believe me, Mr. Black," she said, "I acted entirely out of self-interest. If you look like a fool, then so do I. So do all Halflings."

"All the more reason for us to talk and plan what we're doing next."

She licked her lips, the gesture softening her ice-cold demeanor. She avoided his eyes, managing instead to look everywhere else in the hall. For a moment, he thought she would agree. Then she shook her head, looked him straight in the eye, and said with cold clarity, "I don't think so. We're just supposed to be our normal, charming, half-mortal selves. I think I can handle that without a game plan," she said.

"Charm is on the agenda?" he snapped back. "I'm thinking you may need to practice."

He immediately regretted the words. Not that they seemed to bother her. Isole Frost simply glanced at her wristwatch, then turned away. "My appointment," she said. And then she was gone.

Leaving Mordi to wonder what the heck had just happened . . . and why in Hades he was attracted to such an ice princess in the first place.

It really was a conundrum, and he was frowning, his mind filled with thoughts of Isole Frost, when his holopager beeped. He flipped it open, his frown deepening when Phelonium Prigg appeared on the display. Simpering little beaurocrat twit.

Mordi nodded, hoping his disdain didn't show on his face. "Yes?"

"The High Elder has asked me to inform you of your newest assignment."

Mordi lifted an eyebrow. "Another assignment?"

Prigg ignored the comment, barreling on with purpose. "You are to assist with re-assimilation assessments. A high-level Outcast has applied, and Zephron believes that you should be involved in the process."

"That's really not my field," Mordi said, thinking he'd rather shove toothpicks under his fingernails. "Who's the Outcast?"

"I'm sorry, Zephron asked that I not reveal that information at this time. He's currently in a very important meeting, and asks that you wait for him in his office, where he'll give you the full overview of the assignment." At the words "very important," Prigg stood up straighter and lifted his chin, as if the importance of Zephron's meetings somehow reflected on him.

"Fine. Whatever." Mordi didn't like it, but he could hardly argue. "At least tell me who the counselor is."

"Isole Frost," Prigg said.

Mordi stared at the three-dimensional image. "Frost?"

"Yes. Why?"

Suddenly the assignment didn't seem that terrible after all. "Thanks. I already know Ms. Frost. I'll head on over there now and meet up with Zephron later."

"I really don't think that's—"

Mordi flipped the case on his holopager closed, taking a perverse satisfaction in shutting up the little twerp . . . and anticipating the look on Isole Frost's face when she learned that Mordi was her brand-new assistant.

After being dissed by the girl, he had to say, the afternoon was looking up.

Chapter Seven

Mordichai Black.

Jumping Jupiter, how could she be so unlucky?

Mordichai's reputation was well-known among Protectors. The man had an Outcast for a father (albeit one who might be making amends), and now he was busting his tail nailing traitorous Protectors.

Her own tiny bit of treason flashed orange neon over her head. Every minute she kept silent was an Outcastable offense, and that little fact made her stomach hurt. Oh please oh please oh please . . . don't let him have seen her guilt.

He couldn't possibly have, of course. She'd kept her cool, though she probably *had* been a little more standoffish than necessary. Had he noticed *that*? Had he been suspicious?

Izzy took a deep breath, trying to calm down as the elevator took her even deeper into the bowels of the U.N. basement. Unlike her recent trip to see Bilius, this time she hardly even noticed the elevator. For one, her office was down here, and the elevator ride—though always unpleasant—was somewhat familiar. For another, her mind was too full of Mordichai Black to have any room for her petty phobias, no matter how unpetty they might seem at some other time.

The doors opened, and she stepped out, striding automatically down the hall toward her office. *Calm down, Izzy. Calm down and think.*

Right. Good advice. She paused outside her office, took a couple of deep breaths, then pushed inside.

Everything was as she'd left it. The five case files—including the one on Hieronymous—that had come with her promotion were stacked neatly on her desk. The black leather couch was cleared off, except for two small red throw pillows. An assortment of magazines and newspapers—everything from *People* to *Protector Living*—was fanned out on the coffee table. And her flamingo floor lamp burned in the corner, adding a soft glow and a bit of whimsy to the room.

The familiarity of the room calmed her, and she tucked her purse into the credenza, then made her way behind her desk. She sat in the chair, leaned back, and contemplated her ceiling.

She was fine. Mordi wasn't going to present any problem. She'd picked up on his attraction, true. But she'd been so terrified that he might try and get close—and thus discover her misdeeds—that she'd immediately tried to discourage him.

It had worked, too. No doubt about that.

The thought brought a tiny tinge of regret. Under other circumstances, she might want to see what could develop between her and the likes of Mordichai Black. After all, with his tailored suits and prep-school manner, he certainly had the appearance of an eligible man. But it was those dangerous green eyes and the slightly windtousled hair that shifted his appearance from refined to *very* fine. No doubt about it, in a different time and place, she would definitely look twice at the intrepid Mr. Black. Here and now, though? No. No way, no how.

Which was why she'd put a quick damper on any heated thoughts that Mordi might have for her. Which meant that she'd see Mordichai Black at the committee meetings, but that was that. No planning strategies. No late-night coffee while they opined as to the state of mind of the various committee members. No scrambling to figure out how they could play a role in the negotiations bigger than simply being Halflings-on-parade.

She told herself that was good. She didn't want to see him. But even as she sternly lectured herself, a tiny rebellious part of her wanted to see the man again. Wanted to see heat flush that face, so perfect with its aristocratic nose and sharply defined jaw. Wanted to see those green eyes spark. Wanted—

Jumping Jupiter! What was the matter with her? A good-looking man thinks a few lustful thoughts, and suddenly she's ga-ga for him? She was made of sterner stuff, and she'd do well to remember just how much trouble Mordichai Black could cause her.

With a frown, she glanced at the clock on her wall. Any minute now, Mordichai's father would arrive . . . and he was trouble enough without adding the son to the mix.

And she *was* in trouble. The bump to Level V might technically be a promotion, but the assignment to Hieronymous's case put her in a stress-filled, damned-if-you-do and damned-if-you-don't position.

So, yeah. She had a pay raise and she had a bit more prestige. Enjoy it while she could, because she was about to commit professional suicide.

She sighed and glanced at the clock. Five after two. The Outcast was already late. Either that or he'd gotten held up on the security level.

She sighed again, wondering if she should go check and, if need be, rescue him from the overzealous aides that guarded the Council headquarters' various ports of entry. As a re-assimilation candidate, he'd been granted immunity from his past crimes, meaning he could remain free in the world during the process. He could not, however, wander free in the Council hallways.

As she thought more about her new candidate, she realized that she had to keep as much distance as possible if she wanted to extricate herself from this mess with her professional skin intact.

It really was quite a conundrum. If she determined that Hieronymous was truly intent on reverting to good, many in the Protector world would shun her, forever looking at her as the idiot who reinstated the evil Hieronymous Black.

But if she ultimately determined that he wasn't sincere, then she either had to ruin her father's life and shatter his dreams . . . or she had to keep her secret and risk being Outcast herself.

Quite the pickle.

Once again, she frowned and looked at her watch. Ten minutes late.

Damn it all. Now that she'd got her head on straight, she really didn't want to waste any more time.

Grabbing her case file and security pass, she headed for her door, planning to make the trek back up the elevator to Security Check Point One.

But as soon as she opened the door, she realized she didn't have to.

Hieronymous Black stood right there, an armed Protector in the familiar guard uniform standing at attention next to him.

"Outcast Black to see Counselor Frost."

"Yes. Thank you." Izzy lifted her chin and straightened her shoulders, sliding easily into her professional façade. *Maintaining* the façade wasn't so easy, however. The famous Outcast was even more intimidating in person than his file photo had led her to believe. He had coal-black hair and the same sturdy jaw that she'd seen in his son. But while Hieronymous's eyes were cold and superior, Mordi's had been warm and willful.

Hieronymous stepped past her into the room, exuding a masculine, almost metallic scent that she couldn't place, but which seemed oddly familiar . . . and definitely added to his overall charisma.

Was it any wonder he'd turned countless Protectors, and that his reputation among Outcasts had grown on an almost daily basis?

Realizing she was still standing in the open doorway, she gave the escort a quick nod, her signal that it was okay for him to leave, and then followed Hieronymous inside, shutting the door behind her.

"Alone at last," Hieronymous said.

"Excuse me?" she said, and to her infinite shame, her voice squeaked.

He laughed, the tones almost musical, as he moved to sit on the couch.

"Yes. Please, do sit down."

"You doubt my sincerity," he said.

"Not at all." She took one of the chairs opposite him, happy to be talking shop so soon. *That* she could handle. "I keep an open mind about all candidates." Which was rather easy, frankly, when you could open their minds.

"But you *were* surprised to learn of my application," he said.

"Well, yes. I assume everyone was." She almost said something about her own father, but then realized that he might not know who she was.

"Yes, of course." He fixed his gaze on her. "Too bad they can't all see into my heart."

She swallowed. "Yes, too bad." She, of course, *could* see into his heart. Not all re-assimilation counselors had that skill, and she was certain that her ability had played a big part in getting this promotion. Not to mention being assigned to Hieronymous. She didn't, however, intend to read him right away, even though the re-assimilation process was one of the exceptions to the rule against mind reading. Instead, she liked to get a feel for the candidate first. Mind-exploring could be exhausting, and she found it much more tenable if she already had some familiarity with the candidate's overall sensibilities.

He seemed disappointed that she didn't immediately reach out to touch him, but he covered it well. "Shall I tell you my story? Why I wish to come back to the fold?"

"That would be helpful," she said.

He nodded. "In that case, I'll begin."

She focused on him as he spoke, letting her mind flow toward him, wanting to get a feel for the man himself before she took a closer look at his actual thoughts.

Sincere.

"I suppose it was petty jealousy and youthful hubris that led me to spurn the Protector life in the first place."

Truth.

"After that, I discovered I had quite a knack for making money in the mortal markets."

Reluctant modesty.

"Yes," she said, "you have a reputation for playing the markets and doing exceptionally well."

He bowed his head modestly. "As I said, I seem to have a knack."

"For inventing things, too." She tightened the hold on her thoughts here, seeking to pick up any hint of his mind wandering toward her father.

Nothing. Just pride.

"Yes, that's also a gift." His voice took on a sorrowful tone. "Though I suppose I abused that gift. I do so regret the harm and fear I've caused." He paused, then looked at her with baleful eyes. "I think I was afraid."

She blinked, trying to hide her surprise. "Afraid? Of what?"

"Of mortals. Afraid that they would shun us, misunderstand us." He sighed, the sound low and mournful. "I behaved like a scared child, acting out. And in the end, my own fears of mortals forced me off the Council and into a terrible Outcast existence." He shook his head. "I can only hope that the Council can forgive me. And learn to trust me."

She studied him, not at all sure what to believe. This was Hieronymous Black, after all. She'd grown up hearing the stories about how vile he was, about how he wanted nothing more than to destroy mortals and, if that meant destroying Protectors and the Council in the process, then so be it.

That was the reputation, yes. But was it the reality? Her own powers were leading her to trust him; her initial impression was that he was . . . well . . . *good*.

Could he really have had such a change of heart?

Could everything she'd heard about him have been exaggerated?

More than anyone, she should know not to listen to gossip. She needed to judge a person on the evidence, not the rumors.

But even so . . . this was *Hieronymous*. And rumors and gossip usually started as truth.

Her face must have reflected her doubt, because he leaned forward. "I realize I've shocked many people, coming forward as I have." He shook his head, as if pondering some unsolvable riddle. "You are my only ally," he said. "As my re-assimilation counselor, you

81

are the only one who can ascertain the truth and let the Council know that I'm sincere."

As he spoke, he reached out to clasp her hand. She gasped, surprised by the unexpected touch. A million megawatts of thoughts coursed through her veins. Goose bumps rose on her skin, and a warm flush filled her body.

She'd had no time to prepare, to try to control her abilities or rein them in. And without that time, his thoughts and emotions poured into her without direction or control, racing through her blood, filling her head. She couldn't fight it, didn't want to fight it. This was who she was, what she did. And so she let the thoughts and feelings run their course, and in the end, when she sat in the chair gasping, she could do nothing more than blink at him.

"You did that on purpose," she said, her blood pounding in her ears, as if she'd just run a hundred-mile marathon.

"I did," he said. "I apologize. I was afraid that you wouldn't. And you had to know."

"I would have explored your mind sooner or later. That's my job."

He shrugged. "I wanted it sooner."

"You're sincere," she said, the word emerging as a startled gasp as the tremors of his emotion finally stilled inside her. "You really want to be re-assimilated. You really want to be on the Council." She blinked, certain her face bore an expression of disbelief, but unable to erase it. "You really want to do *good*."

"Of course," Hieronymous said. His black eyes bored into her own. "Why else would I be here with you?"

Chapter Eight

Why else, indeed?

Perhaps because he intended to infiltrate the Council and sabotage the ridiculous treaty negotiations. Perhaps because he was determined to finally prevail in creating a better world where Protectors ruled rather than served, wasting their time helping puny mortals with their insignificant little problems.

Yes, that was Hieronymous's goal. His dream.

And this necessary first step had worked beautifully. Of course, he'd known it would. Being a super genius gave him such an edge. Isole Frost had absolutely no idea that Hieronymous's invention had tricked her, making her see only the happy mortalphile thoughts he'd conjured specifically for the occasion.

He bit back a snort, remembering to keep his face schooled with sincerity. Mortals on a par with Protectors!? The idea was absurd. Any treaty signed between his race and the mortals should have the mortals cowering in fear, slaves to the superior race. Not working together in mediocre symbiosis.

As if the mortals were worthy . . .

Try as he might, Hieronymous couldn't understand how the Inner Circle abided the creatures. *Useless*. The entire lot of mortals were nothing more than useless insects.

Then again, he amended, casting his gaze toward Isole, perhaps not *entirely* useless. Her father, for example, was proving to be most useful indeed. Certainly the balm Mr. Frost had created from Hieronymous's meticulous directions had performed as required. Hieronymous would have made it himself, of course, except that the use of his powers would have blipped on the Council monitoring boards. He'd had to enlist a mortal's aid, and Harold Frost had been the perfect choice.

The balm was performing perfectly, too. First it had functioned well in the test run with that idiot Patel. And now, despite her empathic abilities, Isole Frost, Level V Re-Assimilation Counselor, had absolutely no idea that Hieronymous was anything but sincere.

". . . followed by a series of practical tests." She stopped talking and looked at him, her clipboard on her lap, the absolute height of efficiency.

Hieronymous regarded her calmly. He'd not been listening.

After an uncomfortable bit of silence, she cleared her throat. "So, perhaps Friday would be good?"

"Friday would be perfect," he said, wondering what he was agreeing to.

It didn't matter. Aside from being locked for eternity in the catacombs, he would agree to anything. Anything at all so long as it furthered his cause.

"Excellent." She made a tick mark on her clipboard.

Hieronymous nodded, and tried to affect the appearance of a mortalphile. It wasn't easy.

"Are you staying in the dormitories?" she asked.

"No," Hieronymous said. "The Council was gracious enough to allow me the use of my Manhattan apartment during the re-assimilation." They'd taken it from him, of course. Zephron—that Gorgon's ass—had probably enjoyed the formal divestiture proceeding. And as if that wasn't punishment enough, the Council had actually sublet the penthouse apartment to a *mortal* financier.

The news had burned through Hieronymous's veins like wildfire, relieved only when he received word that the unfortunate financier had met an untimely death. A hit-and-run. Very sad.

Hieronymous would have to remember to commend Clyde once they rendezvoused. Despite Clyde's fugitive status, Hieronymous's former Chief of Guards was still performing his job with admirable skill.

"Perhaps we could hold Friday's session in the penthouse, then. I like to interact with candidates as much as possible in a familiar environment."

"Of course, my dear. Of course."

He smiled, magnanimous and friendly. And why not? Things were going his way even more than expected. In fact, in light of fortuitous recent events, he was even considering revising his plan just slightly. Less risk for him, and the payoff would be exactly the same.

The desktop holopager buzzed, and Isole excused herself to answer it, then turned her back to him and began a long, dull conversation with another counselor about some formal testing procedure.

Really, the things he put up with in order to nurture his plan!

That very plan had germinated with the instigation of the Re-Assimilation Act. And as the treaty negotiations drew closer, Hieronymous realized that he had no time to lose. He had to be re-admitted into the Council's fold; that much was imperative if he wanted to thwart the treaty negotiations.

But how to pull off such a feat? Fortunately, since he was a super genius, determining the best method of infiltrating the Council was a task easily tackled. He would re-assimilate, of course, taking care to ensure that his assigned counselor didn't pick up on any little clues that perhaps Hieronymous was not as sincere as some of his predecessors.

Harold Frost's balm had proved invaluable in that regard. But it was the assignment of the actual counselor that was now making Hieronymous's brain hum.

Isole Frost. Harold's daughter. A Halfling, desperately attached to her mortal father. A daughter who would undoubtedly do anything to protect her father. Anything at all . . .

He'd intended to use her all along, of course, but in a much reduced role. During his planning, she'd been a Level I Counselor, and he hadn't even dared to dream.

Now that the impossible had come to pass, Hieronymous knew exactly what he had to do—or rather, what Izzy had to do. She would, too. If anyone understood the subtle art of persuasion, it was Hieronymous. He'd simply explain in small, easy-to-understand concepts that if she chose not to recommend him for re-assimilation, she would also be choosing to hurt her father.

He didn't doubt the decision she'd make, not even for an instant.

He glanced at her: still speaking to her colleague, her voice calm and assured, without even an inkling of what was in store for her.

Ah, by Zeus, the empath-balm had to be one of his most brilliant inventions. And he, of course, was a brilliant, brilliant man.

For just a moment he considered laying the plan out for Isole the moment she put down the phone. He longed to see her face as she realized that her innate abilities had been thwarted, and then watch surprise turn to anger, then fear, then resignation as he explained why, exactly, she would agree to help him.

And what, exactly, he needed her to do.

But no. Better to bide his time. Allow the Protector and mortal presses to cite him as a hero as he did good deed after good deed after nauseatingly good deed. He would put the pieces of his plan into place even as he built her trust, letting her sink deeper and deeper into believing in him. Only when all the pieces were in place would he drop the bomb.

His plan was, quite simply, perfect. Nothing could go wrong. Nothing.

The thought had barely settled in his head when the door to Isole's office burst open and Mordichai marched in. *His son.* And for the first time, Hieronymous had to admit the possibility that, perhaps, possibly, something could go wrong after all.

Chapter Nine

His father? Mordi blinked, certain he must be seeing things. What the hell was his father doing in the Council headquarters? In Isole Frost's office? And why weren't the security guards dragging his sorry carcass off to the catacombs?

"Excuse me. Uh, Mordichai? Hello? *Hello?*" Isole stood behind her desk, glaring at him. Although he'd been enthused by the prospect of seeing her again, apparently she didn't share the sentiment.

For that matter, his own enthusiasm had waned dramatically when he'd seen her companion. Bumping into his father had *not* been on the day's agenda.

A holopager blipped on her desk—her conversation put on hold—and she had her arms crossed over her chest as she stared him down. "Would you like to explain what you're doing here?" she continued. "You're interrupting my session."

"Session? Who cares about your session?" He pointed an accusing finger at his father. "What's *he* doing here? And why hasn't he been arrested?"

"Son, please." Hieronymous held his hands out in a

gesture of supplication, his voice filled with the kind of warmth Mordi had always hoped to hear while growing up, but never had.

" 'Son,' " Mordi repeated. "You remember that so easily when it suits your purpose, don't you?"

Isole's forehead creased—she was probably concerned about fisticuffs—and her perfectly pressed suit was starting to look a little rumpled. She held up a hand. "Gentlemen . . . please."

Mordi and his father both stayed silent, and Isole nodded approvingly, then switched the holopager back on, set in non-image mode, and told the caller she'd have to call back later. After disconnecting, she turned to Mordi. Her eyes were stern and no-nonsense, but he couldn't help but admire her efficiency.

"All right, Mordichai Black," she said, all traces of her pleasant phone voice erased. "I'll ask you again—what are you doing interrupting my session?"

"Some session," he said. "All I saw was him sitting there and you talking on the holophone."

One perfectly arched eyebrow lifted a millimeter or two. "Considering you walked in unannounced, I hardly think you're in a position to criticize my job performance. But if you must know, I had to take a call regarding another case."

"Re-assimilation not working out?" he asked.

She didn't answer; just closed her eyes and sighed, probably counting to ten. The woman worked in counseling, after all. She probably knew all the tricks for holding her temper.

And he *was* trying to play with her temper, though he really didn't know why.

No, that was a lie. He did know, and he didn't like the reason. He was attracted. She was not. Wounded male ego. Simple as that.

Still, it was a ridiculous subject to attack her with. Of all people, Mordi believed in re-assimilation. He'd never been formally Outcast, of course, but he'd still gone through his own mental re-assimilation.

He cast a sideways glance at Hieronymous, hoping his face didn't reflect the extent of his pain.

Oh, yeah. He'd been re-assimilated, all right. And he never intended to turn back.

Isole sighed and opened her eyes. "Just tell me what you're doing here." The harsh tone was gone from her voice, replaced with an almost sickly-sweet timbre. Frankly, Mordi missed the edge.

"I was assigned to assist you with a re-assimilation assessment. I guess Zephron thought—"

He broke off, suddenly realizing what was going on—and why Zephron had wanted to talk to him before he came barging in here. "*Him?*" he asked, pointing an accusing finger at his father. "*He's* seeking to re-assimilate?" He laughed, the sound harsh and cold. "Oh, come on. Tell me another one."

"I assure you, he's quite sincere," Izzy said.

Mordi glared at her, then focused again on his father. Hieronymous, no fool, was staying quiet.

"Funny," Mordi said, looking her straight in the eye. "I was told you were *good* at your job."

"Believe me," she shot back. "Your sources are quite accurate."

Mordi snorted. "I'm thinking not."

Pure ice burned in her eyes, and she circled the desk. "*You* were sent to assist me?"

"That's right."

"Fine. Then let's start with the ground rules. There are only a few things I require from an assistant. Not insulting me or challenging my competence tops the list."

The comment was so unexpected, Mordi didn't answer.

"And as for the rest of the rules, I think it's best we discuss those in the hallway."

"And leave him in here? Alone with confidential Council files?"

She grimaced and, for a second, Mordi thought she was going to argue again, insisting stupidly that Hieronymous was really good at heart, that he was simply a misunderstood little Outcast who'd seen the error of his ways. Blah, blah, blah.

She turned toward his father. "I apologize, but apparently I have a few administrative things to take care of that are going to eat into our session time. Why don't we call it a day and continue at our next meeting?"

Hieronymous inclined his head, the picture of civility. Mordi fought the urge to punch him. "Certainly, my dear. My apartment, you said?"

"That's perfect."

She buzzed for an escort to lead Hieronymous back up to street level, and they all waited in an uncomfortable silence for the uniformed security agent to arrive.

Moments later, the knock sounded on the door and Hieronymous stood. He nodded briefly to Mordi, murmuring the single word "Son," and then he stepped out into the hallway.

As soon as the door shut behind him, Isole rounded on Mordi, the professional veneer dropping to reveal a fiery temper. "Who in Hades do you think you are?"

"Who am I? I'm the guy who knows better than anyone that Hieronymous Black has no interest in being a good guy. Believe me. It's not his style."

She crossed her arms over her chest and glared at him. "That, sir, is not your call to make."

"It is if everyone else is blind to the truth." He could hear his voice rising with frustration and tried to tamp it down. He wasn't going to get anywhere by ticking this woman off.

"Look," she said, and he could tell from the tight lines of her face that she, too, was trying to keep a leash on her emotions. "You clearly have a conflict of interest. It's not professional. And I refuse to have anyone on the team who might interfere with or compromise my work."

"Your *work*? What about the fact that the man is a raving loon, and he wants you to give him carte blanche to wander the halls of Olympus, not to mention the rest of the world?"

She took a step toward him, obviously seething. She was a head shorter, and now she tilted her head back as she faced him. "My *job* does not mandate me to rubber-stamp candidates, as you seem to believe. I'll analyze his sincerity on a number of different levels. I am an empath, after all. I'm uniquely skilled in determining your father's motives."

Mordi blanched. *An empath*? What exactly did that mean? And—more importantly—did it mean that she'd picked up on how attracted he was to her earlier in the day? The possibility mortified him. His father had spent a lifetime messing with his head; Mordi really didn't need this woman poking around inside it, too.

"If—and only if—I find that Hieronymous Black is both sincere and psychologically cut out to be a law-abiding productive member of the Council, will I enter a recommendation that he be reinstated."

She started in on the specifics of the tests and Mordi tuned her out, schooling his features into an expression of interest while he examined her face, alight now with fury. He realized that he'd been wrong about her looks. He'd thought she had a patrician nose. Instead, it was slightly rounded at the end and just a little too small for her face.

It was a damn cute nose, though, he thought, then

immediately quelled the thought. He wasn't here to think about Isole Frost's nose, or any other part of her anatomy. He was here to—

What the hell *was* he here to do?

He must have frowned, because Isole cut off her diatribe, propped a hand on her hip, and said, "What?"

He shrugged, lifting his hands in silent surrender. "Nothing. Just listening to you."

He didn't think she believed him—considering her powers, she probably *knew* he was lying—but he gave her points for not calling him on it.

"At any rate," she said, "all I'm saying is that this isn't the case for you. Conflict of interest and all that."

"Sorry. Not buying it. Zephron knew damn well who you were working with, and he assigned me to you." Even as he spoke the words he knew he had to be right. *This* was what he was here to do.

He stood a little taller, bolstered now with purpose. "I'd say it's pretty clear Zephron wants me on *this* case. Probably figured the Council needed someone to play devil's advocate to your Pollyanna certainty that Hieronymous is nothing more than a high-strung guy who took a wrong turn in life."

Her jaw worked, as if she was grinding her teeth, and a little muscle near her eye twitched. Clearly, Isole Frost was doing her damnedest not to explode right then and there. "I do not need a babysitter," she said, her voice too calm for comfort. "And I am not a Pollyanna. I'll have you know that I've entered a recommendation against re-assimilation at least as many times as I've—oh, blast it all!"

He started. "What?"

"Why in Hera's name am I explaining myself to you? You spend your days hunting down traitors."

Mordi blinked. "I didn't realize you knew what I did."

"You're serious?" She seemed genuinely perplexed. "How could anyone not know? Every time you nail a new Outcast, they splash your picture up on the Council website—not to mention running some article with a major photo op on the front page of the *Daily Protector*. And on top of that, you happen to be the formerly loyal son of one very notorious Outcast."

"So you admit he's notorious."

"I admit he was. Yes." She stared pointedly at him. "So were you."

Well, hell. He couldn't argue with that. Or rather, he could. He could say he'd reformed. And she'd turn that argument right back around in his face and point out that Hieronymous was trying to reform, too. He didn't know much about Isole Frost, but he knew she was quick.

He liked that in a woman, though at the moment he didn't particularly like *her*. So much for first impressions filled with lust and longing. That was the trouble with relationships—the bloom wore off the rose far too quickly.

He tried a different tack. "You're right. My job does put me in the public eye a lot. But it's the behind-the-scenes stuff that matters here. I know a traitor when I see one."

"Do you? Or are you just predisposed to find the bad in everyone?"

She tossed the words out, merely another volley in their ongoing argument. Mordi didn't think she even realized she'd scored. But she had, and he fought to keep his emotions and his face in check, to not let her see what was in his head.

Because she was right. He *was* predisposed to find the bad in everyone, himself most of all. He knew how hard he'd fought before finally and firmly entrenching himself on the good side of the line in the sand. And he really couldn't believe that Hieronymous was strong enough to win that battle. Or more important, that Hieronymous had any desire to.

He shook his head. "You know what? Let's just drop this. I'm here. I'm helping you. That's the end of it."

He expected another argument, but instead she just pushed a button on her desk. After a second, a voice sounded through the intercom. "Yes, Ms. Frost?"

"Cancel my appointments for today."

"Certainly, ma'am."

She clicked off and faced Mordi. "I'm leaving. It's been a hell of a day."

"I'll go with you. We should talk."

"We probably should," she agreed. "But we're not doing it now, and you're not coming with me." She moved around her desk, gathering her things, ending finally by snapping a leather portfolio closed and tucking it under her arm.

"I'm not going to go to Zephron about you," she said, "although I'm sorely tempted. You're right. He must have had a reason for assigning you, so I suppose you'll be of value at some point."

"Gee, thanks."

"But this is *my* job and *my* case. You're here to assist me. Got that? Because if you don't, I *will* talk to Zephron, and we'll let him sort out what everybody's roles here are."

"No problem," Mordi said. "Sounds great."

She frowned, and he was certain it didn't sound great to her. Not by a long shot. But considering Zephron had made the assignments, she really didn't have a choice.

Mordi stayed silent, not willing to press his luck. He was pretty sure Zephron wouldn't take him off this case, but he wasn't absolutely positive.

His father was up to something. Something bad.

And whether she knew it or not, Isole Frost was wrapped up in it.

Until Mordi could figure out what his father had planned—and put a stop to it—he wasn't about to risk getting booted off this case.

On the contrary, he intended to stay very, very close. And if that meant keeping Isole Frost happy, well, that was a mission he was more than willing to accomplish.

Chapter Ten

"He's applied for *what*?" Jason bobbed in the water, only his head breaking the rippling surface.

Above him, Mordi frowned, leaning over the houseboat's railing and staring down at his half brother. "Re-assimilation," Mordi said. "You know. He wants to rejoin the Council. Be a good guy. All that jazz."

Jason snorted. "And you believe him?"

"No, I don't believe him! But it's not up to me. This girl—" He cut himself off, waving a hand at Jason, who was silently treading water. "Will you get up here? How am I supposed to talk to you if you're bobbing around like a buoy?"

"You look like you're talking just fine," Jason said. But then he held up a finger. "Give me one second. Davy dropped one of his gizmos off the boat, and I told him I'd find it."

As if called by the mention of his name, Davy came charging out the patio door, bare feet pounding on the wooden deck as he yelled, "Daddy, Daddy, Daddy! Did you find it? Did you?"

"Not yet, kiddo." And then, to Mordi: "Hang on."

Down he went, slipping under the dark surface, which smoothed over him, not even a few bubbles to show that he'd once been bobbing there. Frowning, Mordi leaned farther out, trying to find some sign of his brother. Nothing.

Well, hell.

While Jason did his fish-man thing, Mordi leaned against the railing, feeling the eight-year-old's eyes boring down on him.

Mordi shifted uncomfortably. He liked Davy just fine, but they'd had a decidedly iffy relationship, what with Mordi having attacked and kidnapped him at various times over the last few years. He hadn't seen the kid for a bit.

"Mommy says you're a nice guy now." Davy squinted at him. "Are you really?"

"What do you think?"

The kid shrugged. "Dunno." The frown faded, replaced by a bright smile. "You wanna wear my truth detector?"

It was Mordi's turn to frown. "Um."

" 'Cause if you're telling Momma the truth and you're really good, the detector will know."

"Right. Well. I mean, why don't you just believe me without the toy, okay?"

Davy just stared at him. Under the circumstances, Mordi supposed that made sense.

Mordi twisted to look over the rail again. "Your father should be back up by now."

That wasn't true, of course. Jason was more than capable of staying under the water indefinitely; he could turn himself into a fish when he wanted. But that didn't stop Mordi from hoping the man would surface immediately and save him from this interrogation.

"You're a chicken," Davy accused. "I'm going to tell Momma."

"I'm *not* a chicken."

The little boy crossed his arms over his chest, looking dubious. "Yu-huh."

"Come on, Davy. I'm your uncle. You can trust me." Faulty logic if ever there was any, but Mordi wasn't about to let the kid hook him up to any machine.

He told himself it was only that the eight-year-old might have mucked the whole thing up—the machine might fry his brain instead of reading it—except Mordi knew better. Davy was Hieronymous's grandchild, and the kid had inherited the Outcast's superior inventive powers. Give him a battery, some wires, a few sticks of gum, and some string, and the kid could make just about anything.

So, no. Mordi wasn't afraid that the kid's machine would be off. Instead, he was afraid that *he* would be. He was afraid that the machine would see some deep truth that he'd kept hidden even from himself. That somehow, some way, he still wanted his dad to succeed.

He shuddered, blocking the thought. *No.*

"Chicken," Davy said again, and this time Mordi privately agreed with the assessment.

He didn't have to conjure a response, though, because a splashing sounded behind him, and then came Jason's triumphant "Found it!"

Davy jumped, then raced to the railing to see his dad holding a red metal cylinder with plastic straws extending like spiders' legs.

"What is it?" Mordi asked.

"My pet spider robot, Fred," Davy said. "He makes my bed and puts my shoes away even though Mommy says that's my job."

"Oh. I should have known."

Jason had climbed up the ladder, and now he stepped onto the boat, water rolling off him to pool on the polished wood decking. He handed the soggy spider-bot to Davy, who took it and raced back inside, apparently no longer concerned with Mordi's motives.

"Okay," Jason said, pulling a pair of sweatpants on over his bathing suit and then dropping into one of the deck chairs. "So the girl thinks Dad is legitimate. Do you think *she's* legitimate?"

"What do you mean?" Mordi thought about it; shifting uncomfortably.

Jason tossed his head back and laughed. "Let me guess: She's a looker."

Mordi waved the words away. "All right, I know what you mean." Heck, he should. His job was to locate, capture, and prosecute Protectors who were colluding with Outcasts. Jason wanted to know if Isole was a secret traitor. "I did consider that, but she seems sincere. Obviously delusional if she thinks our father is legitimate, but sincere nonetheless."

"And she's a looker."

"That has nothing to do with it." Except that it did, and that simple fact pissed Mordi off. He'd worked his tail off to have his probation lifted and land this position in the Council. If there was even the slightest hint that Isole Frost was turning traitor, he should be zeroing in on her like a tractor beam. He *shouldn't* be blinded by her ocean-deep eyes and frosty-seeming professionalism.

Jason was watching him, and Mordi swallowed. "I'm keeping my eye on her, of course. But my preliminary impression is that she's on the level." He shrugged. "And she's Zephron's niece, too. I'd be surprised if she'd turn." He'd done some quick research on his flight from New York to Los Angeles. The Protector commuter shuttle took only twenty minutes, so he didn't have time to get very in-depth, but he had learned that there were those in the Council who thought she owed her position to nepotism rather than skill. That was a huge motivator to prove herself. Of course, it could also be an impetus for revenge.

"Our father, though . . ." Jason trailed off with a shake of his head. "What do you think he's up to?"

"I don't know," Mordi admitted. "Nothing good."

"Really? No ideas at all?"

Mordi scowled. "I'd tell you. I came to *you*, remember?"

"Sorry." Jason did seem contrite, and Mordi relaxed.

"The only thing I can think of is the treaty," Mordi said. "He's always been obsessed with foiling any Council attempts to get in closer with the mortals. But I don't know what he could have in mind specifically."

"Me neither," Jason said. "Keep an eye on him, though."

"Oh, I intend to." He took a breath; he still had one bombshell to drop. "What's your assignment schedule like these days?"

"Free as a flounder," Jason said. "I'm on a two-month leave."

"How do you feel about an under-the-table assignment?"

Jason's mouth quirked. "Why, little brother . . . is there something you've not been telling me?"

Mordi reached into the pocket of his jacket and pulled out a copy of the note he'd taken from Romulus. He held it out to Jason, who opened it and read it, his expression darkening.

"What's this about?"

Mordi explained how he'd retrieved the note from his quarry, and also explained how Romulus had gotten the note in the first place.

"Clyde," Jason said. "Son of a bitch."

Mordi had never liked Clyde, but his distaste for the Halfling-hating flunkie was mild compared to Jason's animosity. Clyde had been Hieronymous's right-hand man for years; and the Chief of Guards had been complicit in the scheme that had kept Jason imprisoned in a fishbowl for six long years.

" 'Holmes' has to refer to Hieronymous. Clyde isn't literary enough to think that up on his own," Jason said, his voice cold. "They're plotting something."

"I *know*," Mordi said. "But I don't know what. Other than that this re-assimilation is part of it."

"And that's what you want me to figure out?"

"That's right."

Jason nodded slowly, not in agreement, really. It was just a sign that he was still thinking. "Won't the elders assign a team? To investigate the note, I mean?"

Mordi shrugged. "Who knows? Not my jurisdiction. And they may not even believe that 'Holmes' means Hieronymous. I'd hope so, but—"

Jason's face hardened. Jason would never turn traitor, that much Mordi knew. But Jason knew well enough that sometimes the deeply bureaucratic workings of the Council didn't move quickly enough.

"All right," Jason said. "I'll do it." He fixed Mordi with a stare. "And what will you be doing?"

"I'm going to be babysitting the man himself."

Jason nodded. "So Romulus is in the stockade now?"

"Right." He frowned. "Why? What are you thinking?"

"I'm just wondering if that's exactly where Hieronymous wanted him to be."

Mordi considered the possibility and decided that Jason might be on to something. "Though I'm not sure what good it will do him with Romulus behind bars."

"Who knows?" Jason agreed. "But with Daddy-O, it's best not to take anything for granted. Romulus has always been considered pretty upstanding. He'll have powerful friends."

"And who knows how many other Protectors our father has gotten to," Mordi added.

"Exactly."

"Which is exactly why our operation has to be off the books," Mordi said. "Completely unofficial."

"I understand. I'll let Zoë and Hale know, too. We might need them."

Mordi rolled his eyes. "So much for low-key."

"We can be discreet."

"We'd better be."

Jason reached out and brushed Mordi's arm. Mordi stifled the urge to jerk away. "We won't be Outcast for this," said Jason. "It's a technicality-type offense at best. And if we uncover a plot to mess up the treaty negotiations, we'll be heroes." He squeezed Mordi's shoulders. "No worries."

Mordi frowned. He was becoming more confident about the mission by the minute. Something else, however, still preyed at his mind.

He pushed the thoughts away and faced his brother. "So, we've got a plan?"

"Guess so," Jason said. "You heading out?"

"Yeah. I'm going to go talk to Isole. Make sure she's really one of us good guys."

"Dirty job," Jason said.

Mordi grinned. "But somebody's got to do it." He paused, then drew in a breath. "Jason—?"

"You want me to keep an eye on her, too?"

Mordi nodded. "I do think she's sincere. Misguided, yes. But sincere." He inhaled, then let the breath out slowly. "But I could be wrong, and we need to be smart about this. If I investigate, she's likely to get wind of it. Can you—?"

"Just tell me what you need, and I'll do it."

"Nothing yet." Instead of feeling the pride of doing a thorough job, though, Mordi only felt like a heel. "I'll let you know when I've got a lead."

He cocked his head toward the stairs. "I'm going to go tell the kid good-bye," he said. He felt Jason's eyes bore into his back as he headed up.

He maneuvered to the upper deck, finding Davy surrounded by piles of toys in various stages of disarray. The little boy looked up. "You want to use my truth detector." It wasn't a question. The kid was astute.

Mordi met the child's pale eyes. "I want you to know your uncle's one of the good guys."

Davy looked at him uncertainly for a moment, and even though the kid was only eight, Mordi shifted uncomfortably under his penetrating gaze. Finally the kid nodded, then pointed toward a small chair in the corner. "Sit there."

Mordi did, and then the kid plunked a baseball cap threaded with a variety of colored wires on his head. He took the wires and threaded them into a metal cylinder that was attached to a car battery. Mordi frowned when he saw it and twisted around to look at Davy, who was fiddling with a control panel behind him. "This is safe?"

Davy shrugged. "I guess."

Not exactly a rousing endorsement, but Mordi was still inclined to believe the kid knew what he was doing. He hoped so. "Okay. Plug me in."

"It's on," Davy said. "You just gotta say something, and I can tell if it's the truth or not."

"Yeah? My name is Jason Murphy."

The kid giggled. "Nuh-uh. I don't even need the machine for that." Maybe not, but the machine obviously knew its stuff. It made a sound like a raspberry. Mordi twisted back around and saw that a red light was flashing in time with the obnoxious noise.

"Okay, then. Last month I spent three days as a dog."

Green light. And a little trill from the machine.

"You did?" Davy asked. "A collie?"

"Labrador," Mordi said. "I was working under-cover."

"Cool."

"Yeah, well. It's not bad work."

"Uncle Mordi?"

"Yeah."

"Was that really what you wanted to tell my machine?"

Mordi frowned, then cleared his throat. "No. Okay. Here goes." He drew in a breath. This was the truth, by Zeus. So why was he so nervous? "I want my father to fail. I don't want him to enslave any mortals or have some great Outcast empire. And I don't believe he's turned good."

For a moment, the machine was silent, and Mordi held his breath. Then the little trill filled the room and the light flashed green. Mordi exhaled, unreasonably relieved that a pile of metal and a tortured baseball cap had heard the truth in his words.

"Cool beans," Davy said. "I guess Aunt Zoë's right and you really are a good guy now, huh?"

"I guess so, kid." He turned then to face his nephew, and as he did, he saw Jason leaning against the door-jamb. Mordi felt his face flush, but he met Jason's steady gaze. "Just something I had to do."

"It wasn't necessary," Jason said. "We trust you. Now."

Mordi nodded. They still had a ways to go, but at least they were starting out on a solid foundation. "This one I did for me."

And his gamble had panned out. Davy's machine had confirmed what Mordi already knew.

There was still one truth left, though. One that he hadn't challenged with the machine—the simple statement that Mordichai Black no longer cared about his father's approval, much less his love.

That, he thought, was a truth best left unexamined.

Chapter Eleven

Later that day, Mordi stood outside Isole's Greenwich Village brownstone and pondered his current dilemma—how to wangle an invite inside. He knew he shouldn't be here; a Protector's home address was considered confidential information. The Protector could choose to list it on the Internet Information Directory, or could simply list a holopager number without an actual street address. Isole, apparently, was the shy type, because she'd included only her number. Fortunately, Mordi had learned a bit from his father about hacking computer files. Apparently, his genes were good for something.

Of course, since her address wasn't public, Isole probably wasn't going to be happy to see Mordi appear on her doorstep. In an effort to forestall her wrath, he bought a bouquet of carnations from a street vendor. Then, just in case she'd prefer something edible, he popped into an Indian food restaurant and bought enough to feed a party of seven.

Having gone through those procrastination measures, he had no choice but to take the plunge, buzz her apartment, and see if he could talk his way inside. He didn't have long to ponder the question; she shot him down almost instantly.

"*Go away.*" Her voice sounded tinny and thin through the building's intercom.

He stepped back so that he was in full view of the security camera, then held up first the flowers and then the food. Then he moved back to the intercom and punched the button. "I come bearing gifts."

"I'm not hungry."

"Flowers."

"I'm allergic."

"No, you're not."

She sniffed. "I'm developing an allergy."

"Isole . . ."

"Call me Izzy," she said, and he perked up, assuming that giving him her preferred name was a good sign.

He assumed wrong.

"We need to talk," he said after she told him again to go away. "We're working together on two different projects. I think it would be a good idea if we got to know each other."

"I don't see the point," she said. "Besides, I'm busy."

"Doing what?"

"I'm writing a letter to the president of the Society of It's None of Your Damn Business," she snapped.

"Fine. Whatever. I'll see you at the office."

"Good. Good night."

He stood on stoop for a moment, wondering what to do with all that food, and half-expecting her to poke her head out of an upstairs window and tell him she'd changed her mind and to come on up. Why not? That always seemed to happen in the movies.

Apparently he was not in a movie, however. Her head did not appear; and she didn't run out of the front door telling him to wait, she was only kidding.

Time for a new approach.

He passed the food and flowers off to a woman pushing her life's possessions in a shopping cart. Then he ducked into an alley, found a dark corner, and emerged as an orange tabby cat. He did a figure eight between the homeless lady's legs, and she fed him a bit of chicken. Yum.

It took some wrangling, but he finally managed to hop from street level to the fire escape. Izzy's apartment was on the second floor, so it was simply a matter of springing to the next platform, then sitting there, meowing through the window until she noticed and let him in.

Hopefully she wasn't serious about the allergies . . . and hopefully she wasn't allergic to cats.

Lacy white curtains covered her windows, but they did little to bar the view, and he watched her move through her living room in a fluffy bathrobe, a towel wrapped on her head and a steaming mug in one hand. She looked relaxed and comfortable, not at all like the woman he'd encountered at the office. This was the woman behind the cold mask. This was the woman he wanted to know better. So far, he'd only caught glimpses. Now, he wanted to see the whole woman.

The urge to simply sit there and watch her was almost overwhelming. Fortunately, chivalry took hold; he was here to talk with her, not to ogle her outside her apartment.

With that in mind, he meowed softly. Nothing. He tried again, this time a little more loudly. Did she move? Yes. But not toward him. She was heading even further away, toward the kitchen.

Time for desperate measures. He backed up, then lifted himself onto his haunches, pressing his front paws against the window. Then he scratched, mentally cringing at the sound of claws against glass. Unpleasant, yes. But definitely effective, because now she turned around and stared right at him, her eyes going wide and her mouth opening into a little O.

She eased to the window, obviously afraid she was going to spook him, then tapped gently on the glass. He meowed and rubbed up against the window, trying to make it clear that he wasn't going to run and she should just hurry up and get this business over with.

Moving slowly, she eased the sash up. As soon as the gap was big enough, he leapt inside her apartment. He probably should have done this from the beginning. After all, he was supposed to be investigating her. If she was up to no good, she wouldn't do it in front of Mordi. With a cat, however, she might be herself.

She was still cooing at him, but now she plucked him off the table where he'd landed and pressed him against her chest. She made a startled little sound, but recovered quickly and started stroking his belly. Sweet Hera, this was better than ambrosia . . . and it would take a stronger man than him to change back now. Not in the midst of this total ecstasy.

Her fingers smoothed his fur, creeping up to give him a good scratch behind the ears. He couldn't help it; he started to purr.

"Oh, you like that, do you? Well, come here, then." She carried him to the couch, then sat down, pulling him down on her lap, where she proceeded to stroke and pet and scratch until Mordi was absolutely certain that he'd died and gone to heaven.

He was a cat, and his reactions were therefore wholly catlike. But there was enough real Mordi in there that he could feel the slow burn in his soul. He wanted this woman; wanted her to touch him, to stroke him. But he wanted her as a man. He'd been drawn to her from the first moment he'd seen her. And he made himself a promise. No matter what, somehow, he was going to have her.

Her constant attention made him warm and languid, and now she eased him off her lap onto the couch cushion. He blinked, reaching one paw out in protest, but she laughed and stood up. "More later. Right now, I need to get dressed, and you probably need some food."

She headed toward the bedroom and he considered following—he was sorely tempted by the idea of watching her change—but in the end chivalry won out again and he stayed put, instead looking around her small but neat apartment, and breathing deep of the scent of her that clung to the couch cushions.

This had been a bad idea.

He'd gotten in, yes. But he hadn't counted on his own reaction from her strokes and caresses. The urge to change back to human form overwhelmed him, the urge to hold her in his arms and feel those touches on flesh instead of fur.

But that was lust talking. If he changed now, it would be the sting of her palm against his face that he felt, not soft caresses or gentle endearments. Better to remain a cat . . . and to simply keep the memory of her touch tucked away safely in his mind.

The bedroom door opened, and Izzy stepped out, clad simply in jeans and a plain white T-shirt. Her feet were bare and her hair, still wet, was combed back from her face. She wore not even the slightest bit of makeup, and Mordi thought he'd never seen a more beautiful woman.

"Tuna," she said as she moved past him toward the kitchen. "You look like a tuna kind of cat to me."

He heard her rummaging around in the kitchen;

then she emerged again with a china plate topped with canned tuna. He'd planned on something a bit more substantial for dinner, but he was hungry and . . .

She put the plate on the coffee table, but instead of letting him go to it, she picked him up and put him back in her lap. "How about a belly scratch before you eat?"

Not being stupid, he wasn't about to say no to *that*, so he let her flip him over, then sank into another stupor as her fingers worked their magic. "Oh, you're a sweet little devil, aren't you?" she said, and there was something in her voice he couldn't quite place. He was still thinking about it when she flipped him over, then sank her fingers into the thick folds of skin at the back of his neck. "Come here, little kitty-witty," she said as she plucked him up. He blinked, astounded to find his tiny limbs now flailing in the air. By the time he blinked again, she'd carried him to her bedroom door and shoved him into a cat carrier.

What in Hades?

He hissed and swiped, but she snapped the door shut and flicked the lock. Well, wasn't this special?

He should have changed while she'd been carting him across the room, but honestly, he'd been too flabbergasted to react. There was a life lesson in there; something about belly scratches and women and trust. But he was far too worked up now to sort it out.

He gave a few more mewls and spits and swipes of one clawed paw, but Izzy wasn't the least bit impressed. He considered changing back now—the carrier would surely crack against the force of his sudden growth spurt—but he might as well stick it out and see what was up.

She carried him back into the living room, sat him on the coffee table, and peered at him. "I'm sorry, sweet kitty. But if I'm going to keep you, I'm going to have to get you neutered."

Mordi squalled, automatically curling up into a ball and shoving himself into the far corner of the carrier. It was a ridiculous reaction, really, when he could just as easily change back into human form and put a fast stop to this neutering business. But in the face of that particular threat, Mordi had to admit he wasn't thinking too clearly. What male would be?

She bent down to peer at him through the little wire door, and that's when he noticed the devious grin and the hint of sparkle in those ice blue eyes.

What the . . . ?

And then he realized. Damn it all to Hades . . . he'd been caught.

He stretched out, moving away from his corner and holding his head up with as much feline dignity as possible. He kept his eyes on hers, and when he reached the front of the carrier, he pawed at the door, one quick swipe. She opened it, and he stepped out, then shifted back to human form, ending up perched on the edge of her coffee table while she stood in the middle of her living room, arms crossed over her chest, her expression entirely unreadable.

"What the *hell* do you think you're doing?" she said.

Anger, he decided. That unreadable expression was definitely anger.

"Pretending you're a cat and wrangling your way into my apartment?" she continued. "I mean, where in Hades do you get off doing that?" She was pacing, shooting him venom-laced glances with every pass.

He considered spinning an elaborate tale, couldn't think of a thing, and ended up telling her the truth. Well, some of it anyway. "We're both on this committee because we're Halflings," he began, keeping his voice calm and level, as if talking a jumper down from a building. "I just thought it would be a good idea to get to know each other better."

"You *thought*?"

"Well, yes." He cleared his throat, then gave her a tiny shrug.

"And that gave you license to change into a cat and finagle your way into my apartment?" The anger was still there, but she'd quit pacing. Mordi decided to take that as a good sign.

"I tried food and flowers first. Give me *some* credit."

That time, he thought he saw a smile, and even though it passed over her mouth so quickly he couldn't be certain, the mere possibility that she was warming up to him thrilled him.

With a mental groan, he stifled a grimace. *What* was up with him? This was about the job, not an attractive woman. And that was true no matter how appealing she might be.

She cocked her head, examining him. "And that's really it? You're just here because you want to get to know me?"

He swallowed. The woman was an empath, so how much did she know? If he said no, would she realize that he was lying? Would she realize he didn't completely trust her? Even more, would she realize that she intrigued and excited him?

She raised an eyebrow in silent question. Apparently, he was taking too long.

"Not exactly," he finally said. "I . . ." He aimed his most charming smile in her direction, figuring he didn't have anything to lose. "Well, the truth is I think you look damn good in a bathrobe."

That actually earned him a laugh, and he thought he saw a spark of sensual heat light her eyes. "I wasn't wearing a bathrobe when we met with Armistand," she said.

"No, you definitely weren't." He let his gaze drift over her, some bit of male satisfaction fueling his blood when she shifted slightly under his examination. He added, "You look damn good in jeans, too."

She looked down, focusing on something near her feet. "Thanks," she said.

"Truce?"

She didn't answer right away, just exhaled, long and loud. It was a sigh of resignation, and he knew then that he'd won.

"Halflings," she said, her tone musing. She moved to the sofa and sat down, tucking one foot up under her as she grabbed a pillow and hugged it to her chest.

"Halflings," he repeated. He moved off the table to take a seat in the chair next to her. He would have preferred moving to the couch beside her, but he didn't want the miniscule portion of her internal wall he'd knocked down to go back up. "Who would have thought our tainted blood would end up giving us such a political in?"

"Tainted?"

He frowned. "Sorry. That's my father talking."

For a moment, he expected her to argue—something about how his dad didn't really think mortal blood was bad. But she said nothing, just nodded as she played with a bit of fringe on the pillow. After a moment, she looked up, her gaze steady despite misty eyes. "I didn't even know I was a Halfling until I was seven," she said. She blinked, and a single tear ran down her cheek. "My mom died right after I was born, and my dad was never very tied into the whole Council thing. Still isn't."

"What happened?"

"She was on a mission," Izzy said. She swiped the tear away. "She was trying to save a dozen mortal children. There'd been a school bus accident, and she . . .

117

well, she got them to safety. But then there was an explosion. And my mom . . ." She sniffed, then rubbed the back of her hand under her nose, looking all of seven years old and just as innocent. "My mom was killed."

"I'm sorry," he said. He wanted to put an arm around her, to pull her close and comfort her, but that was a foolish urge. Izzy Frost didn't even like him. And Mordi wasn't about to offer himself only to get slapped away for it. Not when he was already on such shaky ground.

Beside him, she was taking deep breaths, pulling herself together. "It's okay," she said. "Sometimes I like to just sit and think about it, picturing my mom as this great hero, you know?"

"Not really," he admitted. "My parents were hardly heroic."

Her eyes softened, and her mouth curved into a smile. "Well, I'd just as soon my mom hadn't been a hero if that would have meant she'd have been around for me more."

Mordi made a buzzing noise. "Nope. Sorry. Thanks for playing. No parents there for Mordi, heroic or not."

She frowned. "Not even your mother?"

He knew what she meant: *Didn't you at least have someone around to counter all the havoc caused by your psycho dad?*

"My mom . . . well, she . . ." He trailed off, considering telling her simply that his mother was dead. But that wasn't the case, and he didn't want to start off with a pile of lies. Not with her. Not anymore than he had to.

"My mom wanted nothing to do with me," he finally said. "As soon as she learned the truth about my dad—that he was a Protector, I mean, not that he was Outcast—she told him to get lost. And then, when my powers started to show up, she got rid of me, too."

"Got rid of you?" Izzy's voice rose, her tone scandalized.

Mordi nodded. "She managed to track down my dad. Left me with him. I was seven."

"Of course you were. That's when Halfling powers really start to show up."

"Yeah, well, I thought mine were a curse. After all, if my powers had never surfaced, maybe my mom would have wanted me. She didn't. I saw her only once more, when I was twelve. She called me a freak."

"Your dad wanted you, though."

"My dad wanted someone to do his bidding. And he hated the fact that I was a Halfling. But I was all he had, and so he sucked it up. When he found out he had another son—a *full* Protector . . ." He waved his hands as if he could somehow wave away the memory. "Well, let's just say that my place in the hierarchy dropped faster than you can say 'favored son.' "

She leaned forward, pressing a soft hand on his pants-covered knee. "I'm sorry."

As much as he wanted her touch, he didn't want anyone feeling sorry for him, much less her. He shifted, pulling his leg out from under her hand as he stood up. Isole clasped her hands in her lap, her gaze shifting toward the window.

Mordi opened his mouth to apologize, and then closed it again. They'd almost connected, and he'd blown it. Now the silence hung between them like a dense fog, and he cast about for something to say, finding nothing.

When she turned back to him, he thought he saw a hint of color in her cheeks, and he felt like even more of an ass for pulling away and embarrassing her.

"At least things should improve between you two now," she said.

He shook his head, squinting at her as he frowned.

119

"Why?" he asked when it became clear that she didn't intend to elaborate.

"Well . . ." It was her turn to frown, and he noticed the little creases on her forehead, the tiny V above her nose. Isole Frost was positively adorable, and Mordi could contentedly stare at her all night.

"Never mind," she said. A shadow crossed her face, and he realized where she'd been going—the relationship could improve because Hieronymous was turning good. Soon it would be all wine and roses, not hard liquor and thorns.

Mordi knew better, but for the moment, Izzy seemed to be buying the crap that Hieronymous was selling. Inexplicable, really. The girl seemed so intelligent and insightful.

"Izzy—"

She held up a hand. "We're a lot alike," she said, apparently relying on non sequiturs to change the subject.

"How so?"

"Both raised by fathers who wanted us in their world, not the Protector world."

"Your father didn't want you to join the Council?"

"Oh, no, I didn't mean that. He was fine with that when the time came. But he never went out of his way about the whole Protector thing. He knew it existed, of course, and he told me where to find information. And he let Zephron visit me and hire a coach so I'd at least have a shot at passing my Halfling exams. But . . ." She trailed off with a shrug.

"But he didn't nurture your talents."

"Not by a long shot."

"My father nurtured mine," Mordi said. "He was determined that I'd be the heir to his empire. Not that he had an empire, mind you. And with every mistake I made, it was as if I'd stuck a knife in his heart and twisted. He hated that I was a Halfling." Mordi shrugged. "Naturally, I hated it, too."

"And now?"

"Now it's not so bad." He moved to sit on the couch, making a huge leap of faith by sitting right next to her. Then he took an even bigger one and reached out to stroke her bare arm. She jerked away, and he let his hand drop, defeated, then cleared his throat. "I enjoy my work. I believe in it. And, hey," he added with a self-deprecating shrug, "I get to work with people like you."

For a moment she didn't react; then her blue eyes warmed and a hint of a grin touched her mouth. She brushed her fingertips over her arm in exactly the manner he'd been intending. "I'm sorry," she whispered, color rising in her cheeks. "It's really best not to touch. Not without warning. And not if you want to keep . . . well . . . your secrets."

"Right," he said. "I wasn't thinking." So she was an empath *and* a mind reader—a woman who could discover every secret of his heart. She was the kind of woman who should positively terrify him, and yet all he felt was relief that she hadn't pushed him away because she didn't like *him*. She'd pushed him away so that she wouldn't take his thoughts.

In response, he reached to touch her again, and this time she didn't flinch. He brushed his fingertips over her cotton-clad shoulder, then traced the shirt's neckline, careful to touch only the fabric and not the smooth flesh beneath. He traced a path down her shirt to her jeans, then drew a line with his fingertip to her knee. Her eyes were closed, and a faint smile played at her lips. When she looked at him, he kissed his fingertips and blew the kiss to her. She caught it in her palm and pressed it to her cheek.

"Thank you," she whispered.

They sat that way for a moment, and then her clock chimed the quarter hour. The spell was broken.

She cleared her throat. "You really did work for your father, though, right? I mean, everyone knows you were a mole, but before that, you worked for your dad."

"Guilty," he said.

"But now you don't."

"Right."

"What changed?"

He didn't answer right away. First he considered what to say; considered how to summarize a lifetime of being the disappointment, juxtaposed against an ever-growing revelation slowed only by his own inability to find inner strength. He *had* found it, though. In the end he'd found the courage to not only walk away, but to betray his father in the name of doing good.

Finally, he said simply to Izzy, "I changed."

"You realized what your father wanted was wrong, and you walked away from it. Your whole perspective changed, and you along with it."

"Something like that."

She nodded slowly, as if pondering some deep mystery. "Was it hard?"

"Yeah." A knife twisted in his stomach.

"But you still managed."

Did she not trust him? He met her eyes dead-on, and nodded. "I managed."

"Then is it really so hard to believe that your father might have changed, too?"

Her words hit him with the force of a blow, violent and unexpected. He sucked in air, then gave her the only answer he knew. The only *truth* he knew. "Yes, Isole. It is."

Chapter Twelve

Surprisingly enough, Mordi didn't spend any more time trying to convince her that Hieronymous was pulling a fast one. Who knows? Maybe she'd managed to sway him with her argument. After all, if Mordi could come over to the good side, then why not his father?

She breathed deep, trying to pick up the scent of his thoughts, but all she picked up on were fluttery bits of attraction. She blushed and focused on her tea, fighting both guilt and flattery—pleased that he liked her, especially since the feeling was mutual; embarrassed for feeling like an emotional voyeur, looking in where other women couldn't see.

With supreme effort, she managed to ignore that scent of attraction. She told herself it didn't matter anyway, she wasn't influenced by it. Women all over the world were astute enough to tell when a man liked them. She just had a tiny little advantage.

What she *didn't* have an advantage in was the down-and-dirty interpersonal stuff. So she found Mordichai Black attractive. So he found her attractive. What was she supposed to do now? Especially since she shouldn't be doing anything at all. This man could mean big trouble for her. Her head knew that.

Unfortunately, the rest of her was having a hard time getting with the program.

Mordi turned to her, a question in his eyes.

"What?"

"So, how did you know it was me? The cat? Or were you really planning on doing . . . *that* . . . to a kitten?"

She laughed, remembering the expression on his face when he'd shifted back to human form. "Touch, remember? You might have been a kitten, but you were still you—and I got a Technicolor view of your thoughts. Surprised the heck out of me, but I think I recovered nicely."

He quirked a brow. "Isn't that against the rules?"

She lifted an eyebrow. "One, I was caught off guard. Two, is a man who broke into my apartment by pretending to be a cat really going to throw some rule back in my face?" She held her breath, hoping she didn't look as nervous as she felt. Because while she was totally in the right *here*, where her father was concerned she was way, way, way out on a limb.

Mordi, however, didn't seem to be thinking about anything else, and looked suitably abashed. "I had planned to ply you with Indian food," he said. "But I ended up giving it to a homeless person."

She laughed, and he shrugged, and the atmosphere in the room shifted: her wariness disappeared, replaced once again by a deep sense of well-being. She felt immediately comfortable with this man. Too comfortable.

"Could we go out?" he asked. "I'd like to take you to dinner."

She wanted to, she wanted to, she wanted to. "I've already eaten," she said, the voice of reason and responsibility.

"Oh."

She heard the disappointment in his voice and felt like a raving bitch. "I could . . . I mean, I have some cookies here, if you'd like some."

What was she doing? She should be trying to discourage him, not keeping him hanging around. He was going to ask more questions. They'd both opened up about their fathers, but he more than Izzy. Now he was going to want to know more about hers. Tit for tat and all that.

Would he be able to tell if she was lying? Or, if not lying, not exactly giving him the full story?

Sweet Hera, she was an idiot. The man looked good in a suit, challenged her, and made her laugh—and suddenly she was falling all over herself?

Damn.

In the end, though, he didn't ask her any personal questions. He just sat next to her on the couch and they watched an *X-Men* video. She suggested the old Christopher Reeves video *Superman II*, but he soundly nixed that idea. So they ended up watching Hugh Jackman and gang (hardly an unpleasant way to pass the time), laughing at some stuff, marveling at the perception of other things. Was the screenwriter perhaps a Protector? they wondered.

Two hours later, Mordi stood up to go, the picture of a perfect gentleman. He hadn't tried a thing, and Izzy wasn't sure whether to be pleased or disappointed.

At the door, though, he paused. "Listen, Isole . . ."

She nodded, silently encouraging him.

"The next session, with my father, it's Friday?"

"Right."

"Afterward, maybe we could grab a bite? I feel like I owe you dinner."

"You don't. I'd already eaten, and we didn't have plans or anything—so you really didn't give away my meal."

"All right, then. I think we should talk about the committee. Discuss the various members and make sure we agree with where they each stand, and come up with a game plan about how we can help them see the value in the renegotiated treaty."

"Have you been practicing that, or did it just come to you?"

"Sorry. I can't reveal that."

She laughed.

"Seriously, Izzy. I'd like to see you Friday night."

She licked her lips. This time, at least, she had an easy out. "I'm sorry. I've already got plans."

"Oh." She saw the displeased shift in his features, realized that he assumed she had a date.

"No, no." She rushed to correct his impression, even though she knew she should keep her mouth shut. An assumed boyfriend was as good a defense as anything against interest from a new man. She paused, thought about it, then pressed on. "My father's getting an award. I'm going to the ceremony."

"Oh." She watched as he processed the information, apparently coming back to the very reasonable conclusion that she was unattached. "*Oh*. Well, in that case, I'd be honored to *escort* you."

She realized her palms were sweating, and wiped them on her jeans. "I, um, don't know if that's such a good idea. I mean, we're working together. Should we . . . well . . . *date*?"

"Who said anything about a date?" He smiled, the gesture full of light and charm. "We have business to discuss, after all. I'll be there at the session with my father, we can talk afterward, and then I'll escort you to your father's award ceremony."

She met his grin, feeling lightheaded and more than a little foolhardy . . . but not caring one iota.

She knew it was bad; knew this traitor-hunter had

126

the potential to really screw up her life. But still, she couldn't help it. She did like him, and she did want to see him again—without Protector business hanging over their heads. They could disguise it all they wanted as "committee work," but they both knew the truth: There was something there, in the air, buzzing between them.

It enticed her as much as it frightened her.

"Izzy?"

"Yes," she said, before she could change her mind. "Yes, I'd love to go with you."

Chapter Thirteen

"So what are you saying?" Zoë asked. "That she's working for Hieronymous?"

Jason shook his head. They were on the houseboat patio, Lane next to him on the settee, the others in scattered chairs on the deck. The morning sun streaked the boat with white gold, and the steady lapping of water against the hull acted as a counterpoint to their conversation. "I'm not saying that. I'm simply saying that we don't know. Mordi's going to try to find out, but he may need our help. And in the meantime, our focus is on this Romulus guy."

" 'Holmes says,' " Zoë quoted. "Weird."

"And ironic," Taylor added, squeezing his wife's hand. "After all, Sherlock Holmes was one of the *good* guys."

"Hieronymous thinks he's doing good," Hale said.

Jason raised an eyebrow, even as the rest of them turned to look at Hale. Their expressions were incredulous. It was Lane who spoke up. "You're not serious?"

"Well, *I* don't think he's doing good," Hale explained. "I'm just saying that I doubt the H-man is going around thinking. 'Hey, gonna do a little evil today.'

I mean, he honestly thinks he's doing some great favor for Protectors everywhere. He thinks mortals are scum."

"So did you once," Tracy said, leaning back and looking smug.

"No, I never—"

"Okay, okay." Jason held up a hand. "We're getting a little sidetracked here. Whatever Hieronymous's motives, the bottom line is—"

"He's one bad dude." That came from Elmer, Hale's ferret. Not exactly a pet. More like a constant—and constantly chattering—companion.

"Exactly," Jason agreed, nodding toward the little rat.

"Bad. Evil. Vile. Major pain in the Protector patootie."

"Okay, okay," Jason said. "We get the drift." To Hale, he rolled his eyes. Ever since Davy had invented the simulated-speech collar for the little guy, Elmer had been talking nonstop. His latest fascination was telling really bad jokes.

Elmer's nonstop talk had given Jason a new respect for Hale. For years, Hale had been the only one who could understand Elmer's incessant chattering. Jason's son had put an end to all that, and although Jason loved the little tyke, there were times when he really wanted to take his boy's invention and drop it into some deep-sea abyss. Oops . . . how on earth did *that* happen?

"So where do we start?" Zoë said.

"Well, wait a minute." Tracy, Hale's wife, spoke up. "Zephron doesn't know that you guys are going to be playing detective? Isn't that against the rules?" Her forehead was creased with worry. Not surprising. She and Hale were supposed to be packing for a vacation in Greece. The idea of her husband getting dragged into an unauthorized mission couldn't be very appealing.

"I didn't say he doesn't know per se. Just that we're working under the table."

Tracy frowned, but it was Lane who spoke up. "In other words, you're assuming that—as usual—Zephron knows exactly what's going on."

Jason shrugged. "He seems to have that knack."

"It's the Mord-man you ought to be watching," Elmer said in his computer-generated voice. *"He's the one who's always working for the Big Dog. Every time you think he's gone straight, he's back on board with his daddy."*

"He was working as a mole, Elmer," Jason said. "You know that as well as we do."

"Oh, sure. That's what he says . . ."

"Elmer." Hale's tone was harsh, no-nonsense.

"Harrumph."

"Look," Jason said. "You guys might have issues with Mordi. But he *is* my brother, and Zephron does trust him. And that means that until I see something to make me think otherwise, I trust him, too."

"I trust him," Zoë said. She half-shrugged, then added, "Well, *now* I do."

"Me, too," Tracy said.

Hale shrugged. "Like you said, we've all had our issues, but he is family. If he's getting scammed by this broad, I want to help him."

"Suckers," Elmer said, then turned in a circle three times and buried his head under his haunches, effectively dismissing them all.

"It's not just about helping him," Jason said. "If Hieronymous is getting to a re-assimilation counselor, then who knows how many other Protectors he has in his pocket. Like Romulus, for example. We need to know what's going on—not to protect Mordi, but to protect the Council. Hell, maybe even to protect the world. Think of Romulus. That—"

131

"What can he do from a holding cell, though?" Taylor asked.

"Who knows?" Zoë answered. "But he's popular and well connected. He may not stay in that holding cell for long."

Hale nodded. "She's right. Things are happening." He drew in a breath and turned to Tracy. "Well? It's up to you."

She grimaced. "Let me think. Lounge on a foreign beach with a paperback and a tall drink, or stay in Los Angeles while my husband goes out and helps possibly to save the world." She pressed a finger to her mouth. "Gee, tough decision."

"Okay. So we investigate." He ignored his wife's amused head-shake.

"And if you do find out that Hieronymous and Romulus have some huge plan brewing?" Taylor asked. "Then what are we going to do?"

"Tell Mordi," Jason said. "Get a group together and then foil whatever plot they're cooking." He tried out a smile. "Shouldn't be too hard," he added, trying to intone the words with an air of confidence. "We've all foiled Daddy Dearest before."

"True," Zoë said. "Let's hope it was skill and not luck."

"Or if it was luck," Taylor added, "let's hope it hasn't run out."

Chapter Fourteen

"This?" Hieronymous's voice rose in incredulity, one hand indicating the tree several stories below him and the kitten trapped in its upper branches. *"This* is how you intend to examine my goodwill and veracity?"

Izzy shrugged, forcing her expression to remain stern and serious. "For starters," she said. In truth, it *was* a rather odd assignment for a superhero, but with the likes of Hieronymous, she thought it best that they start small.

So here they were: she, Mordi, and Hieronymous, standing on the balcony of his penthouse apartment, looking down at Fifth Avenue and the park across the wide street, where a tiny kitten was trapped in a treetop.

She wished she could convince Mordi of his father's sincerity. At the moment, Mordi was standing off to one side, arms crossed over his chest, looking for all the world like this was one big waste of time. They hadn't talked much about it since the other night, and she'd been glad. There'd grown an easy comfortableness between them, a feeling in the air that was decidedly absent now, and she was grateful to have shared a few hours without doubt and disbelief hanging between them.

She didn't begrudge Mordi his doubts, of course. Frankly, had she not felt the change in Hieronymous herself, she never would have believed it. But she *had* felt it, and she'd never once failed where her powers were concerned. She just wished (foolish, really, since she hardly knew the man) that Mordi would trust *her*, even if he didn't trust his father.

From the way he was shooting vile glances toward Hieronymous, she really didn't think that would happen.

The ex-Outcast in question was still at the balcony, his back to them, a pair of binocs in his hand as he peered down toward the street.

"A *kitten*?" he said once again, his voice still reflecting his bafflement. "I'm to rescue a pet?"

"Well, yes." Isole cleared her throat. "We're starting small. Regulations require me to present a series of tests of increasing difficulty. Considering who you are, I think it's best that we follow protocol to the letter. I certainly don't want someone later raising a question as to whether you received special treatment. Do you?"

His face darkened, and she recoiled. But then the shadow passed and he drew in a breath. "You're right, of course, my dear. I guess I'm simply anxious to get to the meat of it. I've been so long without helping mortals, my fingers are itching to jump into the fray. To do some real good."

Mordi had been standing beside her through all of this, a permanent scowl darkening what she'd come to regard—from a purely empirical standpoint of course—as a perfectly handsome face. He had an air of sophistication, even despite his anger. The veneer cracked, however, as he faked a cough, the sound half-disguising a bitter curse, "Bullshit."

She glared at him and turned back to Hieronymous. "You *are* helping mortals. That little girl who owns the cat is devastated."

"Of course," Hieronymous said. "Of course. I only meant—"

"This is absurd," Mordi cut in. "You're not interested in helping mortals, you're—"

"*Son.*" Hieronymous's tone was sharp, cutting, and Izzy straightened in surprise. Mordi, she noticed, had also drawn himself up. But his stance didn't seem surprised. No, he seemed ready for battle.

Need and hatred and disappointment and love meshed together in the air between father and son, like a dense tapestry, so interwoven that Izzy couldn't tell whose thoughts were whose, and she felt a wash of sadness for both of them.

She took Mordi's arm, careful to touch his shirt and not skin, and tugged him back. "We'll wait here," she said to Mordi. Then she looked at Hieronymous. "Go on. Help them."

His face hardened as he stared at his son. She couldn't blame him. Mordi wasn't giving an inch.

"The sooner you rescue the kitten, the sooner we can move on to bigger things," she said.

He blinked, his face clearing as he smiled at her, white teeth shining brilliantly. "Of course, my dear. You'll be watching from here?"

"Right."

Hieronymous drew in a breath and pulled his cloak tight around him, stepped up onto the ledge, and readied himself to jump off into nothingness. Izzy lurched forward and grabbed his hem, tugging him back before anyone down below looked up and thought they were witnessing a suicide.

He whipped around to face her, irritation flashing in his eyes. And why not? She was interrupting him once again. "You, uh, know the rules, right?" she said.

He peered over the edge, then looked back at her. "The elevator?"

" 'Fraid so. Regulation 876(B)(2)(a) is quite clear—Protector powers are to be revealed to mortals only as a last resort. Minimal powers, Mr. Black. Please keep that in mind."

"Of course," he said, then moved back inside, presumably toward the elevator.

" 'Of course,' " Mordi mimicked, his tone undeniably smarmy.

Izzy ignored him, moving toward the railing and peering over, waiting for Hieronymous to appear below.

"You can't possibly believe he's serious," Mordi finally said.

She sighed. "Can we stop beating a dead Gorgon?" She turned away and concentrated on the street below, waiting for Hieronymous to emerge. Where was he?

Mordi moved up beside her, his own binocs in hand. "I'm sorry."

She turned just enough to add him to her field of vision, but didn't say anything.

He exhaled noisily. "For the love of Zeus, at least do me the courtesy of talking to me. I'm your assistant in this, after all."

She still didn't face him, but she did answer. "An assistant, by definition, *assists*."

He backed up against the railing, forcing himself to remain in the periphery of her vision. "You know, I may not have your empathic powers, but I'm still picking up on a little hostility here."

"It's not coming from me," she said, turning to face him.

He had the good grace to at least look a little sheepish. "I don't believe my father is interested in doing good."

"I picked up on that," she said. "But *I* do believe it. I looked."

She spoke the words firmly, and he stared at her for a moment. Then his eyes narrowed, full of suspicion.

"It's against regulations to poke around in someone's head without a mind warrant," he said.

She crossed her arms over her chest. "It's not against regulations if they're applying for re-assimilation."

His eyes burned like emerald fire, and she could see the steel inside him as he examined her. That same steel drove him now to hunt traitors, and it had helped him survive a life with the evil Hieronymous. "And?"

"I *saw*." She didn't bother telling him that Hieronymous had made her look before she'd wanted to. "I saw that he wants to do good."

"You saw wrong."

She stiffened. "I told you. I *never* see wrongly."

He turned away from her, peering out toward the park. "This time you did."

She bit back a rude retort, choosing instead to focus not on Mordi's words, but on *him*—on what she'd seen the other night, and on what she felt now. Deep hunger. Need. Loneliness. And a keen desire to be loved, to be needed.

The swell of his emotions crested over her, so powerful that she had to stifle the urge to put her arms around him, to be the one who gave him the comfort he craved. Fearing her own reaction, she moved away, letting the distance between them grow until the pressure on her chest lifted and she could breathe normally again without getting lost in the scent of his thoughts.

"There's a lot of bad blood between you and your father," she finally said. "Maybe it's coloring your perception. Blinding you."

At first, she thought he wouldn't answer. Then he turned to her, his face hard. "There's more bad blood than you know. But believe me, it's not coloring anything. Not unfairly, at least. I know him better than you can ever hope to. The man has no interest in being on the Council. Not to help people. He's trying to further some scheme."

She didn't need to touch him to know that he truly believed his words, and she fought a stab of pity for this man who'd grown up with only a shadow of a father. Her own had been the center of her world. If it had been different, though ... if he'd failed her at every turn, could she suddenly believe in him now?

She had an inkling of what Mordi was feeling, and without thought she reached out for him, wanting to touch him, to feel the anger that cut through him and to discover if it was tempered with love ... or only hate.

"Don't even think about it," he said.

She drew her hand back as if burned. "Sorry."

"I'm telling you how I feel. What I know. And what I know is, Hieronymous Black doesn't have a good bone in his body. He's evil. Manipulative. He wants something, and I'm going to figure out what."

She nodded, accepting the gauntlet that he was throwing down. "You're right," she said. "He does want something. He wants back on the Council. He wants to make amends. And he's going to pass the tests." She shrugged, wanting to reach some sort of truce with Mordi, the idea that there was a rift between them bothering her more than it should. How could his good opinion mean so much to her already? "Besides, what I think doesn't really matter. I only make a recommendation. He might ace all the tests, and the Inner Circle can still refuse him re-assimilation."

She could see Mordi's mouth twist, but was spared

his retort by the appearance of Hieronymous on the street below. She was certain he'd pass this test—after all, how much easier could it get?

Even so, she held her breath—and that one little bit of doubt ate at her gut. Because, if there was room for doubt, then there was also room for error. Her error. Her power's error.

And oh, sweet Hera, she couldn't afford to be wrong.

Chapter Fifteen

A *kitten*. A tiny little ball of white fluff, and he, Hieronymous Black, was having to jump through hoops to pluck the little creature from the top of an overgrown oak tree.

Ridiculous.

Absurd.

And yet one glance at his balcony and his two little Protector babysitters made it oh-so-clear just how necessary this charade was.

He stalked up to the kitten's owner, who was eyeing the tree dubiously even while trying to comfort a screaming brat. He stood beside her and looked up, calculating the distance to the top branch, wishing he had a few of his tools that would make retrieving the pathetic feline that much easier.

But no, this task had to be undertaken with a minimal amount of Protector skills in order to not scare mortals. It was an absurd rule, which only served to prove his point—that Protectors and mortals couldn't interact normally. As Protectors were clearly the superior breed, mortals should simply learn to bow to their will.

At the moment, his position was not the popular one. Soon, though . . . very, very soon . . .

The woman's gaze had shifted from the tree to Hieronymous, and now she was examining him with that same somewhat bewildered expression.

He did a quick mental inventory, confirmed that he was wearing the proper attire for mortals, then tilted his head in greeting. "Good afternoon, madam," he said. Then, though it pained him to do so, he dropped to one knee and greeted the sticky-faced little brat. "And to you, too, my dear."

The woman's face hardened into a thick mask. "May we help you?" she said, her voice cold.

Hieronymous stood up. So much for being polite. That was the trouble with the world today; no trust, and an appalling lack of manners.

He gestured toward the tree. "I thought perhaps I could be of assistance."

"Oh!" The woman's features softened. "That's very kind of you. We'd certainly appreciate it. Wouldn't we, Amy?"

The brat stuck her thumb in her mouth and stared at Hieronymous, her eyes slightly narrowed. He had the sudden thought that the child was a much better judge of character than the mother.

"Yes, well . . ." He trailed off, examining the tree. Above him, the little feline mewled. He could levitate the thing, bring it gently to the ground, but a quick glance toward his apartment building confirmed that Isole and his son were watching his every move.

Minimal Protector powers, she'd said. A wholly absurd rule, considering he was trying to be readmitted to the very organization that prided itself on those powers.

Still, he couldn't do anything to thwart his reassimilation. He certainly wasn't going to allow one mewling feline to destroy all his careful plotting.

No, this was a necessary first step in his plan, and he would see it through. As much as he hated it, as much as it demeaned him, he *would* see it through.

He'd just never expected that the first step to world domination would involve climbing a tree.

Chapter Sixteen

Hera's handbags! His father had actually saved the kitten.

If Mordi hadn't watched the spectacle with his own eyes, he never would have believed it. But he had seen and Hieronymous had saved, and Mordi wished he'd had a digital image-recording device. *This* he'd love to share with Jason.

Behind him, Hieronymous burst through the door and onto the balcony. "Fabulous!" Hieronymous raved. "I feel twenty pounds lighter. As if I'm walking on air. As if I've just eaten ambrosia and—"

"Cut the clichés, already." Mordi cast both his father and Izzy a dark look. "I mean, at least be original."

Hieronymous's smile evaporated. It slowly returned, but this time the effect was slightly sinister, and Mordi had a feeling the smile was meant only for him.

"Heartwarming," the man said, his voice flat. "So sorry if that seems cliché to you, son, but it is the truth."

"Who am I to argue with my father?"

A pained look crossed Hieronymous's eyes. "I had hoped . . . well, let's just say that I had hoped that my new outlook would bring us closer. I would like to re-build bridges. Son."

His father's words cut through Mordi like a knife. He was saying all the things Mordi wanted to hear, but Mordi didn't believe a word. He couldn't. Even so, he took a step forward, his body seeming to move of its own accord. What was it they said—hope springs eternal?

He caught sight of Izzy looking about ready to melt from the sappy sweetness of it all, and Mordi stopped cold. It *was* sappy. It was also scripted. Hieronymous didn't want Mordi in his life. Not unless he could be used. And a Halfling son? Hieronymous didn't want one. He never had.

Mordi took a deep breath. "Any bridges between us burnt down for good a long time ago. I'm sorry, *Dad*. I just don't believe you."

A familiar fury appeared in Hieronymous's eyes, but it was already cooling by the time he turned toward Izzy. "He doesn't understand. I feel as though the world has opened up to me. As if I've stepped over a precipice and into a different place." He sighed, the sound long and drawn out. "A better place, I think."

Mordi watched as Izzy—supposedly a trained professional with empathic powers—bought into his father's routine. Had Hieronymous truly convinced her? Or maybe he'd invented something that made her see things Hieronymous's way? Mordi ruled that possibility out, though. In the past, Hieronymous might have gotten away with it, but in the last year—as a result of past trouble with the man—the Council had implemented a power-usage tracking system. Now, when an Outcast engaged his unique power, the Council knew.

And nothing had blipped about Hieronymous. Which meant that either his father had truly convinced

Izzy of his sincerity . . . or she was working with him from the inside.

"You did excellent work," Izzy was saying, her face schooled into a professional expression. She walked Hieronymous back toward the French doors that led into his penthouse.

She took a seat on the overstuffed loveseat, and Hieronymous sat across from her in the only chair. Mordi stood, debating whether or not to sit, when sitting would involve a certain proximity to one Izzy Frost, a woman who definitely got under his skin. Lust, suspicion, and a billion other emotions swarmed through him whenever he was around her.

He remained standing. It seemed easier. And safer.

"Now, then," she said to Hieronymous, all but ignoring Mordi as she hauled a leather case onto her lap. "It's time for some of the more mundane aspects of the re-assimilation process." She opened her case, rummaging through as she continued to talk. "This really is a mindless exercise," she said, "so please don't be nervous."

"My dear," Hieronymous said, "I have nothing to be nervous about. My intentions are completely pure."

Mordi managed not to retch when his father dumped that load of B.S., but when Izzy pulled out a series of sturdy white cards with black inkblot images on them, Mordi knew the time had come. He moved nearer, all his attention focused on her, intentionally not looking at his father. "In case you forgot to read his file," Mordi began, forcing his voice to remain steady, "my father happens to have an intellect that's off the charts. I think you can safely assume he's more than capable of faking his way through a Rorschach test."

His tone was haughty, his manner both superior and condescending. And yet the woman didn't even blink. For that, at least, Mordi had to give her a few points.

"I'll make a note of it," she said, then scowled at him as she tapped the cards on the coffee table, aligning their edges. After a moment, she looked back up, her eyes widening as if she were surprised to find him still standing there. "Was there something else?"

"Plenty," he said. "But we'll discuss it tonight." He held his breath, afraid that she was going to back out of their date. Instead, she just met his eyes and nodded.

Mordi turned just enough to bring his father into his line of sight. His sire's brown irises burned like hot coals, and Mordi thought he saw a familiar emotion burning deep in those soulless eyes—disappointment.

He swallowed, then forced himself to walk out of the room. Just one foot, then another, in some ridiculous parody of normalcy. But nothing was normal, could never *be* normal. Once again, Mordi had disappointed his father. And though he knew that he shouldn't care, damn it all to Hades, he did.

And that was why he walked straight out of the penthouse and didn't once look back.

Chapter Seventeen

"Absurd," Hieronymous said, anger burning through him like whiskey. "The hoops that I must jump through . . ." He trailed off, hands clenched at his side. "In the end, I hope posterity will recognize the sacrifices I've made."

He was deep beneath the streets of Manhattan in an abandoned subway tunnel. He'd met Clyde there, and now his former Chief of Guards was standing at attention, his scarred face full of awe and loyalty.

"Your sacrifices will be our salvation, sire," Clyde said with a reverential tip of his head.

Hieronymous snorted. "Fool," he spat. "Perhaps that will be so if I do prevail, but in order to fulfill my destiny and bring about the subjugation of mortals, my plan must go forth without the slightest of bumps."

Clyde swallowed, his throat moving. "Has there . . . has there been a bump, sire?"

"Yes, of course there's been a bump. Why else would I have risked this meeting with you?" He spread out his arm, silently indicating the filthy chamber in which they stood. "And why would I choose such a putrid forum in which to discuss the matter?"

Clyde—wisely—said nothing.

Hieronymous paced along the yellow line bordering the subway platform, his fingers itching for a flat surface on which to drum. Finding nothing, he settled for rounding on Clyde. "A Rorschach test. *Why*, pray tell, was I not aware that I would be subjected to such ridiculousness?"

Clyde seemed to shrink under Hieronymous's wrath. "I don't know, sire. Our intelligence must be faulty."

"Faulty?" he repeated. *"Faulty?"* He moved toward Clyde, watching his second cower in fear. "And do you believe that such a . . . fault is acceptable?"

"No, sire. It won't happen again."

Hieronymous drew in a deep breath and collected himself. He could, after all, be magnanimous when necessary. "I trust that it will not. Even so, there are changes to be made. Precautions to be taken."

He turned away, pacing the platform, his hands clasped before him, his incredible intellect on overdrive.

"Are we abandoning the plan, sire?"

Hieronymous spun around. "Of course we are not going to abandon the plan. I've spent the past year putting all the pieces into place. I have no intention of abandoning the plan now—not even if I must rescue a dozen more kittens and return lollipops to petulant little brats." He aimed a sharp glare at Clyde. "The inkblot test was a minor setback. With my superior cognitive skills I, of course, am certain that Ms. Frost remains entirely unaware of my deception. Even so . . ."

He trailed off. Even so, it would be best to move up his timetable and kick his plan into overdrive.

Once again, he turned to Clyde. "You *do* know what I expect of you?"

"Yes, sire. Of course, sire."

"Good. I shall expect the diversion in four days."

Clyde's eyes went wide. "Four days? I had anticipated a week. Perhaps more."

"What you anticipated is not my concern. I've told you what I expect of you." He turned slightly, meeting his servant's gaze. "Or are you telling me that you are unable to deliver?"

"No, sir. Of course not, sir."

Hieronymous nodded, satisfied. He had no reason to doubt Clyde. The burly Outcast had been nothing but loyal since he'd first sworn fealty so many years ago. He would come through. He had to.

But it wasn't Clyde's loyalty or his skill that preyed on Hieronymous now. It was the lack of loyalty from where he'd expected it most.

Not Jason—he'd lost that connection before it had ever been forged.

Mordichai . . .

Though he hated to admit it, Hieronymous had become complacent, used to his Halfling son's constant presence. For that matter, he had even become resigned to the likelihood that Mordichai would inherit the empire once he himself ceased to be.

Not ideal, of course. Certainly, Hieronymous would have preferred a pureblood offspring. But he'd made do, resigning himself to the unfortunate fact that his heir would be an imperfect recipient of a perfect legacy.

Then he'd learned of his son's deception. Of his treason.

Some things could be forgiven. Betrayal could not.

He clenched his fists, fingernails digging crescents into his palms as he fought to quell the burst of anger. *Control.* Control was ever so important in such matters.

Control over others, and control over one's emotions.

He had such control now. And he knew what he had to do.

Slowly, he faced Clyde who was standing at attention, still awaiting his dismissal.

"There is one other thing," Hieronymous said, taking care to keep his voice blank, emotionless. "My son is proving to be an impediment to my plan. I think it's time that we take Mordichai out of the equation. Tonight. When we acquire the bait." He met Clyde's eyes, saw both surprise and joyous anticipation reflected there. "And Clyde," he added. "I hope you understand that I want a permanent solution."

Chapter Eighteen

The main offices of the Venerate Council of Protectors were located on Mount Olympus, a tribute to the Protectors' heritage as descendants of Zeus and his siblings. Back then, the general populace had assumed the original Protectors were gods. And Zeus, not being a particularly humble sort, hadn't done anything to disabuse them of that notion.

There were times when Jason thought it might be cool to be considered a god, but on the whole he much preferred the current arrangement. The actual getting to Olympus was a hassle, and once there, he couldn't help but roll his eyes at the statues of Greek gods and goddesses—his great-great-great aunts, uncles, cousins, and such—that filled every nook and cranny. The offices in New York and D.C. were much more hospitable, if slightly darker, what with being underground and all.

Now he walked through the sun-streamed hallways, searching for Dionys, the elder in charge of granting visiting privileges to Protectors currently in the stockades. The man wasn't on Jason's favorite-person list, but under the circumstances, seeing him was necessary.

Jason had spent a year on Olympus after he'd escaped his father's clutches. And though Dionys had shown no signs of contempt recently, back then the elders had been more than a little dubious about where Jason's true loyalty lay. Dionys had been particularly cold. His hatred of Hieronymous ran deep, and the elder had held no compunction about warning Jason that, if he should turn out to be aligned with his father, he'd be tossed into the catacombs and never again see the light of day.

The accusation and threat had infuriated Jason then, and it still bothered him now. Not a lot he could do about it, though, so he kept searching for the elder.

Dionys wasn't in his office, and the assistant on duty suggested Jason check in the library.

Jason passed a statue of Zeus, arms wrapped around Hera, then another of his closer relative, Poseidon. Another long corridor, and then finally he reached the double doors of the library. He pushed in, received a stern glare from the librarian, then padded softly toward the back.

He found the elder in a small alcove, seven leatherbound volumes open in front of him, the musty smell of ancient paper and ink filling the air. Dionys was making notes, carefully copying information from the volumes onto sheets of lined parchment with an ornate purple fountain pen. Jason waited for the elder to notice him. And waited. And waited.

Finally, he cleared his throat. Dionys looked up, wire spectacles perched in front of clear blue eyes whose edges crinkled with age.

"Ah, young Jason, is it? What brings you back to Olympus?"

The elder's tone was conversational and warm, but

even so, Jason fought a fresh wave of anger. He took five deep breaths and focused his thoughts. This wasn't about him anymore. Dionys had apparently moved on; so should Jason.

"I was hoping to receive dispensation to speak with Romulus," Jason said. He left it at that. If the elder needed a reason, he had a story contrived and ready to go.

"Dispensation?" The elder looked up, his expression amused. "That's certainly not necessary. Romulus has been released on bail."

Jason blinked. "Bail?"

"Why, yes."

"Who bailed him out?"

"You know perfectly well that information is confidential. But I would hardly expect a Protector such as Romulus to remain in the stockade for any length of time."

"Um, right." Jason frowned, reminding himself he'd expected that very thing. "Is he still on Olympus?"

"He may well be," the elder said. "I don't have that information. Certainly, his bail held no such conditions, and while he did express his gratitude to the elders on the prisoner committee, he didn't tell us where he intended to go." He met Jason's eyes. "Of course, we have his holopager number, so we are able to contact him."

"Of course," Jason said, hoping the sarcasm wasn't showing. "Thank you for your help."

The elder nodded, then picked his pen back up and resumed his work. Jason considered that a dismissal and began walking away, pondering the problem of how he was going to locate Romulus. He'd try a holopage, but the treasonous Protector likely wouldn't answer. And even if Romulus had an address on file, the odds were good he was staying elsewhere. . . .

"Excellent news about your father," Dionys said.

Yanked away from his thoughts, Jason stopped cold. He turned around slowly to face the elder. "I'm sorry. What did you say?"

"Your father," Dionys said, that purple pen tapping a rhythm on his paper. "He's applied for reassimilation. I thought you knew."

"Yeah," Jason said. "I'd heard something about that."

"You don't sound pleased." The elder's faced creased with concern. "I had thought you would welcome your father's return to Olympus."

"Ah, well . . ." What in Hades was he supposed to say to that? "I'm . . . well, I guess I'm a little bit surprised that *you're* pleased about it."

Dionis shook his head, his expression one of amused patience. "Nonsense. Your father and I may have had our differences, but I have issues with *all* Outcasts. Once he returns to the fold, though . . ." The elder trailed off, shaking his head, and Jason found himself truly flabbergasted. Had everyone gone insane?

"This is truly excellent news," Dionys continued. "A powerful Protector like your father with such a strong heritage. And your grandfather's seat has been empty now for over ten years. It's high time it was occupied again."

Jason's blood ran cold. Dionys couldn't mean what Jason thought he meant . . . could he? "My grandfather's seat?" The Inner Council essentially ruled over all Protectors, and the seats were passed down along familial lines, going to the eldest member of the family past a certain age. Jason knew he and Mordi were in line for a spot, but that possibility was years away. It had never even occurred to him that his father might still lay claim to a seat. "Hieronymous could fill my grandfather's seat?"

"Of course. At the right hand of Zephron. The seat would have naturally been your father's, had he not been Outcast." The elder smiled broadly. "And now, of course, it will be his once again."

Chapter Nineteen

As Mordi paused on Izzy's doorstep to straighten his tie, his holopager beeped. He considered ignoring it—he had no intention of getting sidetracked from this date by some Protector emergency—but in the end guilt won out. He jammed the Receive button with his thumb. "What?" he demanded, even before the image could take form.

It was Bilius. "We've had an anonymous tip. An Outcast plot. We're not sure what's going on, but since it's taking place at a mortal forum, we assume the plan is to eradicate one of them."

Mordi groaned, seeing his date go flying off to the wayside. "When?"

"Tonight."

Yup. Bye-bye, Izzy. "Okay. Give me the details."

"The Thomas Edison Inventors Award Ceremony. Our tipster says—"

"Wait. You said the Inventors Award Ceremony? The one here? In New York? Tonight?"

"Is that a problem?" Bilius did not look particularly pleased with the interruption.

"No, sir. No problem at all." Because Mordi already

happened to be attending that particular ceremony. So it really was no problem at all.

In fact, the only problem he foresaw was that Izzy just might be the target. After all, his father had an overwhelming interest in inventors and inventions. And, now that he thought of it, it was quite possible that the woman was in cahoots with Daddy Dearest. It was an unpleasant possibility, but one he couldn't deny. Perhaps that's why Zephron had put him on this case as well.

He sighed. In all honesty, he'd been hoping for a little action this evening. Arresting his date, however, wasn't quite what he had in mind.

Chapter Twenty

Izzy sat in the front row of the ballroom at the Montcraig Hotel in midtown Manhattan, her arm hooked through Mordi's, only their sleeves touching, as she clutched the program for the seventh annual Thomas Edison Award Ceremony. Her father was up on that stage, Mordi was beside her—staying blissfully silent about his doubts regarding his father—and Izzy was in heaven.

The chairman finished introducing Harold, and everyone clapped. Then her father moved behind the podium, and Izzy lost herself in his speech, sharing his moment in the sun.

". . . but most of all, I must give credit where credit is due," Harold said. He fumbled at the podium, papers spread out before him, then shoved his glasses more firmly up his nose. He cleared his throat. "I've been fortunate, recently. The last few years have been inspirational for me, most likely because I've had some income to inspire me."

He paused for effect, then waggled his bushy eyebrows. The crowd laughed, just as they were supposed to, and Izzy smiled so hard her face hurt.

161

Mordi leaned toward her. "He's a good speaker."

She nodded. Her father's natural nervousness was fading as he basked in the glory of finally realizing a lifelong dream.

"Not just financial inspiration, though," he continued. "I need to thank my daughter for her support and her love—"

Izzy beamed, ducking her head slightly as the applause swelled. Beside her, Mordi also clapped, but when she turned to look at him, she saw that he was scanning the sea of faces nearby.

"What is it?" she whispered.

A shadow crossed his face, and she inhaled the earthy scent of guilt.

She frowned, confused. "Mordi?"

"Nothing. I just thought I saw . . . nothing."

She wanted to press him, but her father's words caught her attention, and she was consumed by a little guilt of her own.

"I also need to thank those behind-the-scenes folks who help in so many ways. In ways both bankable and inspirational." He leaned forward toward the microphone and cast his gaze over the crowded room. "You know who you are, but let's just say that an enthusiastic silent partner can be good for the soul."

Again, the crowd tittered. Izzy's father's nose turned slightly red, and Izzy felt a little ill. Reflexively, she tugged at her arm, wanting to extricate herself from Mordi, this man who could so easily destroy her career. He turned to her and smiled. She stayed put, feeling a little weak. In truth, however, she liked being close to him.

Her father plowed on, finishing his speech with a finesse she would never have expected. Certainly, he never could have performed this well before.

Before.

Sweet Hera, did her father really owe this new confidence to Hieronymous? He did. And that, even more than what she'd seen of Hieronymous's soul, convinced her that the Outcast was sincere. Why else would the super villain help a man like her father?

She tilted her head, watching her father on the podium. So happy. So *alive*.

Her whole life, she would have given anything to see his face light up like that. She wanted everything good for her father, for this man who'd raised her and loved her, who'd joked with her and kept her secrets. Without a mother, it had been her father who'd gone with her to buy her first bra—though before setting foot in the store he *had* offered to simply invent one for her. And he'd been there when the very first boy she'd had a crush on ignored her, studiously managing to avoid any recognition whatsoever that Izzy existed.

He'd spent a lot of time in his lab, sure. But when she'd needed him, her father had been there. Always, and without fail.

Her father paused again in his speech, and she applauded enthusiastically. A little *too* enthusiastically, if the sidelong looks from her neighbors were any indication. Mordi, however, only looked amused, and his amusement encouraged her. She threw a grin in the dissenters' direction, then let out a wolf whistle for her father. After all, she wanted him to know she was out here.

And even though Mordi applauded wildly as well—going so far as to toss in a whistle of his own—when Izzy leaned back in her seat, her satisfaction was tainted with regret. Not for her. For Mordichai.

What must it have been like, she wondered, growing up as the son of Hieronymous Black?

Not pleasant. Of that much, she was certain. Hieronymous might be determined to re-assimilate—and his desire might even be sincere—but Izzy didn't doubt for a second that what everyone said about his notorious past was one-hundred-percent true. Even now, he wasn't exactly a warm and fuzzy kind of guy.

She frowned, pondering the current Re-Assimilation Act and her place in it. Some Outcasts could be brought back in, sure. But was Hieronymous really the kind they wanted? Could he ever really be an asset to the Council?

She shifted in her seat, uncomfortable with the direction of her thoughts.

"Anything wrong?"

Mordi's voice, low and intense, startled her, and her heart began to race.

"No. Nothing. Just thinking. About Dad. And . . . stuff."

"Stuff," he repeated, but while she'd expected him to sound amused, he looked deadly serious.

She stilled, sure he was on to her. That he'd heard her father's reference to a silent partner and put two and two together. Oh, sweet Hera, what was she supposed to do now?

"What kind of stuff?" he pressed.

"You know. Stuff." She shrugged, determined not to give anything away.

He didn't appear thrilled by her oh-so-eloquent answer. She decided to elaborate. "Daddy and his inventions and how he used to torment me with all his gizmos and stuff. Just memories."

His eyes narrowed, and her stomach twisted, but she held his gaze dead-on. She sniffed a little, then wished she hadn't. The scent of suspicion was heavy in the air between them, and she realized just what a huge fool she'd been to let Mordichai Black into her apartment last night.

She'd been an even bigger fool to let him into her life.

She lifted her chin. "If you don't mind, I'm trying to watch my dad." She turned back toward the stage and watched with rapt attention as the ceremony finished up.

Her father had switched to a PowerPoint presentation, and was taking the audience through the ins and outs of the Polarity Reversal Prototype, the pocket-sized machine that had landed him this award, and that Izzy absolutely did not understand. Mordi shifted beside her, then pulled his arm free of hers. She stifled a little gasp, fighting an unreasonable sense of loss. She knew she shouldn't, but she turned to him. His features were still hard, but the familiar softness was returning, and she relaxed a little.

"I need to run to the lobby. I'll be right back."

She nodded, and as soon as he slipped down the row and up the aisle toward the lobby door, her face relaxed, and she realized she'd been clenching her jaw. She wanted him back—wanted his arm on hers—but at the moment, she was absurdly glad that he was gone. Her thoughts were too much in a ramble, and even though she knew intellectually that he couldn't pick up on what she was thinking, emotionally she wanted to hide.

She didn't want him to see the truth. Didn't want him to know that she wanted Hieronymous far away from the Council even as much as she wanted him back in, a full-fledged, card-carrying Protector. And none of those desires had to do with the Outcast's intentions or beliefs or motives. Instead, she wanted him on the Council because once he was there, her father would be safe.

With a slow sigh, her thoughts drifted to Mordi. He would hate that—

Mordichai!

Suddenly her mind was filled with thoughts of him,

her senses overwhelmed by his essence. Her heart thrummed in her chest and she sat up sharply, confused and terrified. She was sensing something that was entirely removed from how she felt about Mordi or how she feared he might discover her deception. It was simply about the man himself.

Danger . . . harm . . . deception.

The thoughts surrounded her, the bitter smell of animosity, and she twisted in her seat, trying to find their source. Who? Who wanted to harm Mordichai? She had to find his attacker . . . had to warn him.

She couldn't bear the thought that harm might come to him. And that realization scared her as much as the knowledge that she might already be too late.

Chapter Twenty-one

Jason's holographic image stood on Mordi's holopager, his hands spread wide with agitation. "It was the most ridiculous thing I've ever heard," he said. "*Why* would Dionys be excited about our father's return to the fold? And what's this B.S. about sitting at Zephron's right hand? It's a total cro—"

"One thing at a time," Mordi said. He was in a small service hallway off the lobby. At the moment, the hall was completely deserted. "Did you talk to Romulus?"

"Out on bail."

At that, Mordi took a step back. Apparently, his surprise showed on his face, because Jason's image nodded.

"I know. Another oddity in a truly odd day."

"But it makes some sense," Mordi said. "Maybe he was the one planning something here tonight. But then he saw me and figured he shouldn't press his luck, and that's why nothing's gone down yet."

Jason nodded slowly. "Could be. Or maybe Isole Frost was the one planning something there to-night . . . and you sidled in as her date and blew all her hard-made plans."

Mordi scowled, not wanting to acknowledge the possibility, but knowing that he had to at least keep an open mind.

"Is *anything* happening there?" Jason asked.

Mordi had to assume that his half brother meant something other than the way his blood raced and his body stiffened when he was around Izzy. "Nothing," he said. "Although I do have something I want you to check out."

"Shoot."

Mordi took a breath, thinking about his earlier suspicion that Hieronymous had invented some sort of control device. *He* couldn't do it with the current Protector technology—at least, not using his powers directly—but maybe someone else could. "It's probably nothing, but with Hieronymous being such an invention junkie, I thought it was worth checking out. During his speech, Harold Frost said that he—"

"Mordi!"

Izzy's scream reverberated down the hall, and Mordi dove left just as a burly man smelling vaguely of cabbage plowed into him, sending him crashing to the ground. *What the hell?*

Mordi didn't bother trying to analyze the situation, he was too intent on getting the gorilla off him. He reared back with his fist and landed a powerful punch right in the man's face.

Nothing.

Just . . . squish.

A Henchman.

Henchmen. The vile creatures vaguely resembled squid in their natural form, but they could assume other shapes at will. Unlike Mordi, though, the shapeshift was essentially an illusion, so that when you actually fought a Henchman, it was like fighting a tub of slime. Score one for this Henchman.

The beasts were preternaturally strong, too, even stronger than most Protectors. Score another point for the hellish creatures.

They were not, however, very bright. And it was there that a Protector's advantage really lay. At the moment, though, Mordi wasn't thinking. He was reacting. He whipped his leg out, prepared for it to hit a wall of Jello rather than flesh, and was absurdly satisfied with the thick *slurp* as his leg impacted his attacker.

The creature tumbled backward, and Mordi climbed to his feet, already summoning his power. The thug was back up, though, and Mordi wasn't ready. It lunged forward.

Mordi lashed out, hoping he had managed to gather some fire, but it didn't matter. Before he could even attempt to engulf the creature in flames, the Henchman froze.

Literally.

Icicles hung from the creature's nose, and his illusory pasty skin took on a bluish tint. Mordi blinked, then reached out and poked the thing. Hard as a brick . . . and cold as ice.

Mordi spun, searching for his savior, and found himself face-to-face with Izzy. Her already pale skin was even paler, and she was breathing hard. Her perfectly coiffed hair had come loose and now fell in waves around her shoulders. She smiled weakly, then lifted one shoulder.

"Just trying to help," she said.

He met her grin. "Nice skill you have there."

"It comes in handy when you're thirsty and forgot to fill the ice trays." She glanced at the Henchman. "We should move him. The ceremony will be over soon. People might come back here."

"Right." Mordi bent to retrieve his fallen holopager,

saw that it was broken, and sighed. He'd have to use a real telephone to finish his conversation with Jason. What a pain.

"I've got some cuffs," he said. He pulled them out of his jacket, and tossed them to her.

She held the golden binder cuffs out, her forehead furrowed. "If I move his arms like that, he's going to crack. I'm not a field op, so I haven't memorized the regulations, but I'm pretty sure that freezing people and then breaking them is a no-no."

"True enough," Mordi said. "But he's not a person. He's a Henchman."

She drew in a breath and her eyes went wide, and Mordi was absolutely certain that she was as surprised to hear the news as he was to be attacked. If Izzy was involved with anything bad, it wasn't tied to this Henchman.

"But . . . but . . ."

"My father," he said simply.

A flicker of concern flashed in her eyes, but it was gone before Mordi could be certain. "Hieronymous isn't the only Outcast that uses Henchmen," she said. The Henchmen lived in the catacombs, were the embodiment of all the scary monsters and creepy-crawlies that hid under beds and in dark closets. And because they did the bidding of whoever released them, some of the bolder Outcasts had taken to surreptitiously acquiring one or two as pets.

"This is his work," Mordi said.

Again, Izzy shook her head. "No. He's not here. And I felt someone else. Someone who wanted to hurt you."

Mordi waved a hand toward the Henchman. "Duh."

"No, someone *else.*"

He frowned. "What are you saying, Izzy?"

"I can't pick up on Henchman thoughts. That's impossible. But I knew *something* was happening. That's why I ran out here. To warn you." Her lips pressed together in a thin line as her eyes widened. "Mordi," she finally said, "there's still someone here. Someone who wants to hurt you."

Mordi considered what Izzy said. *Someone else?* Clyde, perhaps. Or perhaps a compatriot of one of the thirteen traitorous Protectors he'd so far locked away. Or Romulus, who was out on bail and probably pissed. Both Mordi's past and his present were dangerous. And here he was, unwittingly dragging Izzy into the danger zone—if she hadn't already gotten there all by herself.

He focused again on her. She was frowning at the Henchman, concern etched on her face.

Was it really concern? Or was it all an act? He didn't like it, but he still couldn't entirely discount the possibility that there was no other attacker and that Izzy was simply trying to cover her own tracks.

The possibility disturbed him, and he pushed it away, mentally filing it in a to-deal-with-later pile. Right now, he had to get this Henchman in the stockade.

Inside the auditorium, applause crescendoed. They were running out of time. "Call in a retrieval team," he said. "And be ready."

While Izzy watched, binder cuffs at the ready, he gathered his power, took aim and—quite literally—fired. The Henchman defrosted, first blinking, then writhing about, bellowing at the top of his quite massive lungs. By that time, however, Izzy had snapped the cuffs on him and jumped back. She looked at Mordi, her eyes wide, and mouthed one word—"Fire."

He nodded. "Ice," he said, his gaze fixed on hers. And he didn't have to say aloud that the two simply didn't mix.

Chapter Twenty-two

"How?" Hieronymous demanded. "How can it be that an assignment—no, *two* assignments—that I was assured would go off without a hitch have yet to be completed?"

In front of him, Clyde again cowered, a rather distressing posture for someone as burly as he was. "Sire—"

Hieronymous held up a hand. "I am tempted to find someone more capable to assist me in these matters. I fear that your success rate lately has been pitifully small."

A muscle twitched in Clyde's jaw and his eyes blazed with murder. Good. Perhaps if his puppet was sufficiently fired up and determined to prove himself, he would succeed where once he had failed.

"The girl warned Mordichai," Clyde explained. "Apparently she realized what was coming."

"Of course she realized! It was absurd to send someone in to oversee the operation without first slathering him with the empath balm and cologne."

Clyde hung his head. "Yes, sire."

Hieronymous turned, his cape whipping out behind

him. He inhaled deeply, the air dank and stale in the abandoned station. "And the man? Frost?"

The silence behind him spoke volumes.

"I already know you failed," Hieronymous said, adopting his most reasonable tone. "What I don't know is why."

He turned, watching as Clyde drew himself up to full attention. "Our recruit, sire. He assessed the situation, determined the high level of Protector activity, and made the decision that the mission shouldn't go forth as planned."

"*He* made the decision?"

"Yes, sire. I wasn't present. I couldn't—"

"*He* made the decision."

This time, Clyde just nodded.

Hieronymous couldn't answer; the rage in his head was too loud, drowning out even the remotest possibility of speech.

One thing, though, he knew for certain. If you wanted something done right, you simply had to do it yourself.

Chapter Twenty-three

"This really wasn't necessary," Mordi said. "Nice, but not necessary." He and Isole were on the stoop of her building, and he tilted his head back and looked up toward her window. He'd taken his tie off and unbuttoned the first two buttons of his pressed white shirt, a concession to having fought a minor battle.

Isole watched him, marveling at this man who had the strength to live the life he wanted despite a terrible past, who had strength in battle and who was still innately tender. She fought a smile, thinking about the previous night in her apartment. Truly, Mordi was an extraordinary man. And the fact that he was desperately gorgeous only added to the positives of the equation. The negative part, of course, was that she was falling (and fast!) for a man who could land her in no end of trouble. Not good.

She followed his gaze up just in time to see her light come on. They'd sent her father ahead, and he'd obviously made his way into the apartment.

"And I should probably get going," Mordi said.

Typical guy. "No. Please. My father's enjoying talking to you." What was she saying? She *should* let him go. She should have let him go a long time ago. Instead, they'd left the ceremony and taken her father for a celebratory dinner at The Pump Room, where her father had oohed and aahed appropriately. Now they were back at her apartment and, despite common sense, Izzy wasn't ready to let him leave. "Besides," she added, floundering for something that would persuade him. "You were attacked. What if someone else tries something?"

He crossed his arms over his chest and leaned back against the railing. "Uh, Iz? Not only am I pretty capable of taking care of myself—what with being a Protector and all—"

He had a point, but she just tilted her head to the side and shot him her very best glare. He grinned. "The truth is, I get attacked just about every week."

"Oh." That really did bring her up short. She'd never worked in the field, and the idea that Mordi was constantly under fire made her both thankful for her laidback life and, absurdly, a little jealous. After all, she was a Protector, too. Or at least a Halfling like Mordi was.

"I probably really should go," he said. "If you're not . . ."

He cut himself off abruptly, and though she tried, she couldn't pick up any definitive scent of what was going on in his mind.

He shook his head and started over. "I could be endangering you. It's one of the perils of chasing traitors. I'm a target of both Outcasts and Outcasts-to-be . . . and so is anyone I care about."

Her heart twisted a little. Was he saying that he cared about her?

Frustrated, she pushed the thought away. She *really* needed to stop thinking about this man. Yes, there was a chemistry, but no, she shouldn't pursue it. And that was simply that.

Which didn't mean she needed to send him home, she told herself. After all, they were working together on two separate projects. It was natural for her to be concerned about him. As a coworker, of course.

"You're coming up," she said, the belligerence in her voice intended for both of them. "And I'm really not interested in hearing any arguments. This may happen to you every day, but I work in an office. It doesn't happen to me, and if you were any kind of a gentleman, you'd be insisting that you come up just to make sure I'm okay."

The corner of his mouth twitched. Then he nodded, his expression stern and serious. "You're absolutely right. Don't even think about trying to send me away. I'm coming up whether you like it or not."

"That's the spirit." She fought the urge to laugh.

He followed her upstairs, and they found that her father had not only already found the wine, he'd found her video collection. He held up an open bottle of merlot in one hand and a copy of *Flubber* in the other. "Celebration, anyone?"

Izzy laughed, and kissed him. She and Mordi had decided against telling him what had happened. Since Harold had never been particularly involved in Protector stuff, there didn't seem any reason to burden him with things that had nothing to do with his award.

If he wanted to celebrate, then celebrate they would.

"So, what exactly does this Polarity thing do, anyway?" Mordi asked as he sipped his second glass of wine. He sat on the couch next to Izzy—a fact that she'd made note of—while her father sat alone in the overstuffed leather monstrosity she'd bought at a furniture consignment store.

"Ah," Harold Frost said. Leaning forward, he automatically pushed his glasses up on his nose, as if he couldn't describe the project without seeing better. "If you have a device that works in one particular manner, my device will allow it to work in the exact opposite."

Mordi just looked blank, and Izzy felt absurdly grateful. She didn't want to be the only one who didn't understand what in Hades her father was talking about.

Harold laughed, delighted to have an audience. He reached into a pocket and pulled out the thing, then handed it to Mordi. "Here. You can try it later."

Mordi took it, a small metal gizmo that resembled a key and hung from a chain.

"Izzy tells me you chase traitors. Perhaps it could come in handy."

Mordi shrugged, dubious, but put the thing around his neck anyway. "Okay. But I'm still not understanding what it does, exactly."

"Well, say you have a convection oven," Harold said. "But you need a refrigerator."

Mordi's eyebrows rose. "I'm not sure how that helps with traitors. But it's pretty neat. How does it work?"

Harold waved his hand. "Simply put the device inside the oven. It will do the rest. Now, if you're asking me about the method by which it works . . . well, I could tell you," he said. "But then I'd have to kill you."

At that, Izzy rolled her eyes. "Daddy!"

"Sorry," Harold said, though he looked more amused than apologetic. For that matter, Mordi looked amused, too, and Isole took a secret pleasure in the fact that he seemed to think her dad was okay. "But it truly would be difficult to explain. Suffice it to say, it took years of research, trial and error."

"Well, thanks," Mordi said. "And congrats again." He took another sip of wine, finishing off his glass.

Izzy lifted her own and followed suit. Then she poured them both fresh glasses. She wasn't about to examine her motives, but the thought of getting riproaring drunk that evening was more than appealing.

"So, what else have you invented?" Mordi asked.

"Yes, Daddy, you haven't told me about anything new in a long time."

She loved to hear about her father's inventions. They were always so funky—things you couldn't imagine actually buying, but that would be more than useful to have around the house. Like the Automatic Back Scratcher he'd made for her twenty-third birthday. Or the Dust-Bunny that buzzed around under the furniture sucking up the dust and debris. *That* one had even been featured on the Home Shopping Network one Christmas season, and even now she noticed it occasionally in drugstores in an "As Seen On TV" display.

"Well, let's see," Harold said. "I've been working with thoughts and feelings a lot lately. For example, the Thought Pen should be quite popular. If you have a story in your head, you simply write with the pen, and the words pour out. Very handy for literary types, I would think. And there's the Breakfast Baker Night Cap, which could be quite popular. You wear it when you go to sleep. It picks up on your thoughts during the night, determines what you'll most likely want for breakfast, and starts the meal in your automated kitchen."

"What if you don't have an automated kitchen?" Mordi asked.

Harold looked troubled. "Well, then, I guess there's no point in having the Night Cap." He waved his hand. "That one was inspired by Izzy, of course. A more recent project was also inspired by her, only backwards."

Mordi caught her eye and mouthed "Backwards?" She shrugged.

"Why am I not liking the sound of that, Daddy?" Izzy asked, but she was unable to hide her smile.

"Well, now, dear, you're always complaining about

how thoughts buzz around you like flies, and how you'd like to block them out entirely sometimes? Well, I'm working on a little something that can do that."

She blinked. "Really? Wow."

Her father preened.

Mordi's mouth quirked and he shot a sideways glance at Izzy. The look was playful and a little longing. "I don't suppose you have it on you?"

Harold laughed. "Son, I'm afraid you're on your own."

"Damn," was all Mordi said.

Though his voice was tinged with humor, Izzy was truly disappointed. Right then, she would have loved to sit and hold Mordi's hands without worrying about taking in his thoughts. That, however, wasn't going to happen. Not now. Not ever.

"So," Harold said, clapping his hands together. "Are we celebrating, or what? Because I've got *Flubber* here, and after that, *The Computer Wore Tennis Shoes*."

"Sounds good to me," Izzy said. She snuggled back into the cushions, keeping an eye on Mordi to see how he reacted. If he bagged on them now, she'd mark him off her list. He didn't have to *like* her dad's old Disney movies, but if he wanted to have anything to do with her, he at least had to make a show of it.

When he settled back, then asked if they should make popcorn, Izzy decided he'd passed with flying colors.

They watched the first movie in silence, but when the credits rolled, Harold got up and excused himself, claiming exhaustion after his big day.

"Your father's great," Mordi said after he'd gone.

Izzy nodded. "I know."

Mordi stood up and switched movies, and when he sat back down, he was a bit closer. He tucked his arm around her, and she leaned into him, careful to keep skin from touching skin. They sat like that through the movie, Izzy arranging her thoughts. She wanted to talk, but she wasn't sure about what. Mostly, she just liked sitting with him. It felt natural. Right.

And by the time the movie was over, she'd slipped into that comfortable place where words really weren't necessary. As she caught a glimpse of Mordi, she realized that was probably a good thing, since if she wanted to talk, she'd have to wake him up.

She twisted a bit, careful not to rouse him, then sat back, watching his face.

He looked innocent, nothing like the man she'd read about: Mordichai Black, rogue Protector—a Halfling who'd joined the Council only to find himself living undercover, a mole in his father's operation; a man tempted by fate and his father's promises of glory and riches.

A man whose father cared more about revenge and power than he did about his own son.

She swallowed, then wiped a single tear away as she thought of her own father, now asleep in her bedroom. He'd been there for her throughout her whole life. Never wavering. Steady as a rock, albeit a somewhat absentminded rock.

She couldn't imagine living a day—much less a lifetime—without her father's love bolstering her. She couldn't imagine it, and she didn't know how Mordi had survived.

And then, as she watched him sleep, she shed a tear for the little boy who, despite terrible odds, had grown up into an amazing man.

Chapter Twenty-four

"Excellent work! Just great!" Izzy clapped, jumping up and down as Hieronymous stumbled under the weight of the child. Beside her, Mordi also offered some praise, but his tone was begrudging, not the least bit enthusiastic.

This morning she'd awakened on the couch, but Mordi hadn't been beside her. He'd left her a charming note saying he had things to take care of and would see her on the job. They'd done nothing the night before but sit on the sofa, watch movies, and talk. Even so, the air between them seemed to sizzle with electricity. And every time she spoke to Mordi, he seemed to go out of his way to think (and think loudly) the most mundane thoughts imaginable. He was baffling her empathy.

She should be frustrated. Instead, she wanted him more than ever.

Not that she had any time to worry about her love life or lack thereof. At the moment, she was cheering Hieronymous on at his latest foray into good.

They'd been patrolling a stretch of Bleecker Street, looking for mortals in peril, kittens to rescue, taxis that might be careening out of control. Mordi had been surly and closed-mouthed, and even Hieronymous, who'd started the afternoon with unabashed enthusiasm, had sunk into a silence that could only be described as bitter.

Izzy supposed she couldn't blame him. Until he performed the required number of good deeds, he couldn't be re-assimilated. And if no good-deed opportunities were presenting themselves . . . well, she was frustrated, too.

They'd been ready to head back, to give up and try again another day, when the cry had rung out: a little girl's voice, shrill and desperate. They'd raced toward the sound, Mordi in the lead, but Hieronymous soon passed him—and Izzy's heart soared as Hieronymous made a beeline for the little girl hanging precariously from the edge of the fire escape, an older girl trying frantically to hoist the child back up.

"Please! Please help!" the girl on the metal grating cried.

The younger girl was about three, and Izzy assumed she'd crawled out onto the fire escape when an adult wasn't looking. There certainly didn't seem to be an adult around now.

The little girl had probably wandered to the edge where the ladder should be, but since there was no ladder, she'd been stuck. Perhaps she'd lost her balance. Izzy didn't know; all she knew was that when they arrived, the terrified child was dangling, and her equally terrified sibling was screaming, trying to clutch the little girl's arms and hoist her back onto the platform.

The little girl, though, was too scared, and her kicking and flailing weren't helping the older girl's efforts. The weight of a three-year-old was probably too much for a seven- or eight-year-old even on a good day. With the three-year-old writhing like a worm on a hook, it really was too much.

"Tammy, no!" the older girl cried. And that's when it had happened—the toddler let go and plummeted toward the ground.

Izzy and crew were still half a block away, and they raced with super speed toward the fire escape.

The timing had been close. The kid was falling fast and—

And then she *wasn't* falling fast.

Thank Hera!

The little girl's descent had slowed, even as Hieronymous's pace had increased. He'd slid to a halt under the child, just as gravity seemed to catch up with her. She landed with a *plunk* in his arms, then started wailing, her cries punctuated by loud, wet hiccups.

Izzy exhaled. From the time they'd first heard the scream, maybe four seconds had passed. It felt more like four years.

"Well done," she said again.

Hieronymous put the child on the ground and patted her on the head. "Nonsense, my dear. Anyone could have helped. It was just a matter of being in the right place at the right time."

And having the right skills, Izzy thought. Had she herself been here alone, that girl would have crashed to the ground.

She looked away, not wanting either Mordi or Hieronymous to see it reflected on her face. No matter how bad he might have been in the past, at that particular moment, Hieronymous had more claim to being a Protector than she ever did. He, at least, had all of a Protector's powers. Izzy had nothing but a freezy finger and an uncle who pushed through paperwork.

Above them, the older girl was gone, and now they heard the alley door slam open and the kid's footsteps as she raced toward them.

The two girls embraced, and Hieronymous smiled. The expression seemed forced, but Izzy supposed that wasn't too unusual. He was out of practice, after all. And it wasn't as if he was displeased by the rescue. She could smell the waves of pleasure, pride, and relief that flowed from his being.

Oh, yes. Hieronymous was undoubtedly happy that he'd rescued the little girl.

Izzy made a mental note. As soon as she returned to the office, she'd update his file. At the moment, though, she had no doubt that Hieronymous would pass all the re-assimilation tests with flying colors.

"Bravo," Mordi said, his voice flat. "A few years ago, you would have just let the kid go splat on the pavement."

Izzy knelt beside the two girls, still locked together in a bear hug, and looked up at him. "*Mordi!*"

He had the good grace to look abashed. "Sorry," he said, in the direction of her and the girls. Then he turned back to Hieronymous. "But it's true." His voice was lower, his tone harsh.

Anger. Betrayal. The emotions clung to him like smoke, tainting the air around him. And more, too. There was a desperate need, one so intense it made her heart ache for him.

"Where's Mommy?" the little girl said.

"Hush, sweetie. Your mommy will be here soon."

As if conjured, the sound of high heels clattering on the pavement echoed behind them. "Tammy? Lisa?" The woman's voice rose with concern, and the footsteps increased in tempo. "Oh, babies, babies! What happened? Where's Amelia?"

The woman was at Izzy's side now, and she moved away to let the girls cling to their mother. Izzy listened, amused, as the older girl told her mom the story, between sobs and great heaving gulps of air, of how their babysitter had gone out and how Tammy had ended up on the fire escape.

"I couldn't hold on, Mommy," Lisa said, fresh tears streaming down her cheek. She twisted in her mom's embrace, just enough to point to Hieronymous. "But he caught her, Mommy. He saved Tammy. He's a hero." The little girl's eyes were wide as she spoke these last words, and Izzy had no doubt that, if asked, she would say that Hieronymous had hung the moon.

Mordi stood off to one side, and Izzy didn't need to examine his scent to tell that he didn't share the little girl's sentiment. His expression said it for him. Fortunately, though, he kept his mouth shut. And Izzy said a silent thank-you that, if nothing else, Mordichai Black had at least an inkling of the meaning of the word "discretion."

Managing somehow to keep both kids physically connected to her, the mother rose—a little wobbly in her high heels—and made her way to Hieronymous.

"Thank you."

He took her hand, his expression reflecting nothing but humble sincerity. "Madam, your thanks is not necessary. I'm no hero. I was simply in the right place at the right time."

"Then thank you for that."

Izzy thought she heard a noise come from Mordi's vicinity, but it could have been her imagination.

Somewhat shyly, the mother said her good-byes, then ushered the girls toward the apartment. "If there's anything I can do to repay—"

"The look on your face is repayment enough, madam," Hieronymous said, then bent to kiss her fingers.

This time, Izzy was sure she heard it: Mordi was gagging in the background.

Chapter Twenty-five

Mordi watched as the mother gathered the two little girls up and ushered them away under his father's beaming stare. For Izzy's sake, he tried to keep a straight face, but it was hard. She obviously believed that these tests would reveal Hieronymous's true character, and Mordi had decided that he simply wasn't going to argue. He knew the truth . . . and sooner or later, Daddy Dearest would screw up. He had to. Mordi knew Hieronymous too well to think that the Outcast could maintain this façade forever.

Still . . . he feared that Hieronymous might be able to maintain it long enough. Hieronymous had willpower. And when he truly wanted something, Mordi knew, he was willing to pull out all the stops.

With a sigh, he leaned back against the brick building façade and watched as Izzy ran down a checklist with his father—she'd be filing a report with the Inner Circle as well as with the MLO, just in case some spin was needed.

Izzy. How he wished she could see the truth. Because, damn it, he hated being at cross purposes with her. She'd gotten under his skin, a dangerous place for her to be, but he couldn't help it. She was a part of his life now, a part he didn't need and shouldn't want. But she was there all the same, and he was at a loss about what to do.

He'd awakened at four with Izzy in his arms, both of them still curled up on her couch. It had felt good. Too good. So he'd bolted, thinking that if he could only put some distance between them, his head would clear. He'd gone back to his own place, but was only able to lie in bed staring at the ceiling, imagining that she was still in his arms.

He'd told her the truth—his job did make a relationship nearly impossible. He had enemies. He had the father from hell. No matter how you sliced it, they just weren't workable.

But until he'd met Izzy, he hadn't really cared.

His cell phone rang, and he answered, surprised to hear Jason on the other end until he remembered that he'd broken his holopager. "Well?" Jason demanded.

"Hang on." Mordi moved back, until he was sure that he was out of earshot of his father and Izzy. Not that either of them seemed interested in him; they were too busy filling out the report to even notice Mordi or his phone call.

He turned back to the phone and gave Jason an update.

"And the Frost girl?"

"I think she's clean," Mordi said, casting a glance her way.

Jason made a low noise in the back of his throat, and Mordi silently acknowledged that, while his brain was in agreement, the bulk of his certainty originated in other parts of his body. "Her father did say one odd thing—I was trying to tell you before the Henchman showed up. Something about a silent partner. Can you check it out?"

"Sure thing. What's on your agenda for today?"

"Going back to headquarters after this. Our darling father just rescued a little girl—"

Jason's raucous laugh echoed through the phone.

"—who was falling out of a window, and I'm sure he's exhausted from keeping up the act. I'll try to poke around a bit on my end."

"Keep me posted," Jason said. "And I'll do the same."

Chapter Twenty-six

"Even you have to admit that he's doing well," Izzy said. They were back in her office, and she was peering at Mordi from behind her desk.

Mordi set his jaw. He didn't have to admit anything of the sort. "If by 'doing well' you mean that he's managed to convince you that black is white and up is down, then, yeah. He's doing remarkably well."

"Jumping Jupiter, Mordi," she said, one hand gesturing toward Hieronymous. "You've seen him—"

"Do nothing but the simplest of tasks," Mordi finished.

"He's saved mortals," she said. "*Mortals*. You remember them? That species that you say he can't stand."

"He can't," Mordi said.

"Then why—"

"I. Don't. Know." And not knowing was driving him crazy. "But he's up to something."

"You're paranoid."

"It's not paranoia if everyone really is after you." Mighty Zeus, he was reduced to talking in bumper stickers. The woman had a way of breaking down his defenses and tying his tongue. He wanted to shake some sense into her. Better yet, he wanted to kiss her so hard and so thoroughly that she finally understood. She said she could feel that Hieronymous was sincere? Well, maybe she thought she could, but he'd show her just how sincere *he* was. And then he'd see what she said.

"Mordi?"

Oh, heck. He drew in a breath, looking at her warily. Did she know what he was thinking? *Of course she does, you idiot. She's an empath.*

"Don't read me," he said. "We're working together. It's not appropriate for you to get into my head." His words came out measured and strong, without a hint of embarrassment. Inside his head, he was kicking himself, mortification rolling off of him in huge waves.

The look she flashed him was one of pure disdain. "Read you? Don't flatter yourself. And besides, I can't read you without touching you. All I can tell by being near you is what you're feeling."

Maybe she was trying to make him feel better, but suddenly he felt totally exposed. "Don't," he snapped, the word coming out harsher than he intended.

Something akin to pain flashed in her eyes, but then the mask fell back into place and she was the perfect professional again. "Don't worry," she said. "I have no reason to read you, Mordi. None at all."

Despite the ice in her words, they cut through him like a hot knife. "Good," Mordi said. "Let's keep it that way."

"No problem," she said.

"No problem," he repeated.

He sat there a moment, fuming and feeling foolish, then stood to leave half-hoping she'd stop him. She didn't, and her silence cut through him as much as her sharp words had.

He went to her door, opened it, then stepped out into the hallway. And as soon as the door closed behind him, he leaned back against the wall and took a single deep breath.

He should be satisfied. She was agreeing to stay out of his head and away from his emotions. And yet he wasn't satisfied. Not at all.

Typical. His whole life he'd always wanted to be closer to the people who pushed him away. His mother, his father. And now this woman.

Mordi, you're pathetic. Just do your job and get the hell away from her.

And that, he thought, was very sound advice.

Chapter Twenty-seven

The man was impossible!

Even after seeing Hieronymous unselfishly help mortals—twice now!—Mordichai was still unconvinced of his father's sincerity, and Izzy was at her wits' end.

She wanted to tell him to take his knee-jerk reaction and go jump in a lake. Except she couldn't. Because a teeny-tiny little part of her wondered if the reaction wasn't really knee-jerk after all. Or if the knee-jerk instinct was wrong.

Images of inkblots danced through her head, but she shook them away. He'd *passed*. Maybe he'd been a little off, a little hesitant, but ultimately he'd passed. Just as he'd passed every test she'd thrown his way.

Maybe it would be convenient for her if Hieronymous was re-assimilated, but her personal concerns were not running the show. She was behaving honestly. She was being completely unbiased and professional.

And her completely unbiased and professional judgment was that Hieronymous was passing his tests.

And all of Mordi's bitching and moaning couldn't change that one fact.

And Mordi knew Hieronymous was passing those tests, yet he *was* bitching and moaning. And she didn't know why. Yes, he and his father had a long and complicated history, but was it just bad blood? Or did Mordi know something?

Granted, she didn't know Mordi well (though she *wanted* to know him better), but he didn't strike her as the type to hang onto an issue simply out of pride. Even more, no matter how much she resented his being added to her team, she knew that Zephron must have had his reasons. Plus, she had her own opinions of Mordi, and while she didn't understand his reaction to his father, she did trust his instincts elsewhere. As far as she could tell, he was completely competent. More than competent, really.

Which left her questioning her own conclusions. Hieronymous might be passing all his tests—he might, empirically at least, be doing well—but even so, tiny little doubts as to his goodness were creeping into her head. She didn't know if those doubts stemmed from her own observations or from Mordi's loud and consistent arguments. She'd backed away from certainty and into a shadowy new area.

And that terrified her even more than her growing feelings for Mordichai.

Chapter Twenty-eight

Mordi rushed through the deserted corridor, glanced at his watch, and then picked up his pace. He'd been up all night poking around on the Internet, trying to locate Romulus, trying to figure out who Harold's silent partner was, trying to determine if any of the traitors he'd caught in the past might be trying to kill him. In sum, trying to get some sort of handle on any one of the fires that were currently burning at the top of his workload.

In the end, he'd accomplished nothing. He had, however, thought a lot about Izzy Frost. About the gentle way she interacted with her father, and the pride she had in him. About her snappy comments and her sense of humor. About the way she could take care of herself. And most of all, about the way she made him feel when she looked at him with those ice-blue eyes.

She'd crept into his mind even when she didn't belong there and—damn him—he'd let her stay.

Now, however, wasn't the time to be thinking about that. Not when he was on his way to see her, for she'd most certainly pick up on any stray thoughts of lust.

He rounded a corner, almost careening into Elders

Armistand and Trystan. "Elders," he said with a small bow. "I didn't see you."

"And where are you going in such a hurry, young Mordichai?" Trystan asked.

"Isole Frost, sir. More testing." He coughed. "For my father." He cringed a little as he spoke the words. Elder Trystan held a particular dislike of Hieronymous, though Mordi didn't know the cause. As for Elder Armistand, he had initiated the Re-Assimilation Act, so Mordi knew he wasn't prejudiced against Outcasts per se, but the word on the street was that he'd never expected the more notorious Outcasts to try to make use of the new law.

"I understand he's doing quite well so far," Trystan said, sounding pleased. "Ms. Frost's initial report was quite encouraging."

For a second, Mordi almost couldn't manage an answer. Then he nodded. "Uh, yeah."

"Excellent," Armistand said. "I'm certain that if he is doing that well, Ms. Frost will recommend complete re-assimilation."

"And the committee will surely approve the recommendation," Trystan added. "I know I will enthusiastically vote yes."

Mordi frowned. The committee—like the treaty committee—was composed of the entire Inner Circle and a few other select Protectors.

"As will I," Armistand agreed. "It will be wonderful having him back on the Council."

"And in the Inner Circle," Trystan added. "Don't forget that."

"Of course, of course." Armistand bobbed his head jovially while Trystan beamed. Mordi wondered if he'd been transplanted to an alternate universe.

A fledgling Protector rushed forward, a clipboard in his hand. "Sirs, sirs! Could I get your signature on these power-use authorizations?" He tapped the paper. "Here, and here. And press hard because the form's in triplicate."

As the flunkie held out the clipboard, Mordi watched as both Trystan and Armistand pulled out identical purple fountain pens. Then they signed the papers with a flourish. Armistand turned to Mordi, as if he'd forgotten he was there. "Well, do run along, Mordi. Surely you have someplace to be."

"Washington, D.C., I believe," Trystan said. "Didn't Bilius tell me you had a meeting this afternoon with Senator Banyon?"

Mordi blanched. *Hopping Hades . . .* was that today?

Chapter Twenty-nine

"It is a question of responsibilities," Senator Banyon said. He was leaning back in his desk chair, Capitol Hill resplendent through the window behind him. His proper and controlled voice contained a thick, syrupy West Virginia drawl. He was tall, dressed impeccably in a tailored blue suit, and his demeanor and bearing screamed successful politician.

Damn, but Mordi hated politics.

"As a member of this committee," the senator continued, "my responsibility is not just to the good citizens of West Virginia—or even the good folks of this country. I'm representing the world on this. And I don't intend to go down in history as the man who unwittingly brought about the end of humanity as we know it."

At that, Mordi started to pay more attention. He glanced toward Izzy, whose features were schooled in an expression of polite interest, and Mordi couldn't tell if she had any clue what the man was talking about.

The treaty renegotiation committee was comprised of a delegation of Protectors—the Inner Circle plus several other Protectors—and a delegation of mortals. Up until now, Mordi had assumed that the mortal committee members all supported the renegotiated treaty, which would allow Protectors to go public with their powers and services. In other words, the need for the MLO spin doctors would evaporate. *The New York Times* could report mortal politics right alongside news of a team of Protectors rescuing a dozen passengers from a crashing plane.

In light of Banyon's comments, though, Mordi had to reconsider his assumptions. Did Banyon not want the treaty to go through? If that was the case, Zephron was going to be supremely disappointed.

Banyon started on another rant, but Mordi held up a hand and the senator stopped in mid-sentence— something about the backstabbing nature on the Hill and how he had to watch every step. "Yes, son?"

"I'm sorry, sir. Could you go back to something you said earlier? The bit about the end of humanity as we know it. You lost me a little on that."

Izzy's mouth twitched. It was a hint of a smile, but it held absolutely no indication whether it meant that Mordi was the biggest idiot to ever live, or that she wanted to kiss him for finally asking the sixty-four-thousand-dollar question.

Banyon was more easily read. He simply looked annoyed. "My understanding was that Zephron asked you two to liaise with this committee because you have a unique understanding of our concerns. Of *mortal* concerns."

Mordi wasn't cowed. He'd spent twenty-five years taking crap from his father. He wasn't going to take it now from this gentleman from West Virginia. "Considering we're half-mortal," Mordi began, looking Banyon square in the eye, "I'd say that there's no question that we understand mortals. What I *don't* understand, however, are your specific concerns. Perhaps you could give us a quick rundown?"

"I'd like that, too," Izzy said, leaning back in the overstuffed sofa and crossing her legs. She wore a black business suit, a white shirt, and black pumps. She looked like a lawyer. And damned if Mordi didn't think she was the sexiest thing he'd ever seen. "If you tell us your concerns now, we'll be sure to avoid any misunderstandings in the future."

Banyon hesitated, clearly irritated at having his little speech derailed. Finally, though, he moved back around his desk, sat, and clasped his hands in front of him, fingers intertwined.

After a brief moment to ensure that all eyes were on him, Banyon began. "I'm one of the few mortals who know about the existence of your kind," he said. Mordi listened intently, trying to find a hint of derision in the words, but he heard nothing except the simple statement of an indisputable fact. "Even at the highest echelons of the government, the existence of the Venerate Council is known only to a select few."

"Are you concerned that the majority of mortals will resent us? Fear us? I thought that was the point of negotiating this treaty. So that mortals-in-the-know and Protectors could go as one to the general populace and explain. You know," Mordi added a bit lamely. "We come in peace, and all that."

Banyon didn't smile. In fact, his eyes narrowed. Apparently, the man wasn't too happy with Mordi's interruption. For that matter, neither was Izzy, who kicked him soundly in the calf, the maneuver disguised as simply crossing her legs.

"It is not the mortals we're worried about," Banyon said, his tone as cold as if Mordi had just said something nasty about his mother.

"You're afraid of some sort of retribution by the Outcasts," Izzy said. *She* got a smile for her comment. Teacher's pet, already. "That they may resent or even

205

try to sabotage mortal-Protector relations by mass attacks."

"Indeed we are," Banyon said. "We're looking to the Council to alleviate those concerns. I, at least, am not yet convinced."

"And you're the committee chair," Izzy said, her expression wry.

"Co-chair," Banyon admitted. "Mr. Adamson does not share my concerns." He spread his arms wide. "Being open-minded, I'm trying to gain a broader perspective." A smile eased over his face, softening the stern features. "Please. I'd like your help. I can see significant benefits to the world by having those of your race act openly. But—"

"But you're afraid that the Outcasts' mischief would never let you actually reap the benefits," Izzy said.

"That's my fear. Yes." He eyed each of them in turn. "As a result of my position, I've been given access to your personnel files." Mordi's insides shifted slightly, but Banyon didn't hesitate. "You each have unique perspectives. I value your input."

Mordi met Izzy's eyes. He wasn't entirely sure what Banyon expected from him, but she seemed to have no similar hesitations. He didn't need her empathic powers to read her fury as she sat up in her chair, chin up and shoulders back, and met his gaze dead-on. "Considering it's the two of us you have here, I assume you're not concerned so much about Outcasts in general, but about one particular Outcast?"

"They are all a threat. It's not—"

"Senator." There was censure lacing Izzy's voice. Mordi bumped her up a notch on his mental scorecard. When she wanted to be, the woman really could be as cold as ice. Judging from Banyon's expression, her air of authority did the trick just fine.

"Fine," he said, and his entire body slumped a little,

just barely perceptibly, as if a tiny bit of air was being removed from a balloon. "Yes. We've researched the most aggressive of the Outcasts and, while there are several, only Hieronymous Black seems to have both the inclination and the connections to, well, to . . ." He trailed off with a series of complicated hand movements that Mordi assumed represented some kind of horrific warfare.

He glanced at Izzy, hoping his expression didn't say, *I told you so*. She didn't seem particularly perturbed.

"Your concerns, while understandable, are no longer legitimate," she said.

Banyon exhaled slowly, then sat back down. His face lost some of its rough edges and took on a quiet, thoughtful appearance. For a moment, Mordi almost liked the man.

"Then it's true," he said. "Hieronymous really has repented? He wants to . . . what? Be one of you again?"

"It's called re-assimilation," Izzy said. "And yes, he's applied."

"And you believe he's sincere?" Banyon held up a hand. "Wait. Before you answer, I want you to make sure you understand my concern. If Hieronymous—"

"Is no longer Outcast," Izzy said, cutting the senator off, "then you don't have to worry about the Outcasts rising up in some violent protest of the treaty. Yes, I understand your perspective. But yes, I think he's sincere."

"You're very astute," Banyon said. He cocked his head ever so slightly. "But I suppose I should have realized that."

"If you had full access to my file, then yes, you should have." Ice laced her voice. It wasn't surprising. Files were maintained on Protectors on two levels. Basic information, including mission history, was public record. A description of specific powers, however, was not. The idea was that ultimate secrecy ensured that Protectors had the full advantage of their unique powers if attacked. If the committee had dumped full reports in Banyon's lap, then things were definitely politically hot. And Izzy had every right to be pissed.

Even though she hadn't voiced the question, still it hung in the air, awaiting a response. Banyon ignored it, turning instead to Mordi. That, he thought, was response enough.

Beside him, Izzy still looked miffed, the tips of her ears and nose taking on a pinkish tint, making her look a bit like an angry attack bunny: adorable, but dangerous.

He put a hand on her knee and squeezed, a silent entreaty to wait until later to express her displeasure. She jumped a little under his touch, but stayed quiet. Mordi kept his hand where it was, telling himself that he simply wanted to gauge her reactions.

He was lying to himself, of course. But that was something he'd wait until later to examine, too.

He realized that Banyon was talking to him. "What?"

Annoyance flashed across Banyon's face, but was quickly erased. "Hieronymous Black is your father, and I understand you two have had a bit of a falling-out."

That, Mordi thought, was putting it mildly.

"Do you agree with Ms. Frost's assessment?" Banyon asked.

He drew in a breath and answered the only way that he could. "Yeah," he said. "I completely agree."

Chapter Thirty

Sometime later, Izzy stood in the shadow of Abraham Lincoln and wondered what to think—about Mordichai, about Banyon, about Hieronymous. About *everything*.

She wanted to talk it out with Mordi, but he'd answered a holopage as soon as their meeting with Banyon ended, and she'd felt like an idiot waiting around for him. She did want to talk to him. She *didn't* want *him* to know that. After their movie night, it seemed even more important that she keep up a nice solid wall. Mordichai Black could get through her cracks too easily . . . and considering she had secrets to keep, Mordi was a complication she really didn't need.

"I thought I'd find you here." His voice. *Right here.*

Izzy jumped, then spun around, heart beating in her throat. "What are you doing, sneaking up on people like that?"

He shrugged. "It's a free country. I'm admiring the monuments."

She stared him down.

The corner of Mordi's mouth twitched, just a hint of

a smile. For some inexplicable reason, that really ticked her off. "Am I amusing you?" she demanded.

"As a matter of fact, yeah." And then he laughed, and instead of lashing out, slapping him, or stomping away in a huff, Izzy found herself laughing, too. Must be nerves.

"Are you going to clue me in?" she asked, trying hard to pull herself together.

"Depends," he said. "What are your other powers?"

She blinked. "Excuse me?"

"Because I'm pretty sure that if I tell you why I was laughing, you're going to wallop me. And if super strength is in your repertoire, I'd just as soon keep my mouth shut."

She bit back a smile. "No super strength," she acknowledged. "And I can't turn you into a toad or give you a rash, or—"

"There are Protectors who can do that? Turn someone else into a toad?"

She flashed an innocent smile. "I'm sorry. That information is on a need-to-know basis only." In truth, she had no idea at all. At the moment, though, she could see dozens of uses for just such a power. "Just tell me."

"You're cute."

"Jumping Jupiter, Mordi, would you just—"

"No, that's what I was thinking about. Earlier. That's what you wanted to know."

She peered at him, totally confused. "That's why you were smiling? Because you thought I was cute?"

" 'Fraid so."

"And you thought I would hit you? What? Did you just assume I can't take a compliment?"

"I'll take the Fifth."

At that, she laughed outright, even though she knew she really shouldn't encourage him. She tried to pull herself together and look stern. "So. Why did you come looking for me?"

"I wanted to talk with you."

"Okay. What do you want to talk about?" Mentally she cringed. She wanted to keep him at a distance, yes, but right now she was coming off like a bitch.

He looked at her as if she'd gone a little nuts. Maybe she had. "Oh, I don't know. The weather. Who's going to win the Academy Awards. Great literature. What in Hades do you *think* I want to talk about?"

She scowled and moved toward Lincoln's plaque, pretending to study the inscription. "There's no need for sarcasm."

"On the contrary, there seems to be every need for sarcasm."

She drew a breath. "Okay. Fine. Sorry. I'm just a little off today."

"Why?"

Genuine concern swirled around him, and she relaxed just a little, waving the question away. "Nothing. Sorry. Just lost in my own world." That was a lie, of course. But while she might know if he was lying, she sincerely doubted that he could read her well enough to have a clue. "What did you want to talk to me about?" She asked only in the interest of politeness. She already knew what he was going to say.

"My father, of course," he said, exactly as she'd known he would. There were times when her particular power really took the fun out of life.

"Why did you agree with me about your father? I'm going to go out on a limb here and guess that you haven't changed your mind since yesterday."

He laughed. "A sad commentary. I didn't realize I came off as so obstinate."

She didn't answer, just stared at him, one eyebrow raised.

"I want the treaty to pass," he finally said. "Banyon's skittish."

"So you fibbed."

"I fibbed," he admitted. "I lied for the greater good. Or maybe I withheld information for the greater good. Either way, my motives were pure." He fixed his gaze on her. "Can you understand that?"

She licked her lips. *Did he know?* "I, um, yeah. I think I can."

"So tell me about the inkblot test." He stared at her, but she sensed no doubt, no underlying question.

She decided to simply state the obvious. "Mordi, the man's passed every test we've thrown his direction." She tossed in a casual shrug, just for effect.

"But?"

She looked up sharply, the question actually coming unexpectedly. He caught the reaction, and she cursed herself.

"Then there is something," he said, triumph in his voice. She realized then why she hadn't picked up on any scents of doubt. He had none. He was just fishing.

She, like an idiot, had taken the bait. "There's nothing," she said. And though she spoke firmly, in truth, she might be lying. She didn't know. Couldn't be sure. And that uncertainty ate at her gut.

Hieronymous had hesitated on two answers. Ultimately, his response had been positive, well within the range she'd hoped, and she'd given him a passing—even high—score on the test.

Something, though . . .

Still, something bothered her. She tried to push the feeling away, but it persisted, nagging at her like an unsatisfied itch.

Was Hieronymous faking?

Was his application part of a huge ruse, and she was merely a pawn?

No. She couldn't believe that. She'd seen his sincerity, felt it with her entire being. She couldn't be wrong. *She couldn't.*

Her empathic abilities had earned her this promotion. Even more, those abilities had gotten her admitted to the Council despite her pitifully lacking levitation skills. She knew that, and because of it, she could hold her head up when other Protectors whispered about her, saying she wasn't quite up to snuff and that her uncle had pulled strings.

She trusted her power, relied on it. And she needed it for more than just her job. She needed it for herself.

Because if she was wrong—if she couldn't trust what she'd seen in his soul—then that meant the mean-spirited whispers were right: She really wasn't up to snuff.

And that was something she simply wouldn't believe.

Chapter Thirty-one

Nothing.

Mordi turned the word over in his head, looking for double meanings.

Nothing.

His father had passed the test, or so Isole said. But Mordi knew that couldn't possibly be right. Everything he believed in, everything he knew, hinged on the fact that his father was a certifiable nut-job.

She couldn't be right.

He knew that and yet, even so, one tiny thought poked at his mind. He tried to push it away—he didn't even want his thoughts going that direction. But it was too persistent: If Hieronymous really was having a change of heart—if he really was serious about re-assimilating, joining the Council, and fighting to protect mortals against the evil that walked the earth—would he finally, *maybe*, be proud of his son?

Mordi pushed the thought away. He knew better than to open the door to hope. He'd wasted too many years tying himself to his father with a fragile thread of optimism. Hieronymous had snapped it every time. The man wasn't a father any more than he was a true

Protector. And Mordi intended to make damn sure that his name never again graced the Council rolls.

Yet Izzy seemed convinced that Hieronymous was turning over a new leaf and wanted to be good. He had no idea if her approbation was genuine, or if she had some ulterior motive, but he was sticking close until he found out.

Right now, she was staring at Mr. Lincoln, her face pensive. He wondered what she was thinking, and the wondering nagged at him, all the more because he knew that with just a touch, Izzy would know *exactly* what *he* was thinking.

Which, of course, meant that he couldn't touch her.

Not a hardship, he told himself. He had no reason to touch her, no matter how much his fingers itched when he stood near her, and no matter how much the lavender scent of her perfume teased his senses.

If he plucked out the pins that held her hair up, would it fall soft and loose over his hand? If he stroked her skin, would it burn under his touch?

He didn't know. He *couldn't* know. And naturally, that made him want it all the more.

"Come on," he said, more gruffly than he intended.

She turned away from Mr. Lincoln to look at him, but didn't seem inclined to move. "Come where?"

"Are you staying here all night?"

She raised an eyebrow. "Are you my chaperon?"

He exhaled, clenching his fists against rising frustration. "Actually, I thought I'd be civil and offer you a ride home."

"Thanks, but I flew."

He frowned, his gaze taking in her tiny purse. "Where's your cloak?"

Her laughter rang out, the light sound echoing off the stone walls of the monument. "American Airlines," she said.

"Oh," he said stupidly. "Well, when's the return? I'll give you a lift to the airport."

"I haven't booked it yet," she said. "I wasn't sure how long we'd need to stay here."

"Then why don't I give you a lift home?"

She blinked at him. "Home? To New York?"

"Sure. Why not? I've got my car. It's not even five. We'll be there by dinnertime."

She licked her lips. "That's getting us in awfully late. I've got piles of work to get through."

"The piles will be there tomorrow."

"I don't know . . ."

His desire overwhelmed him. "Why are we fighting this?" He knew the answer, and still he blurted out the question.

"Because it's a bad idea," she said, not missing a beat.

"Probably," he said. He crooked his arm in invitation. "But can we at least do dinner?"

She frowned but shifted slightly, and he knew he'd almost convinced her. He told himself he simply needed to keep an eye on her—but it was so much more than that.

"Dinnertime's too far away," she said. "I skipped lunch."

"I'll buy you dinner on the way home."

The color rose in her cheeks, and he thought she was the most beautiful thing he'd ever seen. "It's a bad idea, Mordi," she said. "Getting in your car together, alone . . ."

"Probably," he agreed. "Are we going to let that stop us?"

Her mouth twitched. "No," she said. "We're not." She slipped her arm through his. "So long as dinner's still included, I'll accept your gracious invitation."

"Good," he said. And then, because he couldn't resist: "I promise you won't regret it."

Chapter Thirty-two

They chatted about nothing for the first twenty minutes of the drive, then eased into a companionable silence when they hit the countryside. Mordi was taking them some back way, and after they'd passed out of the city, open fields and charming homesteads filled Isole's vision.

Just as well; the silence made it easier for her to hear her own thoughts. And right then, Izzy's thoughts were all clamoring for her attention, wondering what in Hades she was doing accepting a dinner date from Mordichai Black.

And no, she couldn't tell herself that this was simply two business companions dining together. It wasn't. And she didn't want it to be.

Oddly enough, despite the fact that she'd told herself over and over that getting up close and personal with Mordichai was bad news, she felt lighter and happier than she had since the day she'd met him. She'd taken a step, and although the direction might be dangerous, she had to admit she was craving the excitement.

"Any chance your powers include teleportation?"

Mordi's words pulled her away from her thoughts, and something in his tone set alarm bells off in her head.

"Why?"

"We're being followed."

She swallowed. Apparently she'd been right about the danger.

"Don't," Mordi said, closing his hand on her shoulder. She realized she'd started to twist around for a better look. "I don't want the driver to know we're on to him yet."

She considered arguing—she hated feeling out of the loop—but settled instead for flipping her visor down and using the makeup mirror to peek behind them. Unfortunately, she really couldn't see a thing.

Damn.

"Mortal or Protector?"

"Don't know," he said. "I think Protector, but I could be wrong."

She squirmed, slammed the visor back up, frowned, then yanked it down again. Beside her, Mordi laughed.

She glared at him. "You have the rearview mirror," she said. "And I'd appreciate if you wouldn't gloat."

"I'm not gloating," he said, his hands on the wheel. He looked perfectly calm and reasonable.

How could he be so calm? They were in the middle of nowhere, right smack in the kind of wide-open spaces where an Outcast, a Henchman, or a traitorous Protector would have few qualms about attacking. A secluded place.

He turned his head slightly and smiled at her, his green eyes reflecting her concern, but holding another message: *optimism, concern—and a promise of safety?*

Sweet Hera, the man intended to protect her!

The thought should have made her angry. After all, she was perfectly capable of protecting herself. More or less, anyway. But instead of annoying her, she thought he was sweet.

Almost shyly, she turned in her seat to glance at him more directly. And that's when she realized . . .

Feeling bold, she leaned closer, then reached out and stroked his shoulder, taking care to touch only the twill cotton of his jacket. He raised one eyebrow, turning just slightly so that he was watching her out of the corner of his eye. She tried out a slow, sexy smile. The gesture was a little uncomfortable—certainly slow and sexy wasn't in her usual repertoire of looks—but she wanted to put up a good show in case their pursuer had super vision and was getting an up-close-and-personal look. Or, in case their pursuer simply had binoculars and was getting an up-close-and-personal look.

"What are you doing?" Mordi said, his voice holding a hint of amusement.

She leaned closer until her lips were almost brushing his ear. She tilted her head, giving her a dead-on view of the sleek black Porsche following a good twenty yards back. "What does it look like I'm doing?" she whispered, because whoever was in the Porsche might be reading her lips.

"It looks like you're coming on to me," Mordi said, his voice low and rough as sandpaper. "But I have a feeling I'm not that lucky."

Izzy swallowed and flushed. She could feel the hot blood flooding through her body and face. Her instinct was to pull away, but she fought it, instead keeping her eyes on their tail.

She focused her thoughts, willing herself not to sneak inside Mordi's head, then nuzzled his ear, the gesture designed to hide her words. "He's gaining on us," she whispered.

"Yup."

She slid her fingers through his hair, fighting her

own visceral reaction. Sweet Hera, she was losing it here, and this was really not the time to get all mushy over a man. Even Mordi. Especially Mordi. Pulling herself together, she shot one more glance out the back window, then used the press of her fingers against his hair to camouflage her words. "That Porsche is the least of our worries," she announced. In the distance, a hundred or so yards back, a blood-red Dodge Viper was careening toward them.

Maybe a reckless teenager or some hotshot trying to impress a date?

She didn't really believe that.

"No kidding," Mordi said.

She looked up, expecting to see him looking into his rearview mirror. Instead, he was focusing straight ahead. She turned, following the direction of his gaze, and then gasped. Three hulking creatures on motorcycles, clad head-to-toe in black leather, were heading straight toward Mordi's Ferrari.

"Mother of Zeus!" Izzy yelped as Mordi whipped the wheel to the side, sending his car careering up onto the rough shoulder and barely missing one of the cyclists. "Who the devil are those guys?"

"No clue," Mordi said, his mouth pulling into a frown. His fingers tightened on the steering wheel. "Call in a backup team, would you?"

She nodded, then pulled out her holopager. Nothing happened. "It's jammed."

"Try the cell phone."

She grabbed it, flipped it open, but wasn't able to get a signal. "Nothing. We're on our own."

"Hold on."

He floored it, and Izzy felt the rush of acceleration force her back into her seat. She scowled, hating the idea of running, of fleeing, but not really wanting to tangle with five attackers. Five against two were fine odds if their new acquaintances were mortal. But if the five stooges were Protectors or Outcasts or Henchmen . . . well, in that case she had no particular philosophical problems with simply escaping with her life.

Neither, apparently, did Mordi.

The sun was fast setting on Mordi's side of the car, casting long shadows and painting the tall, thin trees by the side of the road in shades of orange and purple. They were beautiful, but Izzy didn't really have time to notice.

They'd sped past the oncoming motorcycles, but now the three were fast approaching again, having braked in unison and spun around, kicking loose gravel up behind their wide tires as the rubber squealed against the asphalt.

Izzy twisted in her seat as one of the cyclists pulled ahead of them. He reached with one hand to push up the visor on his helmet, and the face that Izzy saw gave her chills. Folds of flesh and beady little eyes utterly lacking in humanity.

The thing grinned, showing broken teeth and a blackish tongue.

"Henchmen." She closed her eyes and sighed. "Great. More Henchmen."

Henchmen were stupid and brutal, but they played for keeps. She and Mordi had been lucky at the awards ceremony, but the simple fact was that if someone was sending Henchmen after her and Mordi, that someone didn't want them to survive.

A chill raced up her spine, and she shivered.

"You okay?" Mordi asked, his eyes never leaving the road.

"Yeah. Fine. No worries." But she wasn't. Not really. She'd told herself time and again that she could take care of herself, that she didn't need anybody. But she wasn't a field agent. This wasn't what she did day after day. And right then, she couldn't help but wonder how the hell she'd get out of this mess if Mordi wasn't there beside her.

Then again, if it weren't for Mordi, perhaps she wouldn't be in the mess in the first place. . . .

"One of your old catches?" she asked.

This time, he took his eyes off the road long enough to shoot her a glance. "Maybe someone you turned down for re-assimilation," he shot back. "Or *this* re-assimilation. My father, maybe."

She let out a groan of frustration. "The reason doesn't really matter right now. The question is, what are we going to do?"

"My current plan involves running like hell for civilization. If you've got a better one, now's the time."

She frowned. She didn't have a better plan. So instead of actually *doing* anything, she just sat there, watching the motorcycles advance on them, while Mordi drove like a bat out of hell.

Damn, but she hated being out of control!

"See if you can levitate one of their tires," Mordi said. "I can't concentrate long enough to get a bead, but if we can lose even one of these guys, it'll even up the odds a bit."

Not a bad plan, Izzy thought. With the minor hitch that she couldn't levitate a flea, much less a leather-clad Henchman on a motorcycle that was gaining on them.

She started to explain to Mordi, saw the determined clench of his jaw, and thought better of it. No sense adding to his worries. Instead, she just twisted in her seat, focused on the first cyclist, and muttered, "I'll try."

And she really *did* try. She focused, concentrated, gathered her internal energy, then released it with pinpoint accuracy, just as Zephron had taught her.

Nothing.

Not that she'd really expected something to happen, but hope springs eternal and all that.

"Any luck?" Mordi asked.

Her cheeks burned. "Moving too fast," she said. "Can't get a bead on them."

"Try—what the . . . ? Hold on!"

She whipped back around in time to see the Porsche that had been tailing them whip around a stand of trees and cut off their path. Apparently, the Porsche had been pacing them, following on a parallel dirt road. Even as she realized what had happened, the red Viper careened in behind them, effectively sandwiching them.

Mordi cursed, and Izzy clutched the dash with one hand. His other hand pressed against the door for balance as Mordi spun the steering wheel and shot the car away at a ninety-degree angle, clipping one cyclist and sending him flying. There was no median, just a four-foot-wide dirt ditch separating the north- and south-bound traffic.

The Ferrari raced over the ditch, fishtailing slightly and spewing small rocks and debris. The two remaining cyclists were still on their heels, and so were the cars. Mordi pulled another right angle as soon as they hit the street, and now they were racing the wrong way down the small, deserted highway.

The bad guys were still following, and Izzy bounced in her seat, desperate to do something.

"Of course!" Mighty Zeus, she was such an idiot!

"What?" Mordi demanded.

"Just drive straight," she demanded as she rolled down her window and unfastened her seat belt.

"Izzy . . ." His voice was low, demanding a response. She didn't give him one. Instead, she scrambled onto her knees on the bucket seat and leaned out the window, one hand hanging on for dear life. The other was outstretched, the warm summer air caressing her fingertips.

"Come on, come on, come on." Her words tripped over each other as she willed the two cyclists closer. A little bit . . . a little bit . . . and then . . . *yes! Now!*

She thrust out her hand, sending a rush of focused energy out of her fingertips. A fountain of ice sprang from her fingers, coating the roadway in front of the cyclists.

They hit the patch and immediately went flying, leather jackets catching the breeze, ugly fleshy faces startled into absurdity, tires flying over handlebars in an almost graceful display of chrome and leather. It was a beautiful sight—*evil Henchman wins international ice-cycling competition with triple sowcow maneuver*—and Izzy clapped her hands, delighted with herself as she slipped back into the car.

Beside her, Mordi was grinning like a fiend. "That was brilliant!" he said. "Did you see the look on their—uh-oh."

She spun back around to peer out the window. One of the cyclists was sprawled spread-eagled on the ice, his bike a mangled mess behind him. The second, however, had managed to right himself, and was even now racing—well, *carefully* racing—toward them.

That, however, wasn't what worried Izzy. She was more concerned about the fact that she didn't see the Porsche or the Viper anywhere. And they were coming up on a bridge. The cars couldn't be in front of them—there was no other way across the river. So where had they gone?

"Can you manage more frost?" Mordi asked, apparently unconcerned with those little details.

"Not this soon after," she said. Her euphoria faded as the familiar tinge of uselessness settled back in her bones.

"Maybe a little fire, then," Mordi said. "I mean, they probably caught a chill, right? It's only polite to warm them up."

He sounded so damnably self-confident that she couldn't help but smile. "Sounds like a plan to me," she said. She reached to take the steering wheel so that Mordi could pull his hands free.

He drew in a breath and, when he opened his hand, she saw a ball of fire dancing on his palm. He leaned toward her open window, ready to pitch the dancing flame that she knew would grow into a huge fireball. As he did pitch it, though, an unexpected flash of lightning ripped across the darkening sky . . . and the Porshe careened over an embankment to land right in their path.

Izzy reacted automatically, but it wasn't good enough. If she'd been seated in the driver's seat, maybe she could have succeeded. But she and Mordi were still tangled, and the Ferrari was on cruise control while she operated the steering. She cut to the left, and the car veered toward the pilings that supported the bridge. Ahead, the air seemed to drop away, and the car looked to be headed down, down, down toward the murky water of the river.

"Turn!" Mordi shouted, reaching over to grab the steering wheel even as Izzy was spinning the thing.

It didn't matter. The Porsche doubled back and rammed them from behind, sending them soaring over the embankment. They landed with a horrible splash in the water.

No longer strapped in, Izzy lurched forward, her forehead slamming against the windshield. And the last thing she thought as the car began to slowly sink below the surface of the water was that this really, really couldn't be good.

Chapter Thirty-three

"No!" Mordi grabbed Izzy's arms, shaking her, then slapped her face soundly, trying to wake her up. Nothing.

No, no, no! Everything he'd feared was coming true, and that was simply unacceptable.

He blinked, trying to see past the thick liquid that filled his eyes. Blood. He must have cut his forehead in the accident. Not that it mattered. All that mattered right then was getting Izzy out of the car and to safety.

He thrust his arms under her, then tugged her toward the driver's seat. The nose of the car was completely submerged now, and water was fast rising toward the open window. He needed to get Izzy and himself out of the car before water filled the Ferrari and dragged them under.

The water rose, and the river poured in, filling the space under their feet. He sat on the car door and tugged at Izzy, but her foot lodged under one of the pedals. With a quick glance out the back window—one of the cyclists was dusting himself off, and the other two cars were on the embankment, headlights burning like evil eyes as their engines revved—he scrambled down. If they came, they came. But he had to try to get Izzy free first.

Her foot was completely submerged, but he managed to pry it free. Her ankle had swollen to the size of a grapefruit, but he didn't think it was broken. He didn't want to hurt her, but they had no time for gentleness. As soon as her foot was free of the pedal, he curled his arms around her chest, locked his hands, and tugged.

She made a slight moaning noise, but she slipped along the seat toward him. Up he dragged her, up to be propped on the door. The car was sinking faster now, bobbing at almost a right angle to the water's surface. The river was still invading, flooding the interior with even more purpose than before.

And still, Izzy didn't wake.

The water was up to Mordi's knee now, Izzy's waist, warm and dark and determined to draw them under. Mordi kept a tight hold on her with one hand; with the other, he grappled in the backseat for his cooler. His fingers found the handle and he tugged it forward, then dumped out the sodas and sandwiches he'd brought. They bobbed in the water in the car.

He shoved the cooler out the window, watching as it floated. Good. Then he scooted out the window himself. His legs were hanging in the river, and he stretched, trying to find the bottom. Nothing. He grabbed the door and pulled himself up, then leaned forward at the waist until he had a hold of Izzy again.

He had her halfway out the window when he heard the howling. It was a high-pitched keening sound, one that he knew. He should know it; he'd heard it often enough while working for his father.

It was the sound of a Henchman, changed back into

its native, squidlike shape, and letting out its native yelp . . . right before it attacked.

Hopping Hades, this was not going to be good.

He didn't waste time looking at the river's edge. He needed to get Izzy free of the car; he needed to make sure she was safe.

The car was almost under now, and the extra water actually made it easier to pull her free. She moaned, her eyelids fluttering, as he held her tight around the waist and kicked off toward the cooler. "Hang on," he said, wrapping her arms around it. She started to sink, but the Supra Styrofoam did its job, and she bobbed there, forehead furrowed, eyes fluttering in half-consciousness, her mouth curved into a question.

A *schlurp* sounded a few yards downstream as the Ferrari finally succumbed to the weight of the water. Behind Mordi and Izzy the keening sounded again, echoing across the river. The Henchman had fully transformed, and now he slipped into the water, his squidlike body moving with unusual grace as he swam toward them with undeniable menace.

Anger burned in Mordi's gut, and Mordi fought the urge to swim forward and meet the squid halfway. He wanted to sink his hands and feet into that soft flesh, to rip the creature apart, to do anything and everything to end this episode and keep Izzy safe.

That wouldn't do it, though. The only thing to do—the only *smart* thing—was to swim away. In the opposite direction. To try to get to the far side of the river and then race for safety.

He kicked backward, then grabbed the cooler, clutching it as he kicked toward the far shore. In the distance, he saw the Henchman slither through the water, closing the distance between them.

He'd shoot a ball of flame, and then—

What the . . . ?

Suddenly the horizon was filled with the writhing, slimy creatures. They marched forward, filling the sky, outlined against the setting sun, like something out of *Night of the Living Dead.*

Suddenly, staying and fighting seemed even less like a good plan. Getting the hell out of there seemed the only option. If they could manage it.

"Izzy," he hissed. Nothing. He splashed water in her face. "Izzy. Wake. Up."

She blinked, her eyes opening, groggy and blood-shot. "What? Where are we?"

"You got conked in the head," he said, kicking for all he was worth. "You passed out. But right now I need you to stay awake. I need you to *kick.*"

"The chase," she whispered. Then she peered over her shoulder, saw the Henchmen, and the little color that had remained in her face drained away.

"Fire?" she whispered.

"Not enough. No way can I conjure enough to get us out of this mess."

She started kicking.

It helped some, but not enough. The gap was closing fast.

"Can you shapeshift?" she asked. "Turn into a shark or bluefin or something and swim us the hell out of here?"

He frowned. "I don't do fish," he said. "I can't."

"A whale? A dolphin? Some other water mammal?"

"Sorry." A wash of disappointment filled him. He'd failed her.

Then the corner of her mouth twitched. "Well, no-body's perfect," she said. And idiotically, even though the Henchman was closer and they were still trying to kick their way out of an endless river, he felt better.

Something cold and slimy gripped his leg, and he

was underwater, Izzy's scream echoing in his ears. *Another Henchman*. He'd been watching the first, and somehow another had sneaked up on him.

He twisted and managed to grab hold, his fingers digging into the thing's squishy flesh. The monster flipped him over, and he gulped, swallowing a gallon of water. He struggled to right himself, but a tentacle lashed out, twisting around his leg and pulling him down, down, down.

Mordi shifted, trying to use the squidlike thing to climb out of the water and suck in air, but the Henchman was holding him under. This wasn't a mere threat; the creature meant to kill him.

With a burst of energy, Mordi rolled to the side, pulling the creature with him. Not for the first time, he wished he were more like his brother. Now, though, he simply wished that he could breathe under water. His powers, shapeshifting and fire, were no match for the Henchman. Not here. Not now.

Unless . . .

He'd done it once before, and it had worked. Could he do it now? Did he have the strength to conjure?

Above him, he saw the second Henchman slither along the surface of the water, approaching Izzy. She'd probably strangle him for the thought, but there was no way in Hades that she was able to protect herself. Not now. Not with that knot rising on her forehead.

He was her only chance, and he wasn't about to let some slimy, water-slicked, *smelly* squidman keep him from protecting the woman he loved.

Loved. The word lashed through him, surprising him, but also giving him strength. Perhaps it had started as lust, but it had grown into so much more. He loved Izzy; loved everything about her. Her dedication, her sense of humor, her protectiveness of her dad. Heck, he even loved that wall of ice that she hid behind, the persona that he'd been privileged to glimpse past.

Yes, he loved her. And he would protect her. Even if, in the end, he had to protect her from himself.

The Henchman was gripping his forearms, tentacles wrapped around him and trussing him up like a pig. The creatures were slow and cumbersome on land, but in the water, they moved with terrifying agility.

Still, Mordi was *pissed*. He might not be able to shift into a sea creature, but that didn't mean he couldn't shift at all. With a burst of energy, he lashed out. Relief flooded him as conjured fire enveloped the writhing Henchman. He heard the creature's squeal of surprise, and wasn't about to hang around long enough for the creature to realize that the fire was fake—nothing more than a pyrotechnical illusion.

He shifted, transforming himself into a long, slick snake. Then he dropped like a stone, the Henchman's slimy grip no match for his smooth scales.

As soon as he was free, he shifted back to human form, fighting against the wave of disorientation that always accompanied a transformation. He kicked to the surface, arriving just in time to surprise the other Henchman, who was approaching Izzy from behind.

Mordi dove down, tucking his feet in, then lashed out in an awkward donkey kick. He got the squid-creature somewhere in the gut, his feet sinking with a satisfying slurp into the doughy flesh. The creature howled and rolled away. Then Mordi broke the surface, clutching the cooler as he and Izzy again started kicking for freedom.

"They're still coming," Izzy said.

A booming laugh echoed over the water, and Mordi turned toward the sound, only to see a dark shape standing on the hill above, between the Porsche and the Viper. "It's over, Mordichai. Don't worry about the girl. I promise, she'll be well taken care of."

Mordi strained, trying to place the voice. So familiar, and yet . . . not.

"Go!" Izzy yelled beside him. He turned to her in question, and she rolled her eyes. Evidently she was feeling better. "You heard him. It's not me he's after. It's you. Now *go.*"

"Not happening," he said. "We both go, or we both stay."

She didn't waste time arguing, just started swimming toward a tree stump that poked out of the water about five yards ahead.

The dazed Henchman was still behind them, trailing them on the right. His companion—the one Mordi had surprised with the fire—had surfaced on the left. It too was tracking their progress.

The creatures were dumb, but they obviously weren't stupid. Mordi and Izzy both had powers—amazing by some standards, nothing special by others. But the one thing neither of them had was any particular ability to live in or breathe water. Which meant that the best way for the Henchman to beat them was to keep them in the river . . . and bide their time while their targets tired themselves out.

If he and Izzy wanted to win, they needed to turn the tables. They needed to do the unexpected. And they needed to do it soon.

"Can you run?" he asked, a plan so ridiculous it just might work forming in his mind.

She didn't miss a beat in her swimming, but she did manage to send him a look that suggested she thought he was losing his mind.

"If there was a surface," he explained. "Could you run?"

"I think so." Her brow furrowed. "I don't feel dizzy anymore. Yeah. But what—"

"Ice."

235

For a second, her face clouded with confusion. Then her eyes lit. "Running? More like slipping and sliding," she said. "You ever try to run on ice?"

"Even crawling will be better than trying to fight these squid in the water," he said. "At least we'll have some sort of advantage." He narrowed his eyes, looking at her battered face. "Are you up to it?"

"I can't do the whole river," she said. "Or enough to keep them imprisoned. But yeah. I think I can do enough to get us out of here." She slowed her swim. "For this, though, I'll need both hands."

Mordi nodded, holding her around the waist and kicking like a fiend to keep them both afloat and fleeing. She stiffened. He knew what she was doing; he'd done it enough times himself—drawing the power in so that she could let it right back out.

A few feet in front of them, the surface of the water rippled. But the Henchmen were drawing closer.

"Not to rush you or anything, but . . ."

Izzy nodded, her body stiff and warm in his arms, filled to bursting with power. "Right about . . . *now*." She lashed out, and ice spewed from her fingers, creating a frozen platform in front of them. "Hurry!" she cried. "Hurry!"

They scrambled on, him lifting her at the waist to help her up, and her scrabbling forward on hands and knees as he piled on behind her. Behind them, the Henchmen approached, still in squid form; but as they rushed forward, Mordi saw the change come upon them. Suddenly they were coming out of the water in droves—fat, thin, tall, short, each some mockery of human form, and all as ugly as sin.

"Faster," he said, taking Izzy's hand. They were half-sliding, half-walking on the icy surface. "We need more," he shouted, seeing the water churning in front of them.

"I know. Can you slow them down behind?"

He could. As he and Izzy raced forward, her hand outstretched to become an ice-making machine, he reached backward, all of his power concentrated on melting the ice in their wake. Behind them, the ice crackled and buckled, finally falling off into the water—and taking the following Henchmen with it. The evil creatures floundered, struggling to again change shape.

Mordi and Izzy didn't slow down. They just kept racing along, Izzy building their bridge and Mordi destroying it behind them. When they finally reached the other side of the river, both collapsed, exhausted, onto the bank.

All Mordi wanted to do was rest, to spread out on the soft grass with this woman at his side and watch the sun dip below the horizon.

What he wanted, unfortunately, severely clashed with reality. The Henchmen reached the water's edge, and were even now emerging from the river like bog monsters.

Mordi reached for Izzy's hand, too tired to care that she might sense his desperate thoughts. "We need to move."

"Can't. Pushed too hard." Her voice, thin and weak, barely reached his ears.

He'd pushed too hard, too, and it was so hard to conjure the strength. But he had to. He had to keep her safe. He knew without a doubt that it was him they wanted. Izzy was in the cross fire, but he'd die before he'd let any harm come to her.

Anger spurred his adrenaline, and he rolled to his side, not getting up because he didn't want to waste the energy. His body felt like molten metal: without form, without strength, but with a billion possibilities bubbling beneath the surface. *He* was bubbling. And he only had to harness his strength.

The Henchmen were fully out of the water now, moving closer. And closer. Their heavy footsteps squished against the muddy bank, a thick *slurping* sound punctuating their increasing proximity.

Almost . . . almost . . .

Mordi held his breath, trying to wait until the last possible minute. They'd been too far away before. But now, perhaps, if he just let them come a little bit closer . . .

He closed his eyes, searching for strength and praying for success.

He wouldn't fail. He couldn't.

And then the Henchmen lunged and Izzy screamed and Mordi erupted. Fire enveloped the creatures, their squeals of pain filling the sky. The evil creatures raced round and round in blind circles, then dropped to the ground, rolling as they tried to smother the flames. Too late. Their oily bodies began to melt, and as they burned away into nothingness the flames started to recede.

Across the river, still on the bank, Mordi could see the Porsche and the Viper. Their headlights flashed once, as if in silent acknowledgment that Mordi had won this round. Then the cars backed away. Mordi understood.

This wasn't over yet.

With that final grim thought, exhaustion overtook him, and Mordi collapsed to the ground, holding Izzy close. He forced himself to stay awake, keeping a silent vigil in the swiftly darkening night.

Chapter Thirty-four

Isole awoke in total darkness, her heart pounding furiously and her breath coming in short, shallow bursts. *Where . . .*

"Izzy."

She relaxed, Mordi's soft voice washing over her like a caress. She didn't know what had happened, didn't know where they were, but she knew that she was safe. Mordi had taken care of her.

With a groan, she sat up. Her body felt boneless, and she rolled her neck, trying to will the exhaustion to leave and some semblance of energy to refill her body. Beside her, Mordi shifted, then reached out to stroke her back. She realized that she was warm and dry and sitting on a bed. She frowned. The last thing she remembered, she'd been cold, damp, and set upon by Henchmen.

"I think I need a debriefing," she said.

He gave her a quick rundown. After he'd rested, he'd pondered what the heck to do since their car was at the bottom of the river. In the end, he'd picked her up and carried her up the embankment and to the road. Across the tiny road he found a ramshackle motel, and decided to take advantage of it. He'd checked them in, used the phone to report in at headquarters, then used the last of his strength to hang and dry out their clothes.

"Thanks for that," she said.

"You're welcome."

She licked her lips. "And thanks for saving us. The last thing I remember is those Henchmen melting like the Wicked Witch of the West."

His mouth curved into a grin. "Again," he said, "you're welcome."

His tone was light enough, but she caught the raising scent of something else underneath. Fear, maybe? She wasn't certain. "What is it? What's wrong?"

He grimaced, then lay back down, interlacing his fingers behind his head. "You *thanking* me. *That's* what's wrong."

"Excuse me?" She shifted on the mattress so that she was sitting cross-legged on the threadbare spread, peering down at him. "Why shouldn't I thank you?"

"The fact that I put your life in danger leaps to mind."

She raised an eyebrow, then laughed. "I forgive you." She rubbed her legs, trying to get the blood flowing again.

"Accident of birth," he added.

His voice was low, almost monotone, and a finger of ice raced up her spine. She knew what he was implying, that Hieronymous was the one responsible. They didn't have proof, and she wanted to argue with him, but she knew it would be futile. They'd been down that road before. Instead she simply said, "It could be someone else."

"It could," he said. "It isn't."

His voice held an infinite sadness, and she blinked back tears. How horrible to believe—to really, deep in your gut believe—that your own father could be out to kill you.

Gently, she pressed a hand to his chest. He reached up, his hand moving to grasp hers. "Mordi—"

The hand stopped. "Sorry," he said. "I forgot." He drew in a breath, his chest rising, then falling again. "I'll tender my resignation tomorrow."

"Resignation?"

"As your assistant."

"Oh." Once upon a time, she'd wanted him to leave her alone to do her job. Now, though, his pronouncement only made her feel lost. "Oh," she said again.

"I'm endangering you. Hieronymous knows I oppose his re-assimilation. He wants me out of the picture." Mordi shrugged. "So I'm removing myself. Before you get hurt when you don't have to."

"Mordi," she said. "I've been in his head, remember? You know I don't believe your father is behind this."

"I know. But *I* believe it." He smiled at her, his green eyes warm. "Guess we're going to have to agree to disagree."

She couldn't meet his eyes. "And here they say chivalry is dead. . . ."

"Is that what they say?"

"I don't know. I—"

"Izzy." He took her hand.

Desire. Want. Need. His thoughts, crystal clear, swirled within her, filling her head before she was able to put up any barriers. And underneath it all was one persistent question:

Does she want me, too?

She yanked her hand away, then looked down, unable to meet his eyes. *Yes*, she thought, wishing he could read her as she read him. *Sweet Hera, yes.*

But thoughts were easy. It was words that were hard. And when she lifted her head to look at him again, she saw doubt flicker in his eyes, and she knew that she had to come up with the words. Though it terrified her, she had to say her desire aloud.

She drew a deep breath, as if she could fill her lungs with courage. "Yes. I . . . I want you, too."

Relief. Waves of relief rolled off Mordi, enveloping and bolstering Isole. Relief and heat and desire and—

His mouth closed over hers. He'd lifted himself up and pulled her toward him, and his mouth had closed over hers with a frenzy born of need and pungent desire. Sparks shot through her body as his emotions accosted her, filled her. She'd pulled away before. Now, though . . .

Now he was absorbing her being; she was filling his veins, coursing through his body, becoming this man who intrigued and fascinated her. She opened her mind, wanting to know everything about him. To feel what he felt. To see what he saw.

She anticipated the images: his life, his challenges, his triumphs, his defeats. Everything, it all would fill her soul and memory as if the images belonged to her.

But there was nothing.

Sort of. He wasn't blocking her; it was more that she'd already filled him, and she reeled under the press of images and emotions that were a mix of both of them. Those coursed through her veins.

Her.

Nothing but Isole.

Mordi wanted her. Needed her. And his passion was so great that, at the moment, it overshadowed everything else. She'd completely filled this man, and the knowledge both humbled and excited her.

She melted under his kiss, opening her mouth to him, her arms caressing him, wanting to bring him pleasure. She wanted him to know that, even though he didn't have her powers, in fact he'd filled her, too. And it was the most wonderful experience she'd ever known.

Chapter Thirty-five

Mordi was on fire. Izzy's mouth burned hot under his, a living flame that he never would have expected from a woman whose frosty blue eyes could—quite literally—turn a man to ice.

Iceberg she might seem, but she was melting for him, and the heady realization of her desire for him coursed through his senses like pure energy. This was dangerous, and yet oh-so-necessary.

She broke the kiss, pulling away just far enough to meet his eyes. "Mordi," she whispered, the single word reflecting the emotions that shone in her face—confusion, longing, desire.

He put a finger over her lips. "No words. Not now. Not yet."

She nodded, just a tiny movement of her head, and Mordi slid his finger away, ostensibly releasing her from silence.

He didn't go far, however. With his fingertip, he traced her lips. They were plump and beautiful, and the thought came to him that they were perfectly kissable. It wasn't the kind of thing he usually thought, but he liked that. He liked the way she made him feel, the way she made him think about touches and caresses and not revenge and retribution.

With Izzy, he'd finally let his guard down. He'd found a Mordichai that he'd thought lost long ago. He was a different Mordi, one who didn't look for a hidden agenda in every speech and who didn't expect betrayal from those closest to him.

It was foolish, perhaps, to drop his guard around this woman who only had to reach out a finger to read his innermost thoughts, but with Izzy he couldn't help it. That was what she did to him. Made him a fool.

Right now, he was going to be foolish enough to kiss her again.

Her eyes were still closed, and her lips parted, as his fingers traced the perfect line of her mouth. Her hair was loose, her usually tame curls knotted and wild around her face. She looked like an angel, not the tough-as-nails re-assimilation counselor who ushered Outcasts into her office, and he was almost afraid that when he pressed his lips to hers, she'd dissolve beneath him like so much spun sugar.

It was a chance he was going to have to take.

Leaning forward, he again captured her mouth with his, pulling his finger down to trace the soft curve of her neck. Her lips parted, and he moaned, accepting her silent invitation to sample and taste her with his tongue.

She was even sweeter than he'd imagined, and hotter than he could have dreamed. Ice? Never. Not this woman. She was heat and energy and constant movement.

As if reading his mind—and he had to consider the possibility that she was—she squirmed against him, writhing closer until he could feel the press of her breasts against his chest, until their legs were tangled on the bed and he wasn't sure where he ended and she began.

"Izzy," he whispered, sliding his mouth from hers.

She pressed two fingers to his lips. "Don't say anything. I'm afraid that if we talk we'll change our minds. And I . . . I really don't want to change my mind."

Her words rent his soul. This was more than just heat and passion, and he wasn't going to change his mind. He knew that. He was certain. He'd decided how much he cared for this woman sometime ago. Isole filled and excited him. He wanted this moment, and the next, and the next.

He didn't know what *she* wanted . . . and he didn't dare ask.

"Mordi?" Her brow furrowed, her blue eyes sparkling in the dim lamplight. She brushed the side of her hand against his cheek, her touch as soft as a feather. He had no empathic abilities, and yet he knew one thing that she wanted. *Him.*

His heart lurched. Today, tomorrow, forever? Right then, it didn't matter. For now, he'd take the moment. He'd worry about the next one later.

He slid one arm around her neck, wisps of hair tickling his fingers. Izzy arched her back like a feline, the motion undeniably erotic as her breasts pressed more firmly against his chest. Her eyes were closed, her lips slightly parted, and the tiny moaning sound that came from her mouth was one of pure satisfaction.

Mordi groaned, his body swelling. But this sound wasn't soft. It was low and hungry, almost a growl, and it held a passion so desperate that, did he not release it, he was certain he would explode. His body burned with need, and he drew Isole toward him, needing to consume her, to complete her.

His hands stroked her back, down and down until his fingertips slipped under the thin material of her shirt. Her skin burned under his fingertips, and he stroked her in long fluid movements. She writhed against his hand, finding a rhythm in his caress.

It was slow and sensual, but Mordi wanted hard and fast. He wanted her, and he wanted her *now*.

He grasped the hem of her shirt and tugged it up, pulling it over her head as she lifted her arms. She wore a red lace bra, and the sight of it against her white skin excited him. Her breasts were lush, spilling over the tight lace, their fullness enhanced by the arch in her back and her hands raised above her head.

Oh, sweet Hera, he couldn't take this.

He bent forward and took one firm breast in his mouth. He laved rough lace and soft skin, his tongue stroking and teasing even as his hand found her other breast.

He teased the nub, popping the nipple out to rub between his thumb and his finger. Isole moaned, the desperate sound filling him with an urgent need. "Izzy," he whispered. "I want—"

"So do I. Now. Please."

Thank Hera. He pulled her on top of him, his mouth still suckling her breast as his hands found the zipper on her oh-so-professional skirt. He eased it down over her hips, and she shimmied a little to help his efforts along.

Her hands fumbled for the button of his slacks, and he muttered a soft curse when she couldn't quite manage to release the button. He closed his hands over hers and guided her fingers, then groaned as she slid her hand down, stroking the length of him as she urged his pants off.

"Careful," he said, "or I won't be able to wait."

She straddled him, her eyes cloudy with desire as she unfastened her bra and tossed it aside. "I already told you. Don't wait. Please, don't wait."

Her words ignited his blood, and he took hold of her

shoulder, rolling them both over so that he was poised above her. Except for a tiny pair of white lace panties, she was naked, her skin flushed with the same heat that filled him.

He ran his hands along her shoulder, reveling in the softness of her skin. She tilted her head back, eyes closed, lips parted.

With a fierceness that surprised him, he captured her mouth, wanting to claim her with his kiss. He wanted to cherish her, yes, but he also wanted to *have* her. He wanted to make Isole Frost his own. His, and only his.

"Mordi," she whispered when he broke the kiss. Her fingernails scraped his back, her hands working lower and lower, and then pressing his hips toward her so that there was no mistaking what she wanted. He wanted it, too, and he hooked one finger under the waistband of her panties and tugged them down. She did a sexy little shimmy move, helping him along. He left the panties somewhere near the foot of the bed, his attention focused utterly on the beauty in front of him.

"Izzy," he whispered.

She didn't answer him in words, but spread her legs in a silent invitation—one he wasn't about to ignore. He slipped his hands between her thighs, letting his fingers explore her wet, slick folds, teasing and tempting until he felt her body shudder under his touch and her breathy moan filled his ears.

She lay there, warm and limp, with a satisfied smile on her face, and Mordi knew that he simply couldn't take it anymore. Her body tightened around his fingers, and he knew that she couldn't take the anticipation any more than he could. He lowered himself into her, thrashing and then pounding into her as her hips rose to meet his. It was wild and hot, and all control was fast leaving him.

His blood boiled, the pressure building until he couldn't hold back any longer—until he didn't *want* to hold back. Then, suddenly, the world exploded around him, leaving only him and Izzy at the center of the universe.

Spent, Mordi went limp, shifting his weight just enough that he didn't crush Isole. He lay there, staring toward the ceiling and lying next to her, his bones and muscles liquid. He felt like molten metal and imagined their bodies blending, becoming one.

"Izzy," he whispered after an eternity of simply holding her. He didn't really have anything to say, just wanted to speak her name.

She didn't answer, and he turned toward her. Her chest rose and fell in the gentle rhythm of sleep. Mordi smiled, then rolled onto his side, idly stroking her hair as he watched her.

I want you, Izzy, he thought. *I want you forever. Can you hear me? Do you know how much you've come to mean to me?*

He didn't know if she could hear him or not. Didn't know if she'd heard his soul while they'd made love. He'd opened himself to her in a way he'd done to no one else before, and he felt a closeness now that he'd never felt with anyone.

Oh, he'd fallen hard for this woman. And, Hera help him, he didn't want the feeling to stop.

Chapter Thirty-six

"Mr. Black! Welcome, welcome!" Harold Frost's round face flushed with happiness, and Hieronymous beamed, enjoying his current role of savior and inspiration. Soon, that would be all but erased, the joy in Frost's eyes replaced by fear. Fear and awe. Just as it should be. As all mortals should feel toward those of Hieronymous's superior breed.

He clenched his fist at his side, forcing his thoughts back on track. He already knew what he had to do. Now was not the time to justify—in his mind, or aloud—to someone as low and insignificant as Harold Frost.

Hieronymous's gaze swept over the workbench, and he moved forward, his black cape swishing behind him. *Or perhaps not so insignificant after all.*

"You are finished, then?" he asked. "The second batch is complete? All is in working order?"

"Yes, yes. Of course." The man's expression shifted, and his gaze drifted to the floor.

"You wish to say something?" Hieronymous asked, graciously allowing his minion to speak.

"I, well . . . yes." The little man pushed on the bridge

of his glasses, shoving them more firmly into place. Hieronymous pulled himself up to his full height, looking down at the man from an eighteen-inch vantage point. Intimidating, no doubt. The little man swallowed, bucking up and continuing. "I, uh, just wanted to say thanks. Yes. Thanks. I, um, recently was honored with an inventors award, and if it weren't for your inspiration and financial backing—"

"And helping you with the trickier bits," Hieronymous put in.

"Yes, yes, of course." Frost contemplated his feet. "I owe you much."

"Indeed you do," Hieronymous said. He softened the words with a smile. "Of course, your success has been my pleasure." He crossed to the workbench and picked up one of eight purple fountain pens. He unscrewed the inkwell portion and peered inside at the tiny mechanism, then smiled. "It has been a joy to watch you so deftly bring my ideas to life." Each pen was designed to write the thoughts of its holder. Hieronymous had engineered the implements, however, to be easily manipulated. Instead of simply *taking* thoughts, the pens *emitted* them—capturing a Protector's brain waves and switching his thoughts and beliefs to whatever Hieronymous deemed appropriate.

Unfortunately, the device didn't work on some Protectors. Himself, of course. And also that gargoyle Zephron—or, for that matter, anyone in his line.

"Might I . . . I mean, could I ask a question?"

Hieronymous inclined his head, silently granting permission.

"You have such a knack, such obvious skill. And yet you've chosen to mentor me. Why?"

Why, indeed? Because he had no choice. Because the Inner Circle could discern if Hieronymous utilized his own skill. And because the punishment for an Outcast utilizing his skill was severe, and he could not directly challenge the Council's power. Not yet.

No, that was a risk Hieronymous could not afford. Not now. Not when he'd finally conceived of a plan so brilliant, so foolproof, that it would ensure his ultimate rise to power . . . and the concurrent subjugation of the entire mortal race.

"Mr. Black?"

Hieronymous replaced the smile that had faded during his reverie. He waved a hand in an offhand gesture. "I wanted to help you," he said, once again grateful that Harold Frost, though he had a Halfling daughter, was so utterly ignorant of the Protector world. "It benefited you, and it benefited me." He picked up one of the pens and examined it in the light. "Exemplary work."

"Thank you." Frost cocked his head. "What do you intend to use them for?"

"Ah, Harold, you know I can't tell you that."

Frost nodded, then ran his fingers through his silver-white hair, causing it to stand on end. The little man vaguely resembled a rumpled porcupine. "Top secret. Yes, of course. I'd forgotten. I'd only hoped to have some idea. I mean . . ." He shook his head, trailing off.

"You mean that the device could be altered—so that it doesn't channel the energy in one's mind, but instead controls it."

"Oh, no. I'd never thought of—*what*?" His eyes widened as the import of Hieronymous's words caught up with him.

Pathetic little mortal. Hieronymous had only to make the choice and the little man would be squashed like the pathetic little insect he was. But no. Not yet. There still was a use for Harold Frost.

Hieronymous sidled up to the mortal and wrapped an arm around his shoulder, stooping a bit to make the contact. "I need your help on another matter," he said. "A matter involving your daughter."

"Izzy?" Fear colored the man's voice. "How do you know Izzy?"

"She and I are quite well acquainted, actually," Hieronymous said. "And I intend for us to become more so."

"I . . . I don't understand."

"It's quite simple," Hieronymous said. "You, my dear Mr. Frost, are bait." He held out his hand to grasp the startled mortal. "Shall we go?"

Chapter Thirty-seven

Izzy awoke in Mordi's arms, a shaft of light peeking through the flimsy curtains to illuminate their intertwined bodies. She smiled and stretched, feeling a bit like a satisfied cat who'd just downed an entire plate of cream.

Happy. Content.

And all the happier because she felt the same feelings emanate from Mordi.

His eyes flickered, and she realized he was awake. "Hey," she whispered. "Good morning."

He reached out to stroke her cheek. She'd had plenty of warning now, and she'd managed to turn off her power. She didn't need it, though, to know what he was thinking. It was right there in his eyes—deep satisfaction and a glimmer of male pride so apparent it made her giggle.

"What's so funny?"

"You. The conquering male."

He rolled over, propping himself up on an elbow. He reached out, then, with his free hand, and stroked her breast. Her nipple tightened under his erotic onslaught, longing for a more intense caress. She let her head fall back, and she moaned.

"Yeah," he whispered. "I think conquering is a fair description."

"Uh-huh." It was the only sound she could manage, and Izzy closed her eyes and let herself fall back into the abyss of pleasure.

Mordi's low chuckle teased her senses, and he shifted beside her. Gently, he slid his hand down her body, a slow, sensual journey.

Izzy kept her eyes closed, her body arching back of its own accord into his touch. She heard the rustle of the bedclothes as he shifted beside her, then another hand joined the first, so that he held her by the waist.

His hands were warm and large, and his thumbs met in the middle of her abdomen, stroking her bare skin and working their way down to her belly button.

At first, she felt only the heat of his hands on her, generating a fire in her belly that would surely grow to consume them. She writhed with pleasure, remembering with satisfaction just how fabulous that fire could be. Then the gentle caress of his fingers was joined by the soft press of his lips against her stomach. She gasped as his tongue joined the party, dipping into her belly button.

Sweet Hera, the man was going to drive her mad!

She reached down and buried her fingers in his hair, still keeping her eyes closed as she let the power of his touch carry her away. Her every nerve ending was on fire, her body a mass of heat and energy, and she could feel herself melting into the mattress—warm, languid, and satisfied.

His mouth moved farther south, and a desperate anticipation edged out her languid feeling. Mordi's hands stroked her hips, then moved down over her thighs. His fingers splayed so that his thumbs caressed the inside of her legs. The touch was so maddening—close, but not quite *there*—she wanted to scream with frustration. She would have screamed, too, if his warm mouth hadn't pressed against her in the most intimate of kisses, making her want to cry out with pleasure, not frustration.

He laved her, taking her just to the brink and then pulling away, teasing and gently tormenting her until she thought she'd go insane.

When she couldn't stand it anymore, she begged.

He slid up her body and silenced her with a kiss, his hands stroking her side, brushing against her breast in a maddening caress.

"Do you want to lose yourself with me?" he whispered. "In the heat?"

She wasn't sure she could manage a response, but somehow she whimpered an affirmation.

She had no idea what to expect. What she got was heaven.

Fire.

A tongue of fire caressed her body—hot, ticklish, but not burning. It was a conjured flame, entirely under Mordi's control. It danced over her ankle, then crept up her leg, teasing the inside of her thigh. It skipped along, teasing her with a promise of pyrotechnics to come, and spread out along her smooth belly, moving slowly up to stroke her breasts until her nipples were so sensitive that even the air was torture.

All the while, Mordi lay beside her, his fingertips following in the wake of the blaze, watching the flame to ensure it never went out. The fire danced up over her lips, an erotic kiss of pure heat, then crept back down her body in a slow, sensual wave until it focused into a point of heat that slipped between her legs, infiltrating her core.

It no longer burned like a flame, but was a liquid

heat, and she writhed as her body neared the boiling point. And then, just as she was about to explode, the fire expanded, emerged, spread out to envelop her entire body and Mordi's. She found release then and there, and as the world shattered around her, she was safe in Mordi's arms in a cocoon of fire.

Afterward, her body felt heavy and boneless, and she wondered if she'd ever fully recover. Beside her, Mordi kissed her ear and pulled her close, spooning her against him. She sighed, feeling warm and loved.

Loved?

She swallowed. He *did* love her. She could breathe deep and inhale the scent of it, and his love filled and warmed her.

But did she love him, too? She *wanted* him; she knew that much. She admired him, she craved him. He filled her heart and touched her senses. But how could she love him—truly love him—with so many secrets hanging between them?

"Mordi?" His name emerged as a whisper.

"Hmmm?"

"I . . . I need to tell you something." She drew a breath, intending to tell him about her dad, about why she so wanted Hieronymous to be on the up and up, but the words wouldn't come. She wanted to tell him, really she did, but still she couldn't bring herself to speak.

"Izzy?" He stroked her hair, his eyes filled with concern. "Sweetheart, what's wrong?"

"I just . . . I just . . ." She took a breath. "I was just thinking about fathers. And how much I love mine." She looked down, unable to meet his eyes. "And I wished you had a father you loved, too." She shrugged. "That's all."

The lie came easily, but she couldn't stop the tears. Because if she couldn't tell him, that must mean she didn't really trust him.

Chapter Thirty-eight

The halls of the Olympus facility were mostly abandoned as Izzy and Mordi moved quickly toward the main conference room. They'd used the motel phone and called for transport, then taken the Council shuttle to the Olympus headquarters to file their formal report and meet with Bilius and Armistand. Considering how little sleep she'd gotten and how busy the morning had already been, Izzy was surprised she wasn't half-dead on her feet.

They'd already completed the paperwork portion (in triplicate, in front of witnesses), and now they were heading for the formal debriefing with the elders. They turned into the antechamber that led into the main conference room, both of their gazes drawn to the pale blue crystalline tube in the center of the room.

"Kind of puts everything in perspective," Mordi said.

Izzy frowned, not at all sure what he was talking about.

He nodded toward the tube. "The mortalization chamber."

"*That's* what that is?"

"Yup. You've never seen it before?"

She raised an eyebrow. "As much as I wanted to be on the Council? I would have keeled over and died if I had to see that thing."

He grinned. "Me, too. Different reasons, though."

"Your dad?"

He nodded. "Considering what scum he thought mortals were, I'd be damned if I was going to be one."

She nodded, and they both watched the tube in silence for a moment. It looked innocent enough, but it was pretty sinister to a Halfling. It was fraught with meaning. At twenty-five, a Halfling had to make a choice, picking one side or the other from their heritage. If they chose mortalization, well, then they stepped inside the tube, the power was thrown, and they stepped out a mortal. Not only were they off the Council, but they also lost all memory of Protector life. But even if they opted for the Council, they still had to pass a series of tests.

For most, their skills and powers were developed, and they had no trouble passing all the various tests and whatnot. Izzy, though, had suffered from that little levitation problem. . . .

She'd had quite a fear of mortalization, all right. And it hadn't been unfounded.

Before she could brood any more over the past, the conference room door opened, and an assistant ushered them inside. Armistand and Bilius were already seated, each reading copies of the reports Izzy and Mordi had filled out.

"Quite an ordeal," Armistand said.

"Yes, sir," Mordi replied.

"And you have no idea who your attacker was?"

"No, sir," Mordi said.

Izzy raised a brow in surprise. He *did* have an idea, and she knew it. He was keeping silent only because of her certainty, and that wasn't fair to him or to the Council. She drew a breath. "Actually, Mordichai fears it may be his father."

The elders exchanged glances, then made notes on their forms. Finally, Bilius looked up, his gaze taking in both witnesses. "I understand Mordichai's fear, particularly in light of the history between him and his father, but I'm not inclined to believe that Hieronymous attacked the two of you."

"Nor am I," Armistand said.

Izzy frowned, her gaze drawn to the pens they were both using. The purple fountain pens seemed oddly familiar. "Excuse me, sir, but I couldn't help but admire your pen. Where did you get it?"

Armistand held the implement up. "Ah, yes. Fine craftsmanship. My assistant Patel provided me with it." He turned to Trystan. "You?"

"Young Patel as well. He said it was a gift to show his appreciation for being granted re-assimilation."

"Oh," Izzy said, and Mordi looked at her curiously. "That was very thoughtful of him." Obviously Patel had no connection to her father. The casing must be a common one for fountain pens. Still, it *was* odd. . . .

She had no time to think about it further, though, because Bilius and Trystan had switched back to the original topic.

"At any rate," Bilius went on, "I hardly believe Hieronymous would attack you." He looked at Mordi and smiled. Izzy stifled a gasp as a wash of pro-Hieronymous emotions seemed to roll off the elder—the very same elder who just a few days ago had essentially told her that the idea of Hieronymous applying for re-assimilation made him physically ill.

The turnabout confused her. Even more, it concerned her. She supposed she should be encouraged that the elders were so optimistic about Hieronymous's reformation. After all, as she'd told herself over and over, if Hieronymous Black was good, then she and her father were out of hot water.

She should be happy. Ecstatic. At the very least, cautiously optimistic.

She wasn't, though. Instead, she simply felt a gnawing fear begin in the pit of her stomach.

Chapter Thirty-nine

Plop, plip, plop.

The steady drip of water—at least, he *hoped* it was water—echoed in the dark chamber. His chamber was pitch-black, and Harold Frost could see nothing.

He could hear and smell everything, though, and in this dank place, that was hardly a comfort. Sulphur, as pungent as rotten eggs, filled the air, stinging his useless eyes. Another smell, too. Though it was unfamiliar, Harold was certain that the sharp odor was the smell of burning flesh.

Oh God, oh God, oh God.

Blindly, he reached back, running his hand along the rough stone wall. He was already sitting on the smooth stone bench—the only one in the cell—but before he leaned back against the wall, he wanted to make sure there weren't any creepy-crawlies on it.

They came in the night—or what he thought was the night—slithering around and over him. He shivered at the memory.

He had no idea how long he'd been here, but it was long enough to leave him exhausted and half-starved. When he'd first arrived, he'd tried to pace the area of his cell, but there was no room. If he held his hands out and turned in a circle, his fingers never ceased to touch the walls.

He thought again of his daughter, how she'd hate this place, and the thought gave him strength. She was special. She'd save him. He knew that. In his heart, he knew that his daughter would come for him.

Still . . . it didn't hurt to be practical. And he'd run his hands over every inch of the walls, looking for embedded latches, nooks, secret passageways, *anything*.

But there was nothing.

And all he could do was sit in the dark and wait.

Chapter Forty

"You're not really going to resign, are you?" Izzy propped herself up next to him and snaked a finger along his bare skin. Mordi shivered, fighting the urge to simply roll her over and take her again. It was morning, after all. Time to get moving.

"Mordi?"

He shook his head. "No. I'll stay." He flashed her a grin. "You need a reality checker, anyway."

That earned him a smack with her pillow, and he caught her wrists, pulling her on top of him. His body immediately stiffened, overwhelmed by the sensation of flesh against flesh. Isole's flesh.

He'd come to know every inch of this woman. Every delicious inch.

With other women, he'd had sex. With Izzy, though, he made love.

He'd fallen hard and fast, and it felt right. Considering who she was, she probably already knew. But even so, he wanted to tell her. Wanted to say the words out loud. Wanted to announce his love to the whole damn world.

But, most of all, he wanted to hear the words reflected back.

He drew a breath and took her hand.

"Izzy—"

The sharp ring of his cell phone cut him off. He considered turning the damnable thing off, but duty won out and he answered.

"Where are you?" Jason demanded.

"Good morning to you, too," Mordi said.

"She's bad news, Mordi," Jason said. "Or at least her father is."

His blood ran cold, and he stilled. Izzy frowned at him, a question in her eyes. He turned away. "What's happened?"

"Can you talk?"

"Not really."

"I figured."

"Could you just cut to the chase?"

"Right. Sure." Jason exhaled, as if from extreme exertion. "We had Hale go to Harold Frost's lab to investigate this benefactor thing. Figured he can be invisible without having to keep his hands and arms under an invisibility cloak. And there might be security cameras, so—"

"Jason. Just tell me."

"Right. Well. He found information. Frost and our father. Working together."

Mordi closed his eyes, counted to five. "On what?"

"Don't know." A pause at Jason's end. "Did she tell you?"

"No," he admitted.

"I didn't think so."

"Maybe—"

"She doesn't know?" Jason finished the thought for him. "I thought of that. But maybe she does. You need to confront her."

"I can't do that," Mordi said.

Jason muttered something unintelligible. "Why?"

"Think about it."

"You can't talk."

"Right," Mordi said.

"Okay." A pause, then: "I guess it does make sense. You're on the Protector Oversight Committee. It's your sworn duty to investigate any suspicious or potentially traitorous conduct. And you can't investigate properly if she knows you're watching her."

"Something like that," Mordi said, hating himself as he spoke.

"Just be careful, little brother."

Mordi nodded, his thoughts a muddle, then realized Jason couldn't see him. "Yeah. Of course I will," he said, then hung up without saying good-bye. Everything Jason had said was true. But there was more. Mordi simply couldn't believe Isole Frost was a traitor. Perhaps she didn't know about her dad. Or perhaps there was some other explanation. Either way, Mordi trusted her.

He closed his eyes and took a breath, praying he wasn't wrong. He'd misplaced his loyalty before, wasting years following his father.

Please, Zeus, he couldn't be wrong this time, too. Not about Izzy. Not about the woman he loved. What would he do if he had to arrest her?

Chapter Forty-one

Every television in Circuit City was turned on, and Hieronymous stood in the middle of them, absorbing the information that was funneled toward him from the screens.

Mordi groaned. They'd been on their way to assist a mortal, but the New York City police had arrived first, handily stopping a mugging in progress. With nothing to do at the moment, Hieronymous had suggested the detour, and Izzy had given in.

From what Mordi could tell, his father was now in a state of bliss. Not too surprising, really. Lately he hadn't had a lot of television access. Where once the penthouse had been lined with televisions—each tuned to some financial channel—now it was stripped down, its function replaced with comfort by the Council, who'd been utilizing it as a spare office and lodging for traveling Protectors who might need the facilities.

Without access to his financial reports, Hieronymous seemed at his wits' end. Now the man was glued to these television screens, and Izzy had gone off to look at a replacement computer for her apartment. Mordi had insisted that he wanted to find a new CD, but really, he just needed a moment alone to get his head on straight.

He held up a Sheryl Crow CD and pretended to be reading the track list. In reality, though, he was watching Izzy. As much as he wanted to remain true to his convictions, tiny pinpricks of doubt had entered his mind. Surely she couldn't be working with his—

"Mordichai! Isole! We must go. *Now*." Hieronymous's voice, urgent but full of self-control, yanked Mordi from his thoughts.

Customers turned to stare, probably wondering about the less-than-fashionable cape that fluttered from Hieronymous's shoulders as he moved with near-inhuman swiftness to where Mordi stood, still rooted to the spot.

"*Now*," Hieronymous repeated.

Izzy rushed forward. "What? What's going on?" she asked, voicing Mordi's thoughts.

Hieronymous didn't answer; he merely turned, one finger pointing toward the rows of televisions. Where once they'd been displaying shows—including the financial programs he'd been watching—from a variety of different stations, now each television showed one scene. Each was a different station, each had different camera angles, but all were focused on one impending tragedy—a splintered bridge, bits of asphalt falling into the river, and snapped cables writhing in the wild winds like serpents.

Cars had come to a dead stop, backed up on the bridge. Lights from emergency vehicles flashed red, blue, and yellow across the scene.

And there, at the center of every news camera's image, was the possibility of real, deep tragedy. A school bus, bright yellow and filled to the brim with children, was dangling precariously over the fissure, its two front tires already free from the pavement. It balanced there, seesawing a bit, and every person in the store—eyes fixed on those television screens—knew what Mordi knew. *It was only a matter of time.*

"Where?" he asked.

"Upriver," his father answered. "The Tappan Zee Bridge is collapsing."

Mordi scowled, suspicious, but Hieronymous gestured toward one of the screens. A ticker was running across the bottom, and it confirmed what he'd said.

"We're close. We have time." He drew in a breath, then fixed his father with a stare. "Stay here," Mordi said, then turned to Izzy. "Let's go."

She was already pulling a propulsion cloak from her Council-issued backpack. She flung it around her shoulders and nodded at Mordi, who was doing the same thing.

"Give me a cloak," Hieronymous said.

Izzy hesitated, then dug deep in her bag.

"What the hell are you doing?" Mordi asked. "He can't have that. This is too big, too serious."

"I intend to assist you, son. If I have to take the train, I will most assuredly arrive too late."

"We have it under control," Mordi said.

Izzy, however, sided with Hieronymous. "We can use the help," she said, and tossed Hieronymous a cape.

Her easy acquiescence to his father's presence worried Mordi, but the kids were most important, and there wasn't time. He took off running for the exit, his father and Izzy at his heels.

As he ran, he remembered that the power source for his cloak's invisibility feature had gone dead, and he hadn't changed it. He sighed. A quick glance at his companions, though, showed that they wore basic propulsion cloaks anyway—without such a feature. The three of them were going to be visible, and there was simply nothing he could do about it.

271

The thought went through his head as fast as a blink, and the next moment he was airborne, Izzy at his side and Hieronymous bringing up the rear.

"This is against regulations," he growled to her as they soared off over the Hudson.

"Flying while visible? I know. But we hardly have a choice."

"Not that," Mordi said, certain that Izzy knew *exactly* what he meant. "No Outcast is permitted to have use of a propulsion cloak or other Council-issued device. That includes Outcasts participating in the reassimilation program. Not until they are cleared to return."

Her cheeks flushed pink, and he wasn't sure if the color was from guilt or from the cool temperature at their current altitude.

"He had to come," she said.

He hated the suspicion that bubbled in his gut. "We should have left him in Manhattan."

She twisted, dipping a bit in the air as she turned to look at Hieronymous. "And what if even one of those children perished? What if we saved them all except one, and with your father we could have saved them all? Could you live with that? I couldn't."

Mordi swallowed. He couldn't, either.

"We'll have help," he said. The Council had surely already sent a team.

"Probably. But do you know that for sure?"

He didn't, of course. Izzy was right. On all counts. At least in terms of helping the most people. And since Mordi hated being wrong, he simply kept his mouth shut as she pulled out her holopager and reported in, telling headquarters their location and the nature of the impending tragedy.

As he'd suspected, the Council already knew—newly trained Protectors monitored CNN and the Fox

News Channel around the clock, and others patrolled major cities—and a cadre of Protectors had already been dispatched.

Mordi took no pride in being right, however. From what the dispatcher said, the team would likely arrive on their heels. Mordi, Izzy, and Hieronymous would be the first on the scene.

The wounded Tappan Zee Bridge now came into focus, seeming to grow larger as they approached. Mordi didn't need his cousin Zoë's super hearing now; the screams of terrified children filled the air.

A burst of wind startled him, and suddenly, Mordi realized he was in his father's wake. He met Izzy's eyes, and they both rushed to catch up with the Outcast.

Above them, news helicopters hovered, their cameras taking in and broadcasting the tragedy below. Somewhere in the back of his mind, Mordi realized that those cameras were also filming him and Hieronymous and Izzy in their Fabulous Flying Capes. The thought, however, never really germinated; he was too concerned with how to rescue the children.

"Look." He pointed toward the front of the school bus, the portion still resting on some of the slowly collapsing bridge. "That asphalt is unstable. It's going to break away any minute, and then—"

"The bus will be counterbalanced," his father said. "It will fall headlong into the water."

"You two pull," Izzy said. "I'll push."

They split up, and she headed for the front of the bus. Protectors in general had super strength—at least, they were much stranger than mortals—but unlike in the movies, all Protectors couldn't go around lifting multi-ton buses. A *few* Protectors could, if that was their special skill, and for a brief moment, Mordi thought of Clyde. And he almost wished the creep were there to help.

Izzy would have it the worst, balancing in midair as she was, with nothing to push against or obtain leverage with.

These thoughts zipped through Mordi's head as he planted his feet on the unsteady asphalt behind the bus and grabbed hold of the back bumper. He tugged as Izzy shoved, and the bus moved backward toward safety. It only moved a hair, but at least it moved.

Mordi dug his heels in, preparing for another massive tug. He kicked bits of plastic and metal out of the way, and tightened his grip. Then, as Izzy gave the signal and he pulled, he realized for the first time that he was pulling all alone.

What the—?

From the bus, he could hear the children's terrified murmurs and cries. From a distance, he could hear the approach of the Council team, their arrival imminent.

Of his father, though, he heard and saw nothing. That slimy son of Medusa! He really was going to leave these kids to—

"Stay back!"

Hieronymous's voice echoed in a *whoosh* of wind, and then Mordi was knocked on his back. His father loomed over him, holding a length of cable still connected to the beams above. Mordi blinked at the sight, unable to register his father's actions against the reality of the situation. A fraction of a second ticked by, and before Mordi could react, his father tossed him over the side of the bridge.

No!

Oh, sweet Hera, his father couldn't be planning to sacrifice all those children. It couldn't be possible. And yet, after everything his father had done in the past, he knew that it *was* possible. It absolutely was.

With a massive effort, Mordi kicked his cloak into action and halted his fall. The Council team was almost there, just a few seconds away and near to being in range. Mordi called out for them to help him, to stop Hieronymous.

Below, he saw that Izzy had fallen as well, and now she was braking to a midair halt, her cape fluttering around her shoulders as her feet dangled in the air just inches above the dark water of the Hudson.

Mordi pushed her out of his mind. She was safe. Only the children mattered, and he focused on saving them, kicking his cloak into overdrive. His arms thrust forward as he tried to make himself as aerodynamic as possible. He ignored everything—the helicopters above, the children's screams, the emergency sirens— and focused solely on his goal.

He cleared the bridge and found Hieronymous moving away from the bus, the length of cable secured to its back bumper. "Bastard," Mordi screamed as he landed on the bridge. "What have you done?"

And that was when the explosion hit. The asphalt beneath the bus crumpled, taking Mordi with it. He fell, debris beating against his chest but fortunately missing his head. A large chunk hit his cloak controls, though, and he couldn't fly. The water, now filled with flotsam and jetsam from the collapsing bridge, was rising up to meet him; and he switched tactics, focusing not on his cloak, but on his levitation skills. He could levitate himself and—

Something grabbed him, strong hands gripping under his arms and carrying him up toward the remains of the bridge. There were cables and girders and beams still standing, just much of the concrete had given way.

His father. Mordi started to twist around, started to tell the man he'd rather fall to the river than be rescued by the likes of someone who would condemn a busload of children to a watery grave. But as he looked up, realization dawned. The bus was still there . . . even though the concrete that had been under it was gone. Instead, it was hanging from the cable that Hieronymous had attached. Now it swung, at an uncomfortable angle for the occupants, yes, but it was safe.

The Council team was even now righting the bus, moving it to stable ground.

The children were safe! Hieronymous had done—*what?*

"A bomb," Hieronymous said, answering Mordi's unspoken question. "I recognized the damage when we approached the back of the bus. I feared there was another, and it would go off, so I did a quick pass under the bridge to confirm my fear."

"And there was," Mordi said. It wasn't a question. The answer had become plainly obvious when the bridge had disintegrated under their feet.

"I didn't have time to tell you. I simply reacted. The cable seemed the best bet. It was the only thing I could think of to keep the bus from falling into the river." Hieronymous's breath seemed to hitch. "So I did what I could to keep those poor, innocent children from falling to their doom."

Mordi nodded, too stunned to conjure words. Hieronymous had just saved not only a busload of mortal children, but Mordi himself.

For the most infinitesimal moment of time, Mordi felt a surge of pride for his father, but that pride was quickly vanquished by fear. Because he still wasn't convinced of the man's goodness. If Hieronymous Black was resorting to saving mortal children to win the battle . . . then who knows what he would do to win the war.

Chapter Forty-two

Camera flashes strobed around him, and Hierony-mous turned slowly, not wanting to thwart any of the reporters' attempts to achieve the perfect camera angle. Because they'd been visible during the rescue, he, Mordi, and Isole were now the subject of the news media's collective feeding frenzy. The other Protectors—those who'd been able to vanish under the shield of an invisibility cloak—had already surreptitiously departed.

Now, though Hieronymous knew that the Council elders would prefer silence, the three of them had no choice but to answer questions. The MLO would step in later and clear up the mess.

In the meantime, Hieronymous intended to make the most of this media-op. He had arranged it, after all. He would be a fool to let it simply pass by.

"Mr. Black! Mr. Black!" A reporter cried out for his attention. "Witnesses say you were *flying*. The footage from the news helicopters confirms this. Can you explain it? How did you and your companions accomplish something like that?"

Mordichai stepped forward. "I don't think—"

Hieronymous put an arm out, intercepting his son at chest level. "What my son means, Mr. . . ."

"Branson," the reporter said. "Roger Branson, Channel Two."

"Mr. Branson," Hieronymous acknowledged. "As my son was about to explain, that information is on a need-to-know basis only. If I were you, I'd simply be thankful that such technology does exist, and that it was able to come to the aid of those poor children. *They*, not me or my companions, should be the subject of your cameras."

He flashed what he hoped seemed a genuine smile. He was a little out of practice, but he thought he managed okay. Branson looked suitably chastised and, Hieronymous knew, he himself would come off looking all the more like a hero for trying to deflect the media attention away toward the little brats.

It wouldn't work, of course. The spotlight would remain firmly on him—as it should. But by having tried, he would raise his PR quotient a point or two. And, after all, this was all about perception.

Beside him, he saw Isole sidle toward Mordi. All doubts had left her; of that, Hieronymous was certain. *Good.* He wanted the pathetic Halfling to feel all the more foolish when she finally realized the truth: that she was nothing more than a pawn in a plan he'd been hatching for so very many years.

Reporters shouted more questions, and he deftly fielded them. As he spoke, his eyes skimmed the crowd, looking for any sign of Clyde or others of his soldiers. *No one.* Good. They'd faded back into the crowd, losing themselves in the sea of faces. They'd stay hidden, he knew, until next he called on them.

His mouth curved in the tiniest of smiles. Everything was coming together perfectly. Even the close proximity of his son couldn't spoil his plan or his mood. Hieronymous was a new hero to the mortals. And soon—very soon—he'd be hailed as the most supreme of all Protectors.

And when he was once again swaddled in the warm and welcoming embrace of the Council, only then would he take final action.

And, yes, he would prevail. Failure was simply not an option.

Chapter Forty-three

"We should have shut him down," Mordi said.

Izzy shrugged. She'd thought the same thing at the time, but then dismissed it. Normally, protocol required a Protector to avoid the mortal news media as much as possible. But these weren't normal circumstances.

"The media was already there," she said. "It would have caused a furor if we'd pulled him out." She frowned. "Besides, I think the only way to have gotten him out would be to use some of our powers or our cloaks, or to call in a retrieval team. And any one of those acts would have created just as much of a stir."

Mordi frowned, but he didn't look convinced. They were back in her office, waiting for Hieronymous to finish his debriefing with the Council elders. It wasn't standard procedure by any means, but considering who Hieronymous was, the elders had decided the meeting was prudent.

Mordi and Izzy had retired to her office and drafted their reports, taking turns at her computer. They'd been finished for almost ten minutes, and there was still no sign of Hieronymous.

"It may be a media nightmare, but frankly, I think this may have been the best thing that could have happened," Izzy said.

Mordi blinked, his entire being emitting a total lack of comprehension.

"For the treaty, I mean. You heard what Banyon said. The mortals in-the-know fear the Outcasts, and your father is the biggest Outcast of all. If the emissaries see that he's suddenly rescuing mortal children—"

"Well, sure. Don't you get it?"

"Get what?"

"My father's no hero. He's just as conniving and devious as ever. More, even, since he's actually willing to be *nice* to mortals if it gets him what he wants."

Izzy gaped at him. "You still think he's *faking*?"

"Hell, yes."

"*Faking?*" she repeated, feeling slightly idiotic. But *really*, hadn't he seen the man jump to action?

"Is there an echo in here?"

She drew in a breath. "Look, Mordichai, I understand that you and your father have some issues—"

"*That's* the understatement of the year."

"—but you can't turn your back on reality."

"No," Mordi said, "that's your job."

Anger whipped through her. "Dammit, Mordi. Don't you trust me even a little bit?"

"As a matter of fact, I've been thinking about that a lot lately. I want to. But . . ."

" 'But?' " she repeated, her blood turning cold. Suddenly, it dawned on her. "You think I'm working with him! That your father has some ridiculous plot, and I'm in on it!" Oh, sweet Hera, had he simply been using her? Was she simply a pawn in some giant investigation? And she'd slept with him—*made love* with him—while he was simply doing his job!

"Dammit, Izzy, take a step back and tell me how it looks."

"I *have* told you how it looks. I've seen inside your father's head, and he looks sincere. But you don't trust me. You either think I'm incompetent or that I'm lying, and—"

"No," he said.

She glared at him, but didn't say anything.

"Iz, I know my father. Maybe *you* should try listening to *me*. Or are *you* the one who's not trusting?"

"You know what? I was factoring in your opinion—I really was. But did you miss what happened yesterday? He saved those kids!"

"Posturing."

"I don't agree," she said.

The intercom buzzed, and Isole's assistant announced that Elder Bilius requested her presence in his office. "Thanks," she said into the speaker, relieved to have an excuse to leave. The tension between her and Mordi was impossibly thick, making her usually cozy office feel small, as if the walls were closing in. She needed some time alone, needed to think, to sort everything out.

"Izzy," Mordi said as she opened the door. It was just her name, but his voice held a question. She turned back to him and waited. "I'll pick you up after work?"

Isole swallowed. She'd agreed to go with him to a rehearsal dinner for two friends of his in Los Angeles who were getting married. They were supposed to catch the Council shuttle there, then stay the night on Mordi's brother's houseboat. Now, though . . .

She shook her head. "I'm sorry. I don't think I'm up to it." She looked at the floor, not willing to meet his eyes. "Besides, it sounds like Bilius is going to have me working late."

"You're sure?" Mordi asked, and she understood

that he was talking about more than just the rehearsal dinner.

She wasn't. She wasn't sure at all. But she didn't say anything; she just nodded. And then she stepped into the hall and let the door shut behind her.

Chapter Forty-four

Izzy met with the Inner Circle that afternoon, in an emergency meeting called by Elder Bilius. All the elders were present. All, that is, except Zephron.

"The High Elder does not have time for these administrative details," Elder Trystan said in response to Izzy's query.

She nodded, duly chastised. "You wanted to see me?"

"The treaty negotiations have been pushed forward to tomorrow morning," Bilius said. "The mortals are anxious, particularly after the school bus incident. Their ambassadors want to use that incident as a rallying cry to gain mortal support for the treaty."

"I see," Izzy said, though she didn't see what that had to do with her.

"Obviously, we will also be pushing up the schedule for Hieronymous's re-assimilation," Armistand added.

"Oh." *Now* she understood. "Yes, er, well . . ."

"You do have a positive opinion at this point, do you not?" That came from Bilius, along with a significant scent of hope. She frowned, once again remembering how he'd come a full 180 degrees from his original point of view.

"Well, child?" Dionys said. "We would like your recommendation."

"You can file the formal papers later, of course," Trystan added.

Izzy swallowed. The elders hadn't moved, but it seemed as though they were surrounding her, a tight circle moving closer and closer. She thought about Mordi's doubts and about Bilius's previous distaste for Hieronymous. She remembered the odd metallic smell she'd scented earlier on Patel . . . then remembered smelling the same scent on Hieronymous himself. Did that mean something?

And then, again, she thought about Mordi. He might not trust her, but she was beginning to wonder if she'd made a mistake by not trusting him. Hadn't he known his father better than anyone else? Wasn't this reassimilation coming along a little too easily?

She couldn't know for sure, and that's what finally fueled her answer. "My recommendation is for further testing," she said. "It would be imprudent to admit Hieronymous to the Council at this point. He hasn't completed the tests, and politics should not be the deciding factor."

The elders looked at each other, then Bilius said, "Thank you, child. We shall certainly give your recommendation the utmost weight." He smiled, then, and though she tried to read his emotions, she couldn't. All she could pick up on was a keen desire for Hieronymous's return. The elder waved dismissively. "That will be all."

Chapter Forty-five

When she got back to her office, Izzy found Hieronymous already waiting for her. He looked up, a charming smile on his features, nothing menacing at all.

Even so, she heard Mordi's voice telling her she was wrong. Telling her the man was bad.

This time, she believed him.

She waited for Hieronymous to say something, anything, about his meeting with the elders, but when the silence continued to hang heavy between them, she had to assume he was going to keep those details to himself.

"Mr. Black," she said, moving to sit behind her desk. "I think it's time we had a little talk."

"My dear, I don't know what you mean." He rose from the sofa and moved across the room, finally pulling the guest chair up so that he was only inches away from her desk, his hand resting on its oak veneer. He started drumming a rhythm on the desk. She frowned at his hand, the noise irritating, but he didn't seem to notice her consternation. "Everything is going exactly as planned."

"As planned? Whose plan?"

His smile chilled her to the bone. "Mine, of course," he said, and then began that damn finger-tapping again.

She slammed her hand down onto her desktop, startling him into silence. "Cut the cryptic bullshit, Mr. Black. Tell me what's going on."

A moment passed, and then another, before Hieronymous finally spoke. "I should thank you," he said simply.

Izzy frowned. She didn't want to ask, but her curiosity got the better of her. "Thank me for what?"

"Why, for believing in me, of course. It made everything so much easier." His broad smile transformed the hard lines of his face, making it almost handsome. She stifled a shudder. This was bad. Though she didn't know what, exactly, *this* was. But she did know with absolute certainty that it wasn't good. And she knew that she'd screwed up. Mordi had been right, and the world was about to cave in around her shoulders.

Hieronymous watched her, apparently expecting her to speak. She didn't. It was a tiny defiance, but she took a small amount of pride in it. He might be taking her down, but she wasn't going willingly.

After a moment, he continued. "And, of course, I should thank you for being good at your job. Your promotion was most unexpected, but quite useful to my plan."

She couldn't keep quiet any longer. "I'm not so sure I *am* good at my job. I'm pretty sure I got you completely wrong."

He laughed, the sound utterly without mirth. "Well, my dear. I suppose that depends entirely on your point of view, yes?"

"And what's *your* point of view?"

"At this point, my only interest is in saving the Council from its own foolishness."

She snorted. "Tell me another one."

He turned and walked toward the wall, stopping in front of her bookcase and picking up a glass snow globe with a miniature of Manhattan inside. "What have I done?" he asked, looking at the globe rather than her.

"Excuse me?"

He turned, his near-black eyes trapping her in their steady gaze. "You were convinced of my sincerity. Of my motives. What has changed? Why are you no longer my friend, my ally? Your job is to assist my reassimilation, is it not? Why have you suddenly prejudiced yourself against me?"

"My job isn't to *assist* you in anything. I'm to *evaluate* you."

"And something has happened to make you doubt my sincerity? Was it perhaps the rescue on the bridge? The praise from the mortal media? Or perhaps it was the kudos thrust upon me by the Circle of Elders."

"No," she said, "it was just me."

"You?" he repeated, derision in his voice.

She smiled sweetly. "I suppose Mordichai deserves some credit, too."

"Now who's being cryptic?"

She tilted her head, regarding him. Beneath her desk, she had one finger on the emergency button. "I'm an empath," she finally said. "I trusted my feelings and forgot to open my eyes."

"You're supposed to trust your feelings," Hieronymous said.

"But you'd clouded them."

He stared at her for a moment, then slowly clapped. "Bravo, Ms. Frost. Aren't you the clever one? But I assure you, I'm not nearly the monster you—or my son—thinks I am."

"I think wanting to destroy all mortals, or enslave them, is pretty monstrous."

"Do you?" he asked, sounding genuinely surprised. "Interesting." He waved a hand, as if shooing away the thought. "Doesn't matter. At the moment I am not contemplating the existence of mortals. All I want is for the treaty negotiations to fail. I want the status quo maintained." He spread his hands wide, a smile on his face. "You see? That is not so terrible, is it? Surely you know that I'm not the only one on the Council who feels that way."

"You're not on the Council."

"Not yet. No."

"And you won't be without my approval."

"Be that as it may," he said with a dismissive wave of his hand. "My concern at this point revolves around one who is already on the Council."

She shook her head, not following. "Who?"

"Zephron, of course."

An icy chill tingled up her spine. "What about him?"

"I need your help to ensure that he doesn't attend the treaty negotiations."

She pressed the buzzer under the desk, hoping he didn't notice. "What makes you think I'd help you?"

"You must. It's imperative that he does not attend. The treaty is Zephron's pet project. If he is absent, the negotiations will surely fall through or, at the very least, be postponed." He held his hands out and smiled, the picture of reason and rationality. "The status quo will remain, and no harm will be done."

The man was nuts.

"You're asking help from the wrong person. You might try someone you've already brainwashed."

He smiled, but Izzy only shivered. Then she glanced at the door, expecting a team to burst through. He caught her look.

"They aren't coming," he said. Fear welled in her stomach as he added, "I disabled your alarm system."

She bolted upright. "This meeting is over."

"*Isole.*" She halted, the note of command in his voice causing her to freeze. "You must stay."

She turned to him, hoping every ounce of revulsion she felt was reflected in her face. "I don't think so."

"I don't believe you've yet disclosed the nature of my relationship with your father . . . or that you've been aware of it for some time."

"Oh." *Well, hell.*

"Not that *I'd* have any reason to reveal such an Outcastable offense . . ."

"*If* I help you," she finished.

This time, his smile was warm. "Of course."

"No." She pushed her shoulders back, then repeated the answer more firmly. "No."

"Little fool," he hissed. "Do you realize what will happen to you?"

"I'll get the punishment I deserve for breaking a rule . . . and I'll prevent you from carrying out whatever half-baked scheme you have up your sleeve."

"*Idiot child.*"

She jumped, the force of his words almost knocking her backward.

"Do you not see how pathetic mortals are? This is a great opportunity. I intend to take full advantage."

"No, you won't."

His eyebrows rose. "I won't? And why not?"

"Because I won't let you."

She spoke firmly, with as much authority as she'd ever put into her voice. It didn't seem to faze him. He just laughed and laughed.

She pulled open her office door, intending to race down the hall.

"Close the door, my dear, or your father dies."

She stopped, then pulled the door shut again. "What?" she whispered.

"You heard me, my dear. Your father is gone, and only I know where he is. Foil my plans and you'll never see the dear man again. And on *that*, young Isole, you really should trust me."

She did. "What do you want from me?"

"Zephron, of course. I thought that was clear."

A shiver ripped through her, and she gripped the edge of the table for support. "No. No, you can't . . ."

"I assure you, my dear, I can. And you're going to help me."

She shook her head, unable to conjure words. Hieronymous just laughed.

"My dear, don't be so squeamish. It's not as though I'm going to put the man out of my misery. I'm simply going to temporarily relocate him. And you're going to help me." Again, that smile. "Your father, remember."

She did remember. But she didn't believe that Hieronymous wasn't going to try to kill Zephron. And she *also* didn't believe that Hieronymous's plan was only to maintain the status quo.

What she *did* believe was that her father was—at least for the moment—hidden but safe. And if that was the case, then Izzy knew that Mordi could help her. He'd have to . . . because no matter how much Izzy loved her father, she couldn't sacrifice the world to save him.

A tear ran down her cheek. "No." She whispered the word, and it was all that she could manage.

"Oh, yes," Hieronymous said, his voice holding a world of menace. He lunged, and she threw herself to one side. He was too quick, though, and he caught her. "Tell me," he said. "Tell me what Zephron's weakness is."

She struggled to get free, but couldn't manage it. "What makes you think I know?"

"Romulus has used his invisibility power to infiltrate all the files on Olympus. He found nothing. But I know he has a weakness. We all do. And his notes on your file suggest that he revealed that weakness to you. *Now what is it?*"

"I . . . I don't know."

"You're his niece and a counselor. Forgive me if I don't believe you."

"Yeah? Well, what the hell are you going to do about it?" She was shouting now, anger and fear making her lash out. "I don't know anything, and even if I did, I wouldn't tell you. So, what? Did you invent some machine to get in my head? Poke around and find all my secrets? Use my father's skills to brainwash me or block your true emotions?"

"Nothing that complicated, no." He reached into his cloak and pulled out a hypodermic needle filled with liquid.

Izzy gasped and tried to make another dash for it. Hieronymous caught her handily and tossed her to the ground.

"I thought you would appreciate the irony of me using a mortal method. Sodium pentathol, my dear," he said, and then Isole screamed as he stabbed her in the thigh. "More commonly known as truth serum."

Chapter Forty-six

"She's bad news," Jason said under his voice, then raised his wineglass along with everyone else at the table.

"No," Mordi whispered, taking a sip from his own glass. "Her father maybe, but not Izzy. I can't believe it. I won't believe it." They all were at the rehearsal dinner, but so far, Mordi had hardly been in a festive mood. He missed Izzy. Even more, he knew now that he trusted her. Completely. There was no way she was in cahoots with his father, and he'd been a fool to let her walk away. He intended to remedy that bit of stupidity as soon as possible.

"Don't let a pretty face cloud your judgment," Jason was saying.

"I'm not. But I do love her." He'd yet to say the words out loud, and they felt good. "I love her and I don't believe that she'd betray either me or the Council. Becoming a Protector was important to her. She worked hard to be worthy."

"I've asked around," Jason said. "She's not exactly in the fold."

Mordi nodded. "I know. She told me. She's a

Halfling. Zephron's her uncle. Of course she'd have a hard time because of that. But that hardly makes her a traitor."

"Mordi—"

He lifted a hand, cutting his half brother off. "We're here for Deena and Hoop. Let's just drop it, okay?"

Jason agreed, but he didn't look happy. And for the next hour, Mordi tried his damnedest to look like he was having a good time. Deena and Hoop laughed as their friends told stories about their various escapades over the years. And all the couples—Zoë and Taylor, Jason and Lane, Hale and Tracy, Nicholas and Maggie—looked cozy and content.

Mordi wasn't content. He wanted Izzy beside him.

The waiter brought out the dessert, and Mordi stood up, his mind made up. He had to tell her how he felt. He had to tell her *now*.

"Are you leaving?" Deena asked, appearing behind him.

"Council business. I'm sorry." He moved to give her a quick kiss on the cheek; then he headed out, shooting Jason an I-know-what-I'm-doing look on the way. He reached the front of the restaurant, opened the door, and just about collided with Isole.

"What the . . . ?" He stopped short, getting a better look at her. Her shirt was ripped, her face scratched, and her hair was a wild mass of loose curls. She looked like hell, but a fire lit her eyes.

He pulled her into his arms. "Are you okay?"

"I need your help." She drew a breath. "And we may need your brother and his friends, too."

Chapter Forty-seven

Izzy let Mordi take her back into the private dining room where his friends were finishing up their dinner. The chamber was dark, and they moved to a corner so they could talk privately before clueing in the others. She gave him the rundown, drawing strength from his arms around her as she spoke.

"But why did he let you go?"

"He didn't," she said. "He left some flunky to watch me. When I ran, the guy got a few blows in, but he didn't manage to follow me." She grinned. "Hard to run when your feet are encased in a block of ice."

Mordi laughed. "I imagine." He took her arm as he nodded toward the others. "Come on. Let's fill them in."

As Mordi gave his relatives the rundown on the situation, Izzy sat next to him, holding his hand. She could feel all their eyes on her. The feeling was both uncomfortable and welcome. They didn't trust her—of that, she was sure, though she couldn't figure out why from the scents in the air.

Even so, it was nice in a perverted sort of way. They were looking after Mordi. He'd told her that he'd started life as a loner, just him and his dad. Now, though, he had friends and family. And Izzy couldn't help but wonder if, someday, she'd have friends like this, too. Friends who worried about her. Friends who cared.

She needed them right now. She needed friends to help save her father. But the only friend she had was Mordi.

In her heart, though, she knew that would be enough.

"The catacombs?" Jason said after Mordi finished the story.

"Right," Izzy said.

"My father knows those catacombs like the back of his hand," Mordi warned. "There are two sets, you know. One where they keep the Henchmen, and one for Outcasts who've broken the rules for the very last time."

She licked her lips. "I didn't know that."

"Your father will be where they keep the Henchmen, I'll bet." He shifted, then looked at her, his eyes piercing straight to her soul. "They're closer. And Hieronymous will want him nearby in case he needs your dad's input on one of his little inventions."

All the energy drained from her body. "You knew about that?"

"I learned about it recently."

"And you think I'm involved." She tried to read him, tried to tell from his scent if that's what he thought, but she couldn't pick up any hint.

"No," he said.

"You believe me?" She was full of hope, and fear.

He closed his eyes and drew a breath. "Yeah. I do." His brow furrowed. "Can't you tell?"

"No. I . . . I can't read you anymore." She swallowed, understanding now why she couldn't read him or her father. "I want to tell you—"

"First things first, kids," Jason said. "Your dad."

Izzy turned to meet Jason's eyes. "Do *you* trust me?"

"Let's just say I'm taking everything under consideration."

Isole nodded, but didn't bother to ask the others what they thought. It didn't matter. The only thing that mattered was getting her father back.

"We'll get him back," Mordi said, this time reading her thoughts.

She swallowed and looked at the floor. Mordi had every reason to feel self-righteous. He'd known from the beginning about Hieronymous, and she'd been too blind to see. She'd been arrogant and stupid, and now she was paying the price. So was her father.

His gaze was steady on her, his expression thoughtful. "You once told me that Zephron wouldn't have put me on this assignment with you unless he believed that I could keep an open mind. Do you still believe that?"

She shook her head. "No. I think he knew. I think he had a sense of what would happen, and he paired you with me to . . . to . . ."

"Keep you from deciding that the vilest man to ever walk the planet was really a good guy?" Jason said.

Her cheeks burned. "Something like that. Yeah."

Mordi moved to her side, taking her hand and squeezing. "It's okay, Iz. We'll get your father back."

She looked up into his eyes and saw what she felt in her heart reflected right back at her: love. And trust. "I know you will." She glanced at Jason, including him in the conversation. "But what about Zephron?"

Jason frowned, and she realized Mordi had left out those details when he'd relayed the story. She filled in the blanks with a quick explanation.

"But what could you have told him about Zephron? I mean, the guy's basically invincible."

"Mosquitoes," she said, then explained what Zephron had told her about the frequency.

"It's a long shot," Mordi said. "But if anyone could pull it off, using that to his advantage, Hieronymous can."

"Have you warned him?" Jason asked.

"Yes," Izzy said. "I called him on my way here. He promised to be careful. But if Hieronymous knows his weakness—"

"He'll never stop trying to kill him," Mordi said. He flipped open his holopager and called Zephron. He couldn't reach the high elder, but was assured by his assistant that the elder was safe and sound and in a meeting.

"So we focus on your dad," Mordi said.

"What about the treaty negotiations? I thought Hieronymous was all set to get on the Council and bust those up."

Izzy shook her head. "He won't be able to. The negotiations are tomorrow at eight in the morning. It's already nine. And I recommended that the elders *not* let him reassimilate. Not yet, anyway. Even if he ultimately passes all the tests and they let him in, the negotiations will have already happened. And if Zephron's watching his back, he'll be there to push the negotiations through."

"You entered a negative recommendation?" Mordi asked, looking shocked. "Before all this?"

She shrugged. "Yeah, well, you're the persuasive type."

Mordi's slow grin reflected pure satisfaction. "So, am I allowed to say I told you so?"

"Yes," she said, also grinning, despite everything else that was happening. She turned to Jason. "You're coming, too, right?"

"He's coming," Mordi said. "And bring Davy. We might need him."

"And the others?" Jason asked, nodding toward the table.

"Stay here. We might need some help on this coast. And there's a rehearsal dinner to finish."

Jason went off to tell the others his plan, and to get his son, Davy, who apparently was some big inventor kid who might have some tricks to help them maneuver in the catacombs. He was back in less than ten minutes, and then the four of them were on their way, each clad in a propulsion cloak, soaring through the night toward the catacombs on Olympus.

Actually, Davy, still too young to maneuver a cloak on his own, was strapped to his dad's chest. The boy was squealing with delight, but he was the only one who seemed happy. The others were somber, lost in their thoughts as they rode the wind. Izzy was drowning in worry, afraid that Hieronymous had lied and her father wasn't safe at all.

"He'll be fine," Mordi said. He swooped closer and took her hand.

"Mind reading now?"

"Trust me. I know my father. He won't terminate an asset until he's through with it. Until it has no further value. You're still around, so he's not through with your dad yet."

"I don't understand why he needed my father at all! Hieronymous can invent anything he wants. Why drag Daddy into this? It doesn't make sense." She wanted to lash out, but they were in the air and there was nothing solid to hit.

"An Outcast can't use his powers. There would have been a blip on the Council monitoring equipment. So he had your father make whatever gizmo he needed. Maybe he made some modifications later, but so long as he wasn't actually inventing the thing, I bet it went blip-free."

She just shook her head. "I should have known. I should have known your father wasn't sincere. But I didn't. I believed him. Even more, I believed in *me*." She blinked, and a huge tear fell, dropping down through the clear sky below. "He made a fool out of me."

"Worse than that," Mordi said. He urged her closer, and she tucked herself gratefully against him. "He made you doubt yourself. Now you doubt your own worth. Your own abilities."

She nodded, her tears flowing in earnest. "Yes. And now my father's imprisoned somewhere, and the Council's in danger, and *it's all my fault*."

"That's what he does best, you know."

Izzy frowned. "What?"

"Cuts you down. Makes you doubt yourself. Makes you believe that everything you do borders on incompetent, and that you're little more than worthless."

His words poured over her, and his anger was somehow soothing. He knew how she felt. And yet he wasn't judging her, wasn't blaming her. He understood and, so help her, she was grateful.

"Why did you stay?" she asked. It was a bold question, invasive, even. But she wanted to know how he'd managed to stay centered, to keep his confidence. Above all, she simply wanted to know everything she could about Mordichai Black.

She felt him shrug, then heard the low rumble in his chest as he cleared his throat. "Desperation, I think. Necessity later."

"Desperation," she repeated. "For his approval?"

"And his praise. I guess I just wanted him—once—to say that something I did was right. For him to look at *me*, and not just at the way I could fit into some scheme he had going at the moment."

"Did he ever?" She wanted to move, to see Mordi's face. But she was too comfortable as she was, and so she simply leaned in closer, enjoying his masculine scent and the strong promise of his arms around her as they flew.

"No. He came close once. Even intimated that the fact that I was a Halfling didn't bother him. But by then it was too late. And frankly, I didn't believe him anyway."

"I can't imagine growing up like that," Izzy said. Her own father had loved her with an intensity that was almost palpable. He'd played silly games with her, told her she could be anything she wanted to be, and never once made her feel like she was anything less than fully and completely loved.

She closed her eyes, once again fighting back tears.

"It will be okay," Mordi said. He stroked her hair. "We'll get him out. And he'll be fine."

She nodded, sniffled, and tried to pull herself together.

"I want to know, Izzy. Why did you come to me? I mean, I was in L.A., and we'd said all those things. . . ." His words were soft, his voice husky.

"I . . ." She swallowed. "Because you knew from the beginning. He's your father, and you saw him for what he really is. I needed help, and you—well, it made sense to come to you. It didn't make sense to go to anyone else."

"That's it?" he asked. He sounded vaguely disappointed.

She shook her head. "No. There's more." She licked her lips, knowing how the truth would sound, and was ashamed in advance.

"Tell me."

She met his eyes. "Because you love me."

Something hard and almost sad flashed in his eyes. "Yes, I forgot. You can see my emotions."

She shook her head. "No. I can't. Not anymore."

He frowned. "What do you mean?"

"There are some folks that I can't read because that's part of their Protector skills. And then there are others, like my dad, that I can't read for other reasons."

"What reasons?"

She licked her lips. "Well, I didn't actually know why I couldn't read my dad. And then, today, I realized."

"Izzy." His voice was firm, no-nonsense. "We're almost there. What are you trying to say?"

"I can't read my dad because I love him. I realized that had to be the reason when I stopped being able to read you."

She couldn't look at him, but he didn't let her get away with that. He took her chin in his hands and tilted her face until she had no choice but to either look into his eyes or to close her own. "What are you telling me, Izzy?" he asked, his voice soft.

"I'm telling you I love you." Surprisingly, it felt good to say it out loud. "I love you, Mordi!"

His mouth curved into a smile and he pressed his fingers to her lips. "I love you, too."

"I know," she said. She bit her lip and grinned. "I *did* read you a while back."

"Yeah? Well, in that case, you may have said it first, but just remember who felt it first."

"Always," she said, then squeezed his hand.

"I'm going to get your father back for you."

"I know."

She looked down then and saw the mountains rising up. Jason and Davy were in the sky below, and she and Mordi swooped, following. Mordi pointed to a pile of collapsed stones. "That's the entrance," he said. "The stones are a Protector-generated illusion."

"Where are we?" she asked. The air was thin and cold.

"Someplace mortals never come."

They landed easily enough, and even though these were the very catacombs that housed the Henchmen and many other things that go bump in the night, gaining access was relatively easy.

"Walking through the catacombs isn't forbidden," Jason explained. "In fact, in some situations it's encouraged. Deterrent, you know.

"Anything that can come out and get you is locked up."

Indeed, as they moved through the dank, moss-covered tunnel, Izzy heard cries in the darkened corners. She couldn't see the cells, though, and Mordi explained that all walls were of solid stone.

"How do they eat?" Sweet Hera, her father hadn't starved to death, had he?

"I don't know. But I know the catacombs provide sustenance. How, though . . ." He probably shrugged then, but it was too dark for her to see.

"We'll never find him this way," Jason said. "We have hundreds of levels here."

"Daddy!" Izzy cried out. They didn't have time to search hundreds of levels. "Hieronymous would keep him near the surface," she said to Jason and Mordi. "Easily accessible in case he needs my father."

"She's probably right," Mordi said. Then: "Harold! Harold Frost!"

Jason and Davy added to the cries, and they all called out in turn as they started down the main hallway, feeling their way so they didn't accidentally pass any branches or turns or alcoves.

On the third level, they got lucky.

"Izzy?" Harold Frost's hoarse voice drifted toward her, barely a whisper.

"Daddy!" She raced to the cell and began pounding

on the stone, looking for a pull, a latch—anything. "I'm going to get you out of there, Daddy!"

"I knew . . . you'd . . . come for me." Exhaustion tinged his voice, and Izzy shot a worried look at Mordi. Her eyes had adjusted to the dark, and the lichen on the walls down here gave off a phosphorescent light that gave him a slight green tinge. From his expression, she could tell he was worried, too.

"Here!" Her fingers found a metal box embedded in the stone. She tugged and yanked, but couldn't manage to get it open. "Damn it!"

"Let Davy try," Jason said.

Izzy wasn't entirely certain what the eight-year-old could accomplish, but she wasn't about to argue.

The boy had brought a backpack full of gizmos, and now he pulled out something that looked like a Gameboy, but when he pulled two wires from it and slipped them into a thin slot on the box, she knew the toy must have been modified. There was a *pop*, some sparks, and then the box cover flew off.

"Thank goodness!" Izzy cried.

"It's not open yet," Davy said, his eyes wide and serious behind Harry Potter–style glasses. "That just got the lock box open." He squatted down, then squinted at the inside of the box. "Oh, wow. This is super neato."

"Davy," Jason said, a hint of reprimand in his voice. "Work fast."

"Sorry, Dad."

While the boy got down to business, Izzy leaned closer to the cell and shouted encouraging things to her father. "Any time now, Daddy, and you'll be out of there. We'll go home, have brownies and ice cream, and watch *Flubber* as many times as you want!"

His voice was too weak for her to hear his answer, and she turned to Mordi for moral support. He, however, was watching Jason, who was holding his holopager up to his ear, all the functions except sound apparently turned off.

"What? I can't hear you." He twisted, cocking his head so that the holopager was closer to the ceiling. "The reception is terrible. Say again?"

Izzy watched as Jason's brow crinkled. Finally, he hung up. "What?"

Jason turned, and even in the dim light she could see the fear in his eyes. "Zephron is gone. And Hieronymous has been admitted to the Council. Which means that, come morning, he's going to rejoin the Inner Circle . . . and he'll therefore be the elder in charge of the treaty negotiations."

Chapter Forty-eight

"How?" Izzy asked, and Mordi's head spun. "I recommended *against* letting him back on the Council."

"That's what Zoë said. Apparently, the elders decided to ignore your recommendation."

Izzy slammed her hand into the wall, and Mordi moved to take her in his arms. "It'll be okay. We'll stop this. Nothing bad will happen. We've stopped our dad before. We'll do it again."

"But he's got Zephron," she sniffled. "And he's in the Inner Circle." She pulled back, then, as if she'd just realized what she'd said. "*Why* is he in the Inner Circle?"

"Heritage," Jason explained. "Neither Mordi nor I are old enough, but our family always holds a seat in the Inner Circle. Our grandfather's seat was vacated when he retired. Our uncle, Zoë's dad, would have sat there, but he retired before he reached the Age of Elder and declined the place. Now that Hieronymous is back in the fold, the seat automatically goes to him."

"Automatically?" Izzy asked. "Even after everything he's done?"

Jason met Mordi's eyes. "Apparently, no one's filed a formal complaint."

"The fountain pens!" Izzy said, her voice nearly a whisper. "I just realized. That's how Hieronymous did it. He altered my father's fountain pens."

"What are you talking about?" Mordi asked, though something tickling the back of his mind made him think he already knew.

"The elders all have had these purple fountain pens. And they said that Patel was distributing them. My dad said the pens were special, designed to perfectly get all your thoughts out. What if Hieronymous altered them to put thoughts *in*?"

"Possible," Mordi mused. He thought about it a bit more. "Yeah. That's very possible."

"Except that Patel was one of my re-assimilation cases. And I touched him." She held up a hand before Mordi could protest. "I know I wasn't supposed to, but I wanted to make sure he was okay. And he was."

"Maybe he was blocking your powers." That from Davy. "Like with something that goes on the skin, so that when you touch them—"

"That coppery smell." Izzy banged her head with the heel of her hand, and Mordi felt a bit like a slow student. Isole continued. "My dad said he'd made some sort of balm, and that I'd find it useful. Something to block my powers." She shook her head. "Hieronymous really did a number on me and my dad."

"That's his specialty," Jason said.

Isole turned to face Mordi, and he pulled her into his arms, wanting to hold her there forever. Wanting to keep her safe. Wanting to make her forgive herself.

"Got it!" Davy's voice echoed through the cave. They turned and, sure enough, part of the stone wall had pulled away, opening on some invisible hinge.

"Izzy." Harold's feeble voice rang out, and he

reached a hand up toward his daughter. His skin was sallow, his limbs shaky.

Davy stood up, blocking his path. "Don't do it, mister," he said. "There's a booby trap."

Izzy's eyes met Mordi's, and he saw the fear reflected there. He asked the question she couldn't. "What is it, Davy?"

"It's keyed for his DNA. If he leaves, these catacombs collapse and we'll all be squashed. You know, all gooey and—"

"Thanks, kid. We get it." *Hopping Hades, and damn Hieronymous!* "Can we do anything? Leave some blood behind? That's got his DNA."

"I don't think that'll work," Davy guessed. "It's set up to need a whole person." He bent back down to look at the control panel.

Izzy had broken away from Mordi and was now near her father. "Daddy. Daddy! Can you hear me?"

Harold Frost groaned, but he didn't actually speak.

Izzy turned to Mordi, pain in her eyes. "He's sick. Oh, Mordi, he's really sick. We've got to get him out of here. He'll die otherwise."

"Right. Okay." He spoke, but he didn't have a plan.

"She can stay," Davy said, looking at one of his devices, and they all turned to him.

"What?" Mordi asked.

"In his place. She's got the right kind of DNA. He can leave and she can stay."

"No," Mordi said.

"Okay," Izzy said at exactly the same moment.

"Sweetheart, you can't."

She looked into the dark cell, and he saw in her eyes just how true his words were. But then she stood up straighter and nodded. "Yes, I can. You have to go stop your father. And after you save the world, you can come back and save me. Deal?"

311

Her eyes were full of love and trust, and his heart twisted, awed by the depth of her faith in him. Still, though, he couldn't bear leaving her. "I'll stay with you. Jason can take your father to safety, then he and Zoë and Hale can search for Zephron. They'll find him. They'll—"

"No." She pressed a finger to his lips, then kissed him. "No. You can stop this. For some reason, I think you're probably the only one who can. But you need to go now. The negotiations start at eight."

"Go? Go where? What the hell can I—" And then he stopped. Because she was right.

All of a sudden, he knew exactly what he had to do.

Chapter Forty-nine

Mordi's kiss still lingered on her lips as Isole stepped into the cell, timing the movement so that she was inside as her father, weak and thin, stepped out. All four Protectors waited a moment, but the catacombs stayed stable. No shifting, no falling. There was no sign at all that the place might collapse around their ears.

"Go," Izzy said, looking Mordi in the eye. "Go save the day. And then come back and save me."

"I will," he said.

She turned to Jason. "You'll help Zoë and Hale with Zephron?"

Jason nodded. "We'll get your dad to safety first. I promise. It'll be okay."

She tried to smile, but couldn't quite manage. "So, you trust me now?"

He leaned forward and kissed her on the cheek. "I trust you," he said. "I have to. I have a feeling we may be family someday."

His words both warmed and shocked her, and her gaze darted to Mordi, half-afraid he was going to look embarrassed or, worse, angry. Instead, he looked delighted. And determined.

"I have to go now," he said.

"I know. Go. Hurry."

"And we have to close the door. If Hieronymous sends someone to check up on . . ."

She nodded. This time, though, she couldn't manage words.

"I'll be back," Mordi said.

"I know," she said. And then she backed into the cell and closed her eyes.

She heard the sound of stone against stone, and when she opened her eyes, it was just as dark. She held out her hands and realized that she could feel every wall. The room really was the size of a coffin.

She started to shake, cold chills covering her body. She knew he was coming back for her, she *knew* it. But though her head might have a clue, the rest of her was scared to death. A small space. A dark space. This was worse than an elevator, with nothing but her and the walls and the dark.

She managed to fight it until she was sure that Mordi and Jason and the rest were gone. She didn't want to risk them coming back. They had a mission, after all. And then, when everything around her was silent and still, Izzy collapsed to the floor, drew in a breath, and screamed.

Chapter Fifty

He'd won. Finally, he'd won, and it was worth the wait. The years of torment. The agony of defeat at his own sons' hands. But he'd finally won. And, oh, what a victory it was.

Hieronymous took his seat at the head of the negotiation table on Olympus. He smiled at the members of the Inner Circle, at the Protectors who were on the renegotiation committee, and at those ridiculous mortals who'd come planning to dictate terms of a new treaty. No. That wouldn't be happening. Not today.

He'd made sure that every place setting had a mind-control pen. That was probably overkill. There were sufficient numbers in the room without every individual having one, and already the chamber was filled with the silent hum of mind control. Unfortunately, the devices didn't work on mortals. That was okay, though. They'd be witnesses soon enough to their own fate.

"Shall we begin?" he asked.

Bilius nodded. "Of course."

"Shouldn't we wait for Zephron?" one of the mortal plebes said.

"Yes," said another. "Where is the High Elder?"

"Apparently *I* am the High Elder today," Hierony-mous said. "Zephron was unavoidably detained." He allowed the slightest of smiles to touch his lips, re-membering with extreme pleasure the surprise on Zephron's face when the stealth mosquito—quickly and capably engineered to Hieronymous's specific specifications by his underlings—had attacked and taken out the elder with a hefty dose of sleeping po-tion.

Now the elder was in the farthest catacombs, and there he would remain. It was safe to say that Zephron would be there for eternity.

What a lovely thought.

"And now, to get down to business." He picked up the itinerary that some flunkie had prepared, flipped through it, then tossed it behind him. It hit the wall just as the mouths around the table dropped open. "New plan," he said. "Mortals are out. Protectors are in." He took a deep breath and spread his arms wide. "Ah, but it felt good to say that."

"What the—"

"You can't—"

"Are you mad?"

"We came here in good faith! These negotiations must—"

He held up a hand, and the sputtering stopped. "I believe I'm in charge here."

"*No*." A familiar, authoritative voice echoed from the doorway. "Actually, I'm in charge. And we'll be sign-ing the treaty as it was negotiated."

Zephron!?

Chapter Fifty-one

Mordi strode into the room, his bearing regal, just as Zephron's would be. He'd assumed the High Elder's form. He moved to the head of the table, took up one of the binders that contained the treaty's terms, and turned to page one.

"We will be signing this today," he said. "The treaty will go forward."

"I believe a vote is in order," Hieronymous said, pure hatred burning in his eyes.

"Indeed it is," Mordi replied. It took every ounce of strength in his body not to spit in his father's eye. "The vote will be between me and the mortals."

"And the Inner Circle!" Hieronymous protested, as the Protectors voiced similar thoughts.

"Am I not the High Elder? Do I not have supreme veto power? We can skip the voting. I assure you, any indication that the Council intends to set aside the treaty will be vetoed by me."

"But Zephron—" Bilius stated, rising to his feet.

"*Silence!*" That from Hieronymous. He spoke so brashly and loudly that even Mordi cringed.

Hieronymous turned to face his son dead-on. Mordi

stood straight, remembering—telling himself—that he was the High Elder and he wasn't about to shrink from the likes of his father.

"I'll do nothing that you say," Hieronymous said, his voice low and menacing. "And neither will these men."

"Oh, but they will. I am Zephron. The High Elder. And in the end, they'll have no choice."

"Perhaps," Hieronymous said, and something in his voice gave Mordi pause. "Perhaps that would be true if you were in fact the High Elder." And then, without warning, he leaped forward, grabbing Mordi's arms and hooking them behind his back. "Be still, *son*," he said. And Mordi felt his plan fall to pieces.

Hieronymous's grip tightened on his arm, and the other Protectors moved closer. Damn it to Hades, he hadn't considered that he'd be fighting half the Council! Damn his father and that ridiculous mind-control pen!

"He's brainwashed you," Mordi howled. "The pens!"

The Protectors all looked blank, but Senator Banyon apparently got it. He started grabbing pens off the table, presumably planning to toss them out the door. Hieronymous let go of Mordi long enough to attack Banyon. The senator flew threw the air, landing in a heap in the corner, the pens scattering everywhere.

Mordi drew in a breath, then shifted back to his normal appearance.

"*You*," Hieronymous sneered. "You are not my son."

"Actually," Mordi said, "I am. And for the first time in my life, I'm glad of it."

Hieronymous stared at him, baffled, and Mordi waved toward the pens. "You're genetically not affected," Mordi explained. "And, as your son, neither am I." He smiled and said a silent thank-you to his nephew, who'd given him a theoretical rundown on the mysterious fountain pens as they'd raced from the catacombs.

"You will not best me," Hieronymous said. "Not this time. Not ever again. You aren't worthy of my blood, and you are certainly no match for me. You're a pathetic Halfling."

For the first time, Hieronymous's personal attacks didn't draw blood, and Mordi stood tall against his father. Even so, he had to agree that the odds were against him. In an effort to increase his chances, he jumped on top of the table and raced toward the door. Hieronymous was at his heels, and his father practically flew into the antechamber just as Mordi did.

Mordi ducked and rolled, and Hieronymous tumbled over him. Mordi raced back and locked the door, effectively trapping the other Protectors inside. Hopefully, they were too mind-muddled to use their powers to escape without Hieronymous there to guide them.

He didn't have much time to worry about it, though, because his father was on him. Usually, the man had Clyde do the dirty work. Mordi had only seen his father fight once, and in that instance he'd slunk away pretty quickly—plus, Mordi had had the benefit of weapons.

As it turned out, though, Daddy Dearest was quite the fighter. He lunged at Mordi, tackled him, and then the two went down, rolling over and over. Mordi drew in a breath, gathered his energy, and conjured enough faux fire to engulf his father.

The ploy worked, and Hieronymous leapt back, howling as he beat at the flames. His eyes brimmed with anger when he realized the fire was fake. The anger seemed to fuel his strength, and Hieronymous raced toward Mordi, shouting a battle cry as he clutched Mordi's shoulders and pushed him back. He moved so fast that Mordi couldn't even keep his feet under him.

They slammed against a wall and rolled against it, then crashed into the glass side of the mortalization tube. Mordi saw the moment the idea hit Hieronymous, but there was nothing he could do; his father had him in his grip, and he shoved Mordi soundly into the cylinder.

Mordi's head struck the inside of the tube, and he blinked, slightly dazed. He moved forward, trying to grab his father, but Hieronymous slammed the door and locked it. Mordi howled, then banged against the bluish glass, but Hieronymous only smiled.

"This is for the best, son," Hieronymous said. "Trust me."

And then, as Mordi's nerves fractured and frayed, Hieronymous went to the control panel, turned the dial, and pushed the button.

The mortalization tube kicked into high gear.

Chapter Fifty-two

Hieronymous couldn't stop laughing. It was beautiful. *Beautiful!* His Halfling son—the one who sympathized with mortals—was now a mortal himself!

He doubled over, feeling not quite himself, but certain he was simply giddy from the wonderfulness of it all. He reached out a hand, prepared to use telekinesis to flip the lock and allow his army to emerge, but nothing happened.

Damn. The fight with Mordi had sapped his powers. He pulled himself upright and headed for the door as Mordi watched from inside the blue tube. *Fool*, he thought.

He reached the door, felt the lock in his hand, and then—

"Not so fast, Hieronymous." *Zephron!*

Hieronymous recovered fast and whipped around. "This really is getting old. I've had about enough of you today."

Zephron strode into the room, his cape fluttering behind him, his eyes twinkling. "And *I* have had just about enough of *you*."

Hieronymous's other disappointment of an offspring,

Jason, tromped in after Zephron, looking smug as usual. Hieronymous's meddling niece and nephew—Zoë and Hale—brought up the rear.

"I knew I should have hidden you in a deeper cata-comb," he said. He waved a hand in dismissal. "Doesn't matter, though. You're too late. I *will* win this time. And you have already lost." He gestured toward the mortalization tube, then saw Zoë's eyes go wide. She rushed forward to open the door. Zephron, sur-prisingly, didn't look disturbed. Then again, the man had an uncanny ability to keep a straight face, even when faced with the most direst danger.

Zoë opened the tube, and Mordi stepped out. At first, he looked confused, then he lifted his head, faced Hieronymous, and smiled.

"I think, Father, that it's you who has lost." And then the little bastard held up a small metal box on the end of a chain. He let loose with a puff of flame from his other hand, engulfing his father.

It wasn't until Hieronymous had fallen to the ground and snuffed the flames that he realized both truths: 1) His son had used imaginary fire again; and, 2) he should have realized, should have seen the trap. After all, he'd see *Superman 2* over and over and over. Hieronymous knew the trick. He knew it well. But he hadn't forseen. Somehow, Mordi had reversed the power on the mortalization tube. Mordichai had been safe all the time.

And now Hieronymous was mortal.

Chapter Fifty-three

Mordi left the others cleaning up the mess and unbending the other Protectors' minds. He wanted everything to be okay, but he had to get out of there and had to save Izzy. That was what he truly wanted.

And Zephron and the others were all there now, they could handle everything.

As Mordi left, Hieronymous climbed to his feet. Mordi had to give him credit. The guy wasn't giving up easily. Harold Frost's Polarity Reversal prototype may have sucked the super heroism right out of him, but Hieronymous didn't cave.

"You think you can save him?" he asked, and Mordi realized that his father must still assume Harold was in the catacombs. He'd guessed his son's intentions. "You can't. If he leaves, the catacombs will collapse, sealing themselves forever. The cells will open long enough to let my little pets escape, but certainly no mortal will make it to the top in time. Some of those Henchmen will be free to do my bidding, and their prison will be sealed off, with no one ever again getting in or out."

Hieronymous smiled, thin and deadly. "I like to call it a little insurance plan."

That didn't sound good, and Mordi raced from Olympus, desperate to get to Izzy's side. He didn't yet know how they would get her out, but he knew he was going to stand by her while his brother and Zephron and Zoë wrested the secret of unlocking the cell safely from Hieronymous.

He refused to believe they couldn't find a way. They had to. He didn't intend to ever leave Izzy ever again. And he really wasn't looking forward to a life spent in the dark of the catacombs.

The entrance was still open, the illusion of the rocks still firm. The thick stone door hung above the threshold, a visual barrier if not an actual doorway. Mordi didn't believe it had ever closed—but now Hieronymous said it would, sealing him and Izzy inside. And at seven feet thick, the door was impenetrable even for a Protector. It if closed while Mordi and Izzy were inside, they would be, well . . . screwed.

He drew a breath and hoped Zephron and the gang would call soon with the key to getting her out. Barring that, the plan was to rally a large team of Protectors to build an infrastructure in order to keep a path open when the catacombs collapsed. Because that plan would require pulling Protectors off official duty, they were waiting to put the team in place until they were sure Hieronymous wouldn't talk.

At the moment, though, Mordi wasn't as concerned with how or when they'd get Izzy out. He just wanted to get *to* her. He raced toward the cell where they'd left her, not stopping until he could press his hand on the cold stone.

Silence.

His heart raced, fear pounding through his brain. "Izzy?" His call was barely a whisper. He was too afraid of calling out to her and having her not answer. What if something had already happened to her? What if he opened the chamber only to find—

"Mordi?"

His entire body sagged with relief, and he pressed his ear to the stone, desperate to hear her sweet voice again. "Iz? Izzy, can you hear me?"

The words she spoke—"I knew you'd come back"—cut through his soul. "Hang on," he said. "I'm going to get you out of there."

Davy had shown him how to work the lock, and he had the door open in no time. Izzy raced forward, but he held out a hand, stopping her at the threshold.

"What's wrong? He's not—"

"No. Everything went great. Everything except . . ." He trailed off, not entirely sure how to phrase it.

"The DNA thing?"

"Afraid so. We don't have an answer to that yet."

She licked her lips. "Oh. Yeah. So, um, what do we do?"

"Zephron's on it. Don't worry. I expect an answer any second now. We'll be home in no—"

Beep, beep!

Thank Hera! "Give me some good news," he said, flipping on the holopager and talking before Jason could get a word in edgewise.

"Sorry," Jason said, his expression about as morose as his words.

"What?" Mordi's tone was sharper than he intended, but, dammit, how long did they expect Izzy to remain stuck in that cell?

"If there's a key, Hieronymous isn't talking. He even told us where the schematics are located, and Hale flew Davy there to take a look. The kid can't find a back door."

"It's got to be there," Mordi said. "Hieronymous couldn't just take Harold and lock him away forever. He'd have no bargaining power."

"I agree with you," Jason said. "But we can't find it, and our father's not telling." He swallowed, looking away from the transmitter so that it appeared to Mordi that he was avoiding his eyes. "There's more. . . ."

Mordi's chest twisted. "Tell me."

"He duped us. The sorry old bastard duped us."

"What are you talking about?"

"Thirty minutes," Jason said. "When Davy pulled the schematics out of the cubby hole, it triggered a fail-safe device Hieronymous had hidden. The catacombs will collapse in thirty minutes. And if Izzy crosses that threshold, the collapse will come that much sooner. I'm sorry, Mordi. There's no way we can get a team there in time."

Mordi clicked off without saying good-bye and caught Izzy's eyes. Her expression was one of stone determination rather than fear. His heart swelled. By Zeus, he loved this woman.

"I got the general gist of that," she said. "Tell me the rest."

He drew in a breath, then told her about how Hieronymous had rigged the place. "He said mortals wouldn't make it."

"We're not mortal," she said.

He thought about that. The lady did have a point. "So our plan is to run like hell?"

Her mouth curved into a sad smile. "Even if we don't make it, I'd rather be running with you than trapped in here." She waved an arm behind her to indicate the tiny cell. "Just say when."

"No time like the present," he said. "On the count of three?"

She nodded, and he counted, and on three they took off, racing up the corridor. At first nothing happened, and Mordi had to wonder if perhaps his father had lied: The place hadn't been booby-trapped, and that had simply been an elaborate ruse designed to knock down Mordi's morale. But Davy had said. . . .

The walls started to collapse around them.

The harsh grating of stone against stone echoed through the shadow-filled chamber as the individual cells opened, freeing all the Henchmen and other imprisoned beings. And that sound, coupled with the high keening of the creatures, gave the dancing firelight on Mordi's fingers an even more unearthly—and ominous—appearance.

All around them, Mordi could hear the *schloosh, schloosh* of Henchmen heading for the exit. He and Izzy had to get there first! They had to get there, get out, and prevent any of the Henchmen from getting out, too. Because Mordi was damned if he was going to loose these creatures on the earth . . . or if he was going to be spending the rest of his days tracking the damnable things down.

They rounded the last corner . . . and ran smack into two hulking Henchmen, their squidlike bodies filling the hallway. Considering the Henchmen barely even moved at the sight of them, Mordi had to assume they'd surprised the creatures.

"Keep going," Mordi cried, holding tight to Izzy's hand as they raced down the final stretch. He punched a Henchman in the gut—or at least, in a gutlike area—and it toppled to the ground. He and Isole kept on moving; he could see a shaft of sunlight slanting in under the slowly closing door. The walls shifted, rocks tumbling toward them, and he lurched sideways to avoid one that fell in their path.

Behind him, Izzy screamed, and he realized that he'd lost his grip on her. He turned to find a huge shower of rocks separated them, and he saw her kicking at a Henchman. The thing was half-buried, but its tentaclelike arm clasped to her ankle as she tried to pull herself forward. She lashed out, dosing the creature with a rain of ice, but he jerked her arm as she aimed, and she froze the ceiling instead. Only a few bits of hail landed on the monster.

"Izzy!" Mordi raced toward her.

She twisted, her face contorted with pain, and he realized her ankle was perhaps broken. "No! Go! Get out of here."

"Are you crazy?"

"The door's closing," she screamed. "You'll be trapped. Now *go*."

"I'm not leaving you." He tried to scramble over the pile of rocks that now was grown between them, and as he did, he turned just enough to see the exit. The door was about eighteen inches from the ground. There was no way they could escape now anyway. Not unless—

"Damn you, Mordichai!" Isole twisted, throwing her body forward and straining against the Henchman as she reached up at an awkward angle. He had no idea what she was doing . . . and then he saw the ice. It covered an entire overhead mechanism, completely freezing the pulley system that operated the door!

"It won't hold for long," she said. "The motor will melt the ice. Mordi, there's no time to get me over to your side. *Go*," she said again as she turned and punched at the Henchman.

She was right, of course. There was no way to get her free of that Henchman, get her through the barrier of rocks, and reach the exit. Not before the ice melted and it closed.

No way at all.

He drew in a breath and drew himself a little bit further up the pile. "I'm not leaving you, Izzy. It's just not happening."

Chapter Fifty-four

Izzy screamed at Mordi to go, to run, but the idiot wasn't listening to her. She couldn't see him anymore. More of the avalanche had completely blocked the corridor except for a tiny area up top where the door mechanism was, and the shrinking hole through which she'd seen him come back for her—and through which she'd seen the door straining to close.

"Dammit," she yelled. "For the love of Hera, go!" Tears streamed down her face, and she kicked against her captor, and punched him again, but was unable to free her foot. The door was going to close soon, and she'd be damned if Mordi was going to be trapped in here, too. He'd saved her from that horrible little cell. It was her turn to save him.

"No!" he screamed from the other side of the dirt. In her incapacitated state, she'd never survive with the frenzied Henchmen. Even if he could escape and break back in with a Protector team, it would be too late. "I'm not leaving you. You're either coming out with me or I'm staying with you, but *I am not leaving without you*. Do you understand me?"

She did. She'd known he loved her; she'd read it in

his soul. But now she knew what love meant to Mordi. He would die for her . . . and she wasn't about to let that happen. She didn't know what they could do, but she was willing to try anything.

Above her, Mordi's eyes and head emerged at the top of the rock pile. And just seeing him gave her hope.

She flashed him a smile. "You're crazy, but okay. What do you want me to do?"

"That's my girl," he said as she kicked once again at the Henchman's gut. He dug his way through the dirt. "I'm going to burn that Henchman, and when I do, you need to jerk free and scramble here faster than you've ever run before."

She nodded. "I can do that," she told herself. The thing made another grab for her waist, and she kicked again, once more feeling her foot sink into something the consistency of Jello. Sweet Hera, these creatures were disgusting.

"There's one other thing," he said.

"Why—"

Kick.

"—am I not—"

Kick, kick.

"—surprised?"

Kick!

The Henchman's slimy grip loosened around her thigh, though it still had a tight hold on her ankle. "Okay," she said. "What?"

"The door."

Cold filled her. She loved Mordi. She could no longer read him. But even so, she knew exactly what he was going to say. "What about the door?"

"Can you see it? We have to make it hold a bit longer. Take a good look before you run, and hold it in your mind. Once that ice melts, I need you to help levitate it. I can't do it on my own, and I'm still weak from my

Zephron impersonation a few hours ago. And I'm going to need much of my strength for the fire."

Sweet Hera, she'd been afraid of this.

She drew in a breath, started to speak, then stopped. How could she tell the man she loved he was about to give up his life with her? She couldn't.

She *wouldn't*.

He was right. There was no other way. They'd either manage it—*she'd* manage it—or they wouldn't. And as foolhardy as it seemed, with Mordi's love to bolster her, she felt stronger than ever.

Just to prove it, she walloped the Henchman good. She even managed to free herself, and just as she was about to yell to Mordi that it was okay, that they didn't need his fire and he could hold the door open, two things happened at once: The ice holding the mechanism melted, and five other Henchmen pounced on her.

"*Now!*" Mordi shouted.

She gathered her energy, pictured the door in her mind, and reached out, feeling its weight, its density, trying to become the door. Nothing happened, though, and she had to fight tears—fight to concentrate—because she would *not* disappoint Mordi.

Then everything felt hot and red, and she realized that Mordi had let loose with his fire. She jerked forward, suddenly free from the squealing Henchmen, and scrambled up and over the rocks. She didn't think about where she was going. She only concentrated on diving through the gap, or moving—and on keeping that door in her head.

The pulley strained and groaned above, its terrible noise echoing through the catacombs as she reached Mordi. He was obviously spent, but he grabbed her arm. "It's heavy. But you can do it."

Behind them, one of the Henchman—now a shrieking flaming mass—was clamoring up the rocks behind them.

"Come on," she yelled, and they ran toward the door.

There were only about twelve inches of clearance now, but she concentrated with all her heart and soul, stronger with the knowledge that Mordi believed in her.

And it worked. She couldn't quite believe it. In fact, she was so amazed that she almost came to a dead stop, but Mordi tugged her on. They slid under the heavy stone, pushing their bodies beneath; her moving more slowly on her bad ankle, and the burning Henchman right on their heels.

"I can't hold it anymore," she cried. She heard the squeal of the pulley, fighting to let the stone descend.

"I'm clear!" Mordi shouted, and then his hands curled around her underarms and he pulled. She shot forward into his embrace, and into the clear, just as the stone door finally crashed to the ground. It destroyed the last, persistent Henchman, cutting him in half with a satisfying *squish*.

Izzy's breath was ragged as she collapsed against Mordi. She pressed her face into his chest and simply breathed in his scent. "I knew you'd come," she said again.

"Always," he said, stroking her hair. "Forevermore."

She pulled away, just enough to look in his eyes, then smiled. "So, you didn't manage to pull all that off at the end just so you wouldn't have to spend eternity with me in a catacomb, did you?"

His smile matched hers, and he pulled her close. "You know, now that I think about it, eternity with you in close quarters sounds pretty darned appealing."

For her part, Izzy completely agreed.

Epilogue

Mordi had never been a particularly sentimental sort, but even he had to admit that Deena and Hoop's wedding was beautiful. Deena glowed, and a tuxedo made even Hoop look dashing. And through the entire ceremony, Mordi wasn't able to do anything else except imagine what he'd look like in a tux . . . and what Izzy would look like dressed all in white.

The band was playing now, and the bride and groom were dancing. "Shall we?" Isole whispered, leaning over so close that Mordi caught the delectable scent of her hair. He'd awakened that morning to that clean, soapy smell.

He wanted to awaken that way *every* morning.

"Mordi?" Izzy prompted. Her blue eyes were wide, sparkling with anticipation of a spin around the dance floor.

"Let's sit this one out, okay?"

She frowned, but didn't argue. "Okay." She touched his arm. "You seem distracted. Is something wrong?"

At that, he couldn't help but smile. "Just the opposite. Everything is perfect. I just want to sit here. With you."

She seemed to understand, and she scooted closer, then took his hand. They sat like that for a few minutes, watching their friends move across the dance floor, just soaking in the atmosphere of celebration and love.

When the band took a short break, Zephron came over and put his arm around his niece. "I will say again what excellent work you two did."

Color rose on Izzy's cheek; she didn't seem to take compliments well. She'd have to get over that, Mordi thought. He intended to shower her in them.

"I'm glad you came to the wedding, Uncle Zephron," Izzy said. "I've heard all of Deena and Hoop's stories, and even though they're mortal, they've helped save the world so many times. I know they're honored you're here."

"And I'm honored to be invited." He handed over a small folder of papers. "Since I knew you would be here, too, I decided to take this opportunity to once and for all disabuse you of certain notions."

As Mordi watched, Isole flipped through the papers, her expression first confused, then shifting to wary joy. "Is this true?" she asked, and he had to fight not to ask what they were talking about.

"It was never me," Zephron said. "It's true, you weren't able to acknowledge levitation on your affidavit, but the committee considered your application without any regard to your familial relationships."

Mordi frowned, not understanding. "You can't levitate? I *saw* you levitate."

"Yeah, well, it's not so much of a problem anymore. And I think I'm over the claustrophobia, too." She handed the folder back to Zephron. "It's sweet of you to do this, but it wasn't necessary. I finally proved my worth. To myself, at least. And that's what counts."

Mordi squeezed her hand, and she squeezed back.

He wasn't entirely sure what they were talking about, but he of all people knew just how much it meant to be able to prove—really prove—that you belonged where you wanted to belong.

"What happened to my father?" he asked.

Zephron almost smiled. "For Hieronymous, I'd say a punishment worse than death. But you already knew that, and it wasn't what you were asking."

"No," Mordi agreed, "but you're right."

"Because of the nature of that reverse-polarization device, the memory-swipe feature didn't engage. Thus, your father still is somewhat dangerous, as he knows many of our secrets. His intellect, however, has faded, and I'm not entirely certain he would know how to launch a full attack even if he wanted to. We will keep an eye on him, of course. Clyde and Romulus are still at large and may try to contact him. But I don't consider him much of a threat anymore. And right now, we're simply trying to instruct him on the basics of mortal life. After that—" Zephron held out his hands in question. "After that, we're not sure. Though there are some excellent training programs at many of the finer mortal fast-food establishments."

Izzy laughed, then quickly became serious again. "And Patel?" Izzy said. "Is he in a lot of trouble?"

"Frankly, no. Hieronymous captured his sister just as he'd captured your father. The placement of the pens was an exchange. Patel should have handled it better, of course, but his punishment will not be as severe."

"Good," Izzy said.

"And the treaty negotiations?" Mordi asked. "Still stalled?" So far, every morning the *Daily Protector* reported the same thing.

"Officially," Zephron said. "But I can tell you in confidence that I am highly optimistic."

"Good," Mordi said. "I'm not terribly political, but I'll admit to wanting the revised treaty to pass just because it would tick off my father."

This time, Mordi was certain that Zephron smiled. "I cannot say I share your motives," Zephron said. "At least, as High Elder, I cannot say that in public."

Mordi and Izzy both laughed, and then the band started up again. Mordi nodded briefly to Zephron, then laid a hand on Isole's arm. "If you'll excuse us," he said to Zephron, "I think they're playing our song."

He led her onto the floor, and she clung to him as they swayed in time with the music. Zoë and Taylor were out there as well, along with Hale and Tracy, who had Elmer perched on her shoulder. Jason and Lane were sitting this one out, and Jason was massaging Lane's swollen ankles. Deena's brother Nick was sipping a Scotch by the bar, his wife Maggie drinking a glass of milk.

For so many years, Mordi had been removed from this group, distanced by his own foolish choices. He was here for good now, though, and at the moment, Mordi was certain that he'd discovered the real meaning of happiness: dancing in a room surrounded by friends and family, with the woman he loved in his arms.

Because, really, life couldn't get much better than that. And to prove the point, he bent down and kissed her.

She kissed him back, her enthusiasm equal to his own. And as he lost himself to the kiss, Mordi learned a new lesson in physics—fire and ice each equaled the other out . . . and when he and Izzy kissed, all that was left was the love.

Aphrodite's Secret

JULIE KENNER

Jason Murphy can talk to creatures of the sea. He also has other superpowers like all Protectors, but none of them really help his situation. The love of his life doesn't trust him anymore. Sure, she has her reasons: When she needed him most, he was focusing on his super-career. But that is all over. He vows to reel her back in.

It won't be easy. His outcast father is still plotting world domination, and Jason's other Protector friends fear his commitment to justice. And though Lane still loves him, how to win her hand in marriage seems the best-kept secret ever. Soon Jason will swear that beating up the bad guys is easy. It is this relationship stuff that takes a true superman!

- -

Aphrodite's Passion

JULIE KENNER

Aphrodite's Girdle is missing, and Hale knows the artifact will take all his superpowers to retrieve. The mortal who's found and donned it—one Tracy Tannin, the descendent of a goddess of the silver screen—wasn't exactly popular before the belt. Now everyone wants her. But the golden girdle can only be recovered through honest means, which means there is no chance for Hale to simply become invisible and whisk it away. (Although, watching Tracy, he finds himself imagining other garments he'd like to remove.) Maybe he should convince her she is as desirable as he sees her. Only then will she realize she is worth loving no matter what she is wearing—or what she isn't.

___52474-0 $5.99 US/$7.99 CAN

Aphrodite's Kiss
Julie Kenner

Crazy as it sounds, on her twenty-fifth birthday Zoe has the chance to become a superhero. But x-ray vision and the ability to fly are only two things to consider. There is also her newfound heightened sensitivity. If she can hardly eat a chocolate bar without convulsing in ecstasy, how is she to give herself the birthday gift she's really set her heart on— George Taylor? The handsome P.I.'s dark exterior hides a truly sweet center, and Zoe feels certain that his mere touch will send her spiraling into oblivion. But the man is looking for an average Jane no matter what he claims. He can never love a superhero-to-be—can he? Zoe has to know. With her super powers, she can only see through his clothing; to strip bare the workings of his heart, she'll have to rely on something a little more potent.

___52438-4 $5.99 US/$6.99 CAN

Dorchester Publishing Co., Inc.
P.O. Box 6640
Wayne, PA 19087-8640

Please add $1.75 for shipping and handling for the first book and $.50 for each book thereafter. NY, NYC, and PA residents, please add appropriate sales tax. No cash, stamps, or C.O.D.s. All orders shipped within 6 weeks via postal service book rate. Canadian orders require $2.00 extra postage and must be paid in U.S. dollars through a U.S. banking facility.

Name_____
Address_____
City_____State_____Zip_____
I have enclosed $ _____ in payment for the checked book(s).
Payment <u>must</u> accompany all orders. ❏ Please send a free catalog.
CHECK OUT OUR WEBSITE! www.dorchesterpub.com

KATE ANGELL
DRIVE ME CRAZY

Cade Nyland doesn't think that anything good can come of the new dent in his classic black Sting Ray, even if it does happen at the hands of a sexy young woman. He is determined to win his twelfth road rally race of the year.

TZ Blake only enters Chugger Charlie's tight butt competition to win enough money to keep her auto repair shop open. What she ends up with is a position as navigator in a rally race. All she has to do is pretend she knows where she is going. All factors indicate that the unlikely duo is in for a bumpy ride . . . and each eagerly anticipates the jostling that will bring them closer together.